ANJI,

A DAKOTA HUNT NOVEL

Book Two

DEB D. DONOHUE

Deb D. Donohue
www.flourishingpenpublishing.com
Revised Edition 4: May, 2024

Dakota Hunt and Private Detective Dakota Hunt are trademarks of Deb D. Donohue and Flourishing Pen Publishing, LLC.

ISBN 978-1-7359371-6-8 (Paperback)
ISBN 978-1-7359371-7-5 (E-book)

Cover design by author.
Cover images by artists, legally purchased by author.

Please also see First Book in Series:
Jillian, A Dakota Hunt Novel Book One

1

Anji

On an early, frigid morning in mid-January, we were huddled together on the porch snuggled up in cozy, winter parkas mesmerized by eerie northern lights dancing above us. Wavy shades of green, brilliant blue and plum purple lights vigorously flashed and whirled across the sky. Icy prickles crept up my spine and a surreal uneasiness completely overwhelmed me. When the aurora borealis is this sensational, my papa believes that spiritual beings are offering significant warnings of some sort and that something tragic will soon occur.

Absorbed in the phenomenon, Papa kneeled down on the ground with his hands in prayer, whispering to the spirits, begging for more information. Even though I don't really accept most of my family's mystical beliefs, I have to admit that it did seem as if some kind of spiritual entity was making its presence known. Suddenly, a peculiar, stealthy raven with its enormous wings spread wide, swooped down then swirled above our heads, startling me into brief hysteria. As I gazed at the dreamlike scene unfolding before my eyes, a surprising form appeared in the center of the mystifying illumination. The raven began encircling us with alarming haste and a hair raising shriek flew out of my mouth. As my eyes stayed fixed on the familiar image, I suddenly recalled a mysterious incident that had occurred in Anchorage almost a year ago, a scene that I have tried desperately to forget. I shivered in horror as sadness and remorse reduced me to an emotional wreck. If I had let out a blood curdling scream and sprinted toward the young woman, could I have changed her fate or would I have unintentionally altered my own?

The curious raven glared down at us, then agitatedly bobbed its head as if it was trying to communicate with us. I stood frozen in my stance, suspecting that there must be a connection between the raven and the mysterious image. The northern lights displayed more energy than I had ever recalled seeing and I felt entirely unnerved. I covered my eyes, but the image continued to thrust itself into the forefront of my mind. I bowed my head and whispered, "Forgive me." I felt ashamed and tears flooded my eyes as I realized that I should not have kept what I had witnessed undisclosed.

Was the face of the young woman some kind of mystical projection from the spirits? I glanced at the others, wondering if they too were affected by the bewildering image, but they made no mention of seeing anything other than the extraordinary animated lights and the mysterious raven. I closed my eyes tightly and shook my head, attempting to force the entire scene out of my mind, but the disturbing vision of the woman stubbornly remained, appearing vividly real as if I could reach out and touch her.

Papa had explained many times before that continuing to connect with the spirits of our ancestors provides a path to profound truths and personal reflection, ideals that he learned from his Inupiat friends. In the past few years, I have begun to question Papa's spiritual beliefs, preferring to rely on the scientific world to provide the truth about everything in life. In particular, I've been struggling with mystical concepts, because I like my world factual, ordered and controlled. I have worked very hard for many years educating myself, planning and studying the truth about things. If I can touch, hear or smell something then it's real, so how is it possible that there is a supernatural explanation for anything at all?

When Papa felt satisfied with the communication he received, he stood up and put his arms around us as we moseyed back into our safe, warm home. We sat together by the hot wood stove, thawing out our frozen limbs. The warmth of the fire on my skin soothed me and the uneasiness I felt just moments before, vanished into the glowing, flickering flames. With a disturbed expression and moist eyes, Papa cleared his throat. "Although the message was obscure, insightful spirits presented us with the raven to help us discover the danger that lurks in the shadows. We must stay together in the upcoming months and protect each other when out and about. Team up when you have to run deliveries and errands in town and be home before dark."

Papa is a strong, compassionate, protective man which has always been comforting and his words made sense however, I shivered as anxiety overwhelmed me once again. He did not mention seeing the image of the young woman. I considered that the mystifying vision I observed, might have been revealed to me only, now charged with bringing some kind of clarity to the mystery. I drew in an enormous breath and sighed as I pondered what to do.

My grandparents and parents have grown to accept many mystical ideals so completely that the lines between reality and spirituality are most certainly blurred. My wise, perceptive grandpapa was given the name Tulugaak, meaning Raven, by his Native Alaskan friends. They believed he was born with a special intuitive gift, the ability to perceive things that most people could not. Papa, named Ethan, shares the gift as well which has proven to be true time and time again throughout our lives. Because of his extraordinary perceptive nature, he has been able to prevent many disastrous incidents from occurring, which could have adversely affected the safety of our family and home out here in the vast, untamed wilderness.

On one occasion, he predicted the arrival of a group of grizzly bears in close proximity to our home, which could have resulted in harm to our family, dogs and the destruction of our vegetation Quonset huts, caribou and fish smokers. Normally grizzlies are solitary animals, but they sometimes gather at streams and rivers where fish are plentiful and would surely act aggressively if other beings threatened their delicious feast. Papa organized a scout team to verify his concerns and sure enough, the scouts observed a group of bears fishing in a tributary north of the Noatak River, about thirty miles from our home. Noting that each day the bears rambled closer, he was able to encourage the bears to alter their journey by building a small damn in the tributary river, creating a delectable fishing pool. Papa and a few friends continued observing the bears until they ambled back up the river rather than downstream, crisis averted.

Grandpapa cleared his throat to capture our attention and spoke in an ominous tone. "The raven is a bearer of magic, the messenger beyond time and space, symbolizing where everything originated and into which everything eventually goes. The raven deity is the creator of light and has the power to draw secrets from the shadows." He held my eyes and narrowed his own. "The raven can also represent a shapeshifter to those of us who possess the enlightened sense of insight." He left me to ponder his enigmatic words. I stared into Grandpapa's perceptive eyes, trying to determine if he too had witnessed the mysterious vision. Though even if he had, I was not prepared to discuss the incident which was most likely the cause of the spiritual manifestation, if that's what it was.

Mother studied Grandpapa's eyes, most likely wanting a reason for his mysterious words and I knew that she also needed an explanation for Papa's concerned behavior. They both nodded and returned her gaze, letting her know that they would speak with her about it in private after my sisters and I retired to our rooms. I shook off my apprehensions, yawned and sauntered off to bed.

I tried to sleep, but the surreptitious image and Grandpapa's puzzling words whirled in my mind. After a while, I finally fell asleep, lulled by gusty winds whistling across my window. A few hours must have passed when I found myself thrashing and turning side to side. Suddenly, I sprang from my bed completely entangled in my sheets and fell to the floor with a noisy thud.

I laid on the floor staring up at the shadowy ceiling, trying to recall the details of my mysterious nightmare. In the dream, an enormous raven darted out of a dark, dense fog and soared toward me at a shockingly hasty pace. I let out a hair-raising shriek as the bird wrapped its long, velvety wings around me like a swaddling cloak. A few seconds later, it clutched my shoulders with its long, curved talons, lifting me off the ground with alarming swiftness. Moments later, the raven glided to the edge of the forest and gently set me down on the frigid, icy tundra. Darkness surrounded me and fear seized me completely. My heart thrummed with such ferocity that I could barely think or move. I knelt on the ground and wrapped my arms firmly around my body as the raven swooped up and perched on a nearby branch. Suddenly, a misty, dense fog emerged out of the dark, shadowy forest and the image of the girl returned with vivid clarity. I closed my eyes tightly, ingraining every detail of her that I could possibly recall and would keep her image closely guarded in the forefront of my mind.

Confusion overwhelmed me as I untangled myself from my bedding and stood in disbelief. Was the spirit of the raven urging me to find the young woman and help her somehow or did my guilt-ridden mind conjure the whole thing up? I realized that my disconcerting memory would haunt me forever if I continued to try to dismiss the scene as nothing, so I decided to discuss the matter with my grandmother to unburden myself. I thought that maybe she could help me decide what to do about it.

2

Anji

I am Anji Sauveur, eighteen years young and have finally figured out how I want to begin my adult life. After I graduate this spring, I will eagerly prepare to go to college in the autumn to study botany and ecology. The scientific study of plants, including their physiology, classification and economic importance has been my main interest for the past three years. I have received invitations to attend Colorado State University, Oregon State University and University of Alaska Anchorage, which is where Mother wants me to attend to be closer to home. I like the idea of remaining close to my family, but I also have the desire to explore other parts of our country.

I'm quite brave and not at all afraid to explore other environments, but I will always consider Alaska my home even if I study elsewhere. I take solace in the peaceful splendor of my inspiring, safe world here, but I also have a particular interest in Colorado because of the spectacular, mammoth mountains, lakes, rivers and diversity of the flora and fauna.

My family and I live in Miki Tarniq, a small, remote town located in northwest Alaska. A dense cluster of white spruce trees surrounds our little town which sits dwarfed on the edge of the vast open tundra. Our home is about 200 feet from the peaceful, meandering Noatak River, where northern pike, Arctic grayling and Dolly Varden fish are abundant and make up a large percent of our diet.

My brother Kaya, two younger sisters, Alina and Joie and I help our parents with many vital daily chores which must be attended to in order to sustain a safe, healthy living here in such a harsh, untamed environment. Papa flies our small bush plane to Kotzebue for food and supplies even though we live primarily off the land. We fish, hunt and grow our own vegetables and herbs in small Quonset hut style greenhouses which is truly rewarding work.

My mother, Hana and grandmother, Sophia keep our home schooling programs very organized and Papa picks up our books and curriculum from the school in the city of Noatak. We visit our Inupiat friends there when we attend exam sessions which I love, but lately I have been preoccupied with my studies and plans for college.

As I sat daydreaming on my bed while gazing out of the window at the extraordinary view of the icy river and snow-covered mountains protruding on the distant horizon, I suddenly questioned how I could possibly be considering leaving my beautiful, pristine home environment. I must be half out of my mind, but curiosity urges me to venture out to experience what I have only read in books. The only unnatural noises we hear way up here in the great frontier are occasional snow mobiles, wilderness planes or ATVs, headed into the wilderness to fish, hunt or explore. Of course, there are the summer tourists who laugh, play and marvel in delight as they experience the magnificence of such a remote environment and I like that sound, the thrilling sound of joy and excitement.

My thoughts suddenly flashed back to the image of the girl with terror in her dark, wide eyes jolting me upright. Papa's concerned words repeated in my head like a broken record. I wondered if we'll be hearing laughter and merriment this summer or if we'll be hiding in fear from dangerous villains skulking in the shadows.

There are only thirty-six people living in our remote little town, though hundreds of people reside in villages not far away. Thinking about our close friends gave me some comfort. We love to visit with them and they often check on us, which is quite sociable and considerate. We have always been compassionate and respectful to our native Alaskan friends and they likewise. Papa and Kaya are always invited on hunting trips which has been immeasurably important in maintaining good relations.

My great grandpapa fought in WWII, when Canada joined the war effort in Britain on September 10th, 1939. He became great friends with several Inupiat men who he served with in the military. After the end of the war,

Amarug Nanook invited our family to live on his land. My grandparents bravely packed up everything from their home in the Northwest Territory, Canada and moved to northwest Alaska, establishing what would be our home for generations. Their compassionate friends taught them how to live in such a wild, remote environment and how to survive the harshest conditions.

At certain times of the year, we see hunters, fishing enthusiasts and other visitors who arrive to explore the Noatak Wilderness or who stop to visit our little town during their adventurous river float trips. The infamous Noatak River is 450 miles long, flowing westward right past Miki Tarniq, Noatak and finally toward Kotzebue Sound at the Chukchi Sea. I feel safe here in our tiny town and don't believe that there will be any tourists arriving with harmful intentions, but could the message from the spirits be informing us to stay away from the larger Alaskan cities? I felt the hair raise on the back of my neck. My sly intuition possibly revealed the truth, but I pondered what it all might mean. I suppose it's possible that witnessing the mysterious scene in Anchorage was a wake up call meant for me to experience, since I will soon be journeying brazenly into a densely populated, unfamiliar environment.

I tried to clear my mind and visualize the pieces of the puzzle falling effortlessly into place. With no success, I grunted with exasperation and shook off the mysterious conundrum. I asked myself out loud, "How could I possibly wake up every day feeling concerned that something tragic might occur?" I blew out a huge puff of air and tried to find an optimistic resolve, even if temporary.

Until we learn more about Papa's concerns, I'll ask Kaya or Alina and Joie to come with me when I want to hike and explore. We all appreciate the blooming treasures and collecting berries can be an amusing chore when done as a group. We all enjoy silently observing wild animals such as musk ox, moose and caribou roaming and grazing across the meandering river tundra. We often see grizzly bears fishing or exploring, but we keep our distance and we surely don't provoke them.

To work off the mounting anxiety, I decided to bundle up and run the sled dogs with Kaya. I thought the vigorous workout might calm my unsettled mind so that later, I would be able to clearly express my fears and frustrations with Grandma Sophia. She has a remarkable way of comforting me when I am troubled and I usually walk away feeling like a whale has been lifted from my shoulders.

We have two dog sleds that we use to get around in the winter, which are pulled by half Siberian Huskies and half Alaskan Malamutes. I found Kaya already out in the barn harnessing the dogs. "I'll run the other team this morning."

He turned toward me, catching the disturbed look in my eyes. "Are you okay? You startled me when you screamed this morning. What in the world caused you to freak out like that?"

I bowed my head and narrowed my eyes. "I saw a frightening form in the northern lights and then the raven startled me swooping down like it did. I don't know. I haven't been myself lately and now Papa has me looking over my shoulder every few minutes. I swear I'm hearing and seeing things that aren't really there."

He chuckled. "Just relax a little until we find out why Papa is so concerned. Like he said, we'll stay together when we go out."

I already knew a bit about why Papa was concerned, because I had overheard Grandpapa and him talking last night. I sighed with a sheepish grin and began harnessing the dogs. I forced myself to relax, shoving my dark, ominous thoughts to the back of my mind for now and began humming a light and lively tune. I find delight in many different kinds of music including the traditional Native Alaskan rhythmic music that we grew up hearing, jazz, new age or an inspiring classical piece. I recalled a time when Mother was listening to a classical composition one day and I joined in her merriment, humming and dancing around the kitchen. I asked her what instrument I was hearing during a lively string solo. She said, "That is a violin, the sweet, lustrous sound of autumn wind whooshing through trees and lovers dancing closely, wrapped in each other's arms." I asked her if I could have a violin to play like the wind. She laughed as she twirled me around the room and three months later, I was learning to play. With a lot of hard work, I began to enjoy the mysteriously sweet sound resonating from the strings. I drew in a deep breath and smiled at the pleasant memory.

Kaya and I started off at a fast run which felt absolutely exhilarating. The swooshing of the briskly moving sled on the icy snow, sounded like the percussion of an orchestra. The wind was my violin, the pounding feet of the huskies completed the drum section and the excited howls of my team were the vocals in my opera. I smiled widely, absorbing the energy of my musical journey through the wilderness valley. Seemingly on que, enhancing my melodious excursion, two ravens glided through the air currents above us, swirling like fanciful dances in the sky. I laughed heartily. I needed to laugh, to sing and to return to the harmonious place in my mind that I have worked so diligently for years to create. I have realized for some time that I don't do so well when confronted with unpleasant or disruptive experiences and I believe that is my downfall that I must overcome. I will have to learn to think clearly when facing challenges or malevolence so that I won't react hastily leading to unwise decisions.

Kaya and I sledded through the snow packed Noatak Wilderness for over an hour and were approaching the western slopes of the Brooks Range at the edge of the Wildlife Preserve. The preserve lies at almost 4,500 feet in elevation, encompassing 6,500,000 acres of undisturbed ecosystem and is one of my favorite places to explore. Our family travels to the preserve often, usually on all day ATV excursions or camping trips in the warmer, sunnier months.

I often find myself becoming lost in the beauty of my home environment, especially in the summer when the sun never sets. I frequently lose track of time when I venture out on my own and have worried my family on many occasions. There are just so many exquisite things in the wilderness to explore and I feel safe and comfortable here, because I understand and treasure every living thing. But since the daylight is so dim at this time of the year, I have to admit that I felt comforted knowing Kaya was with me today.

When we reached the edge of the forest, we stopped

to give the dogs a rest. Strong gusty winds whistled eerily through the evergreens causing the dogs to whine and howl. Out of the corner of my eye, I noticed some movement in the shadows of the forest. At first glance, I thought it might have been a wild animal, though as the figure approached, I realized who it was. "Look Kaya. That's the girl I told you about last autumn, Anya, over there by the trees. Let's go talk with her."

"From where I'm standing, I don't see anyone. Are you sure it wasn't a wild animal?"

"No, it's definitely Anya." I began trudging through the thick, heavy snow which I quickly realized was much too deep to get through. I stood frozen in my tracks as Anya began to hike toward us, but she suddenly stopped, turned on her heels and disappeared into the darkness of the forest. I called out, but she did not respond.

"Anji, the snow is too deep and we ought to head back before the wind picks up. The sun is setting fast and I don't want to sled through a blinding whiteout."

Reluctantly, I trudged back toward Kaya, turning every few feet to try to catch another glimpse of the girl, who I felt sure was Anya. I shivered as icy prickles rushed up my spine. I whispered to myself, "What was she doing there, maybe hunting with her papa again?" I shrugged as I clutched the handle bars, sprinted to gain momentum and jumped on the sled rails. The dogs were excited and energized, transporting us home in record time.

3

Anji

When Kaya and I returned from our outing, I noticed my grandmother in the living room and I asked her if we could have a conversation about unknown environments and other crucial survival skills. I also asked her how she and my great grandparents lived and managed when they first arrived here, knowing I would be fortunate to receive an extraordinarily detailed story rather than a few short answers.

Grandma began, "Anji, I was very much like you when I was a young girl, inquisitive with a tremendous thirst for knowledge and full of energy, but we all spent most days working hard to survive. Your great grandfather took your grandpapa with him every time he went hunting until he was satisfied with his skills and bravery. When old enough, Tulugaak continued the tradition, hunting for days along with a large group of men, each having particular functional skills. They would always bring home caribou, walrus, seal or whale, and I, alongside six or eight women would labor tirelessly preparing the edible portions for cooking and storing and the hides of the animals for clothing and blankets. It was and still is of course, very important to utilize every part of the animal leaving no waste."

Grandma sipped her spiced tea and smiled reflectively as if she was reliving her past memories right here and now. "While our men hunted, highly skilled women from several nearby towns and villages including yours truly, used seine nets to catch hundreds of fish, which we always shared with several villages. The work was tremendously tiresome, but rewarding as you are well aware. We would begin our work early in the morning and stay out until our boats were so full that we had to move slowly through the river to stay afloat."

I smiled, delighted to hear Grandma's stories. I have gone seine fishing with Mother and Grandma many times, but with school and all of my other chores, I don't accompany them as often as I used to.

She went on to say, "Carefully fabricated hide and fur clothing was and still is very important as you are well aware. The fur around our hoods had to be thick enough to cover as much of our faces as possible, shielding us from the bitter cold, gusty winds."

Grandma paused, searching my eyes as if she already knew why I really wanted to speak with her. She is extremely perceptive, although she loves to reminisce about the extraordinary experiences of our family. She continued. "And Anji, we always ventured out into the wilderness in groups or with at least one other, because you never know what could happen in the wild. We always carried a pack with food, water, a strong knife and other weapons for protection." Her warm eyes lingered on mine, knowing I am fearless or maybe careless, since I am not always prepared for the unexpected.

"Yes, I understand and I'll be more cautious." I decided to discuss Anya with her to observe her response. "I have a friend named Anya, who I meet with sometimes near a hunting camp in the preserve. She accompanies her papa and uncle on hunting excursions several times a year."

Grandma gazed at me inquisitively. "I know all of the families here in Miki Tarniq and in the nearby villages and I have not heard of Anya. Where does she live?"

"Anya told me that she and her family moved around a lot, staying here and there depending on what provisions they needed. She and her papa have a log cabin somewhere near Pt. Hope.

Grandma searched my eyes and observed my puzzled expression as if she sensed my bewildering dilemma or as if she knew something about Anya that I didn't. "Anji, do you have something to tell me?"

I love talking with her or rather listening to her as she is so delightfully wise and calm. She listens to my questions and concerns and then responds in ways which are meant to coerce me into thinking about my troubles thoroughly and contemplatively, perceiving them from other perspectives in order to find solutions to my problems myself. When I don't get in my own way, I usually figure things out myself, but Grandma gently nudges me in the right direction. I did have more to speak with her about concerning Anya, but not yet. I wanted to have another talk with Anya first. I plan to ask her next time I see her, if she wants to visit and stay here in Miki Tarniq while her papa and uncle hunt. "No, I just wanted to tell you that I have a friend who keeps me company while I'm exploring out in the wilderness, so that you know I'm not always alone."

"Even if you are meeting with a friend out there, you are still venturing out alone and you are still journeying a long way by yourself. What if you slip and fall or what if you happen on a bear or a hungry wolf pack? Can you defend yourself or get away quickly? It is much safer to go with Kaya or your papa."

"I am not afraid of wild animals. You know that all of my life, I have ventured out alone, wandering and exploring. I mean, I have respect for wildlife and the animals seem to have reverence for me, since I don't disturb them and I keep my distance. I am more worried about the human animals that are up to no good in the larger cities. How can I defend myself from them? Grandma, is the world out there safe?"

I sat patiently while she studied me perceptively. She is a lovely, petite woman with silky, white hair that she wears in a long braid down her back and compassionate, mocha eyes. "Again, Anji, you must find someone to accompany you, like a buddy system. You will make friends when you are away at school and you must choose them wisely. The girls that find themselves in risky situations have not taken the time to plan, to consider the consequences of journeying down one path or the other and they make poor decisions. Plan. Use your head. You have a good one." She snickered.

"Okay, I promise I will keep my wits about me. I hope I make friends, since I am different than others are, particularly since I live out here in such a remote environment. I hope I meet others who like people that are uncommon. You are aware that I am usually quite confident and have never cared before what people think of me and that's because I am surrounded by people who are similar to me, but I see the way some of the tourists look at me and it just makes me wonder what they are thinking. Am I pretty at all or just odd looking?" Our family heritage consists of a combination of mostly French Canadian and small percentages of various European people.

"Anji, grasp my words, you are one of the loveliest girls I have ever seen. Your features are strikingly beautiful and if people stare at you, it's because they are taking in your exquisite, rare beauty, not because they are thinking you are odd. Your bronze eyes sparkle with wonder and sunshine, your long sable hair is silky and healthy, you are tall and strong. I know in my heart and soul that you will have no trouble making friends who will probably be envious of you. How will you treat others who are different?"

"I know in my heart that I am a compassionate person and will never treat others unkindly no matter what they look like, unless they try to harm me and then, I will defend myself."

"Okay, good. You must remember this conversation when you are meeting others. You must also remember what ego means. An inflated ego is the worst character trait anyone can have. It makes men self-righteous and controlling and women catty, self-centered and manipulative. Those are the people who have trouble finding real friends. They hold themselves so high up on their own pedestals that they don't realize that people are offended by this mannerism. People soon find that trying to befriend an egotist is too challenging or disappointing, so they give up. Real friends appreciate and respect each other but most importantly, they have a real interest in each other and in what they like and do. They are also true to each other. It's a horrible feeling when someone who you thought was your friend either lies to you or belittles you, refusing to be happy for you when you accomplish something you have worked diligently for. She might criticize you unnecessarily or act uninterested. When this happens, you will feel hurt, cutting you deeply within your heart which may change the way you behave around her and you will keep her away from your interests."

"You are talking about my old friendship with Mara, aren't you?" Grandma nodded. "I wasn't aware that you noticed the change in our relationship. Well, I haven't asked her to visit in a long while and we don't spend time together anymore, not that we ever did share quality time together. Our aloof relationship was always disappointing but I was able to move on, refusing to let her or anyone else have the power to suppress my strengths and creativity. Grandma, I am absolutely okay with constructive criticism like you, Mother and Papa have given me in all of my current and past endeavors. You all have had a real interest in what I've been doing and for that, I am truly grateful. I hope I find a friend while attending college who knows how to care like you do."

"You will. Have faith. And until then, count me as your best friend." She hugged me tightly.

"Oh, Grandma, I love you tremendously. Thank you for your kind and wise words. You are my best friend and I know you will always have my best interests at heart."

I sauntered out of the room with a delighted smile across my face, feeling confident again. I wanted to talk more about Papa's latest concerns, but maybe tomorrow. While in my room listening to Yanni, an extraordinarily gifted new age piano musician, I began thinking about the things I love about living here in Miki Tarniq. I've been reflecting on my life experiences lately, since I will be leaving soon.

With Papa being so worried lately, I'll have to watch the time more closely when I'm out exploring. Kaya likes to explore as well and we often play games when we are out there together. One of my favorites in the spring and summer is seeing who can find the most plant species, which goes along with gathering berries for Mother. I love to collect plants and flowers in the wilderness and often near the river, which I then compare to the genus previously identified. I'm always searching for a new species that has not been recognized yet. I usually bring my camera to take photos of native flowers such as the Parrya nudicaulis, usually called the Naked-stemmed Wallflower, one of my favorites. The flower has beautiful, light pink or purple blooms and often grows among fields of crowberries.

I carry a special woven case in my backpack when I'm out exploring so that I can gather berries, especially black crowberries, a staple food of Alaskans. We call the berries, 'Fruit of the North'. I have been studying the Latin names of plant and floral species so that when I begin my studies at the university, I will already have a head start.

Fascinating Native Alaskan history is embedded in the landscape, so another favorite game is to find buried treasures and depressions of house pits set on the riverbank. Since northwest Alaska is a remote, arctic environment, people had to design the spaces of their homes specifically for necessary functions, such as foraging for plants and herbs, hunting and fishing preparations, storage and tanning of hides and furs to make warm clothing. Our home is designed in the same way since we basically live off the land. I feel like my life has been splendidly enriching and I hope I don't begin to take advantage of it as I move to the lower forty-eight states, where everything needed is purchased at enormous stores.

I swiveled in my puffy, green chair, pondering my future journey. I could feel my face grimace as I thought about my safety among other people in unfamiliar cities. What will I do if I find myself in an uncomfortable situation, alone in a loud, raucous city where malicious strangers might be lurking? I feel distressed that my well-balanced, perfect world might have to change, because I'm not completely sure that I want it to. Can't I go to school in another environment with everything functioning flawlessly and everything continuing to be safe and ideal? Do I have to choose between my quiet, harmonious home and a life in an unsafe chaotic world, out of control?

4

Anji

Even though Kaya is my brother, I also feel that we are good friends. He is a down to earth, real person and would never hesitate to tell me what he thinks, but with caring constructive criticism. He has always shown an interest in what I find fascinating and I likewise. I will talk with him about my concerns, since he will be leaving as well to attend college.

When we are out hunting for berries and herbs for Mother, another game that Kaya likes is searching for caribou hunting lookouts which can be seen if we stay alert, because some of them are marked by cairns on top of mountain ridges or are tall towers. We like to see who finds a lookout first. Papa would scold us harshly if he ever found out that we were near the lookouts, since hunters may be present, tracking caribou, elk or moose and we could be in imminent danger of being in the line of fire. But we are always careful and alert and I like the covert investigative feeling I experience when stealthily searching for something in particular in the dense, shadowy forest.

I have seen Anya standing near the edge of the woodlands or near a lookout and have wanted to go to her, but Kaya doesn't like to bother people while they are out on the hunt. The last time we were out there, he said he didn't see her anyway which I thought was curiously odd, since she was standing there as clear as day, observing us. Kaya said I was imagining things, but I know what I saw and I will prove it when I bring her home soon.

When Kaya goes hunting with Papa, he is always proud to show him a new lookout that we had previously discovered. The largest caribou herd in Alaska, about 490,000, travels through the Noatak Wildlife Preserve during its migration in autumn. Papa and Kaya always bring home caribou when they hunt together, some of the most treasured experiences they share. They both talk about things, revealing their feelings and concerns and with victuals, hides and furs in their packs and sleds, exhausted but happy, they trudge back to the house whistling, singing and laughing. I often catch Mother smiling at them when they are in such joyful, satisfied moods. She loves to see them interacting and taking time to nurture their relationship.

Our family is very close and we all care for and help each other whenever it's needed or wanted. I like to help my family make hide and fur clothing which is necessary in arctic climate, even though I don't like to hunt. I prefer to quietly observe wild animals and snap photos of them for my journals. The animals here in the great northwest are such peaceful, beautiful creatures although, they also like berries and they sometimes eat more than their share, I think, when I arrive at an area where I usually find berries, but there are none.

We harvest berries, roots, herbs and florals and hunt for sheep, moose, elk, caribou, wildfowl and fish. Mother is a tremendous cook and has shown me how to cook delicious recipes such as my favorite, halibut over a bed of spinach and herbs with a scrumptious garlic, lemon sauce drizzled over the top. She also taught me how to cook elk steaks served with spicy apple chutney, fresh greens and savory herb rosemary sweet potatoes. So tasty.

I love to help Mother make chutney and jams, which we store in jars for use throughout the year. A family favorite delicious chutney consists of a savory blend of crowberries or salmon berries, crabapples, spicy peppers, raisins, onions, sage, garlic, cinnamon, and sugar, all boiled down to a thick, scrumptious mixture.

We enjoy wild blueberry, black crowberry or salmonberry jam every morning with breakfast. What brings Papa out of a snoring slumber are Mother's homemade light and flaky biscuits with fireweed honey drizzled over the top. She often cooks caribou sausage and scrambled eggs with her preferred delicious mixture of scallions, herbs and peppers to go with the biscuits. I'm very grateful that Mother is highly skilled at doing so many things. I truly feel that I have learned from the best and will someday be able to provide for myself, my future husband and family.

Papa owns Sauveur Home and Hardware, a hardware, hunting and fishing supply and animal feed store, where he spends most of his time every day. Kaya and I work there after school, helping customers, unpacking boxes, stocking shelves and making deliveries to customers who can't travel easily to and from remote locations. We bundle up the goods on our four wheelers or sleds and off we go, no matter how severe the weather is. When there is snow on the ground, we usually use the sleds, mainly because the dogs love and need the workout and they are very good at navigating through stormy winter conditions. We wrap ourselves up in heavily insulated parkas, gloves and hats with fur edging shielding our faces from the icy winds. The travel is usually quiet and peaceful. When we deliver the goods to our customers, they are so very grateful which makes the journey worth it. Sometimes they give us homemade cookies or other treats and tips for our service which if I'm honest, is another reason I'm willing to go during the frigid winter, when I'd rather bundle up in a blanket in our cozy home in front of the blazing wood stove.

Mother is a gentle calm soul and has a lovely, kind face and warm, chocolate eyes. Her silky-smooth, ebony hair is hip length with white streaks at her temples. She usually wears the front pulled back at each side, joined with a beaded leather clip. I think she looks like a hippie and I tell her this often which makes her giggle. She is highly skilled at creating not only fur coats but also incredibly beautiful quilts, pottery, mukluks, fur hats and gloves. I work with her on the weekends to help her fill her orders. She sells her finely crafted goods in Papa's shop in the household and gift section. Many tourists and villagers visit the marvelous shop and to my infinite delight, they love her creations. She is extremely meticulous and will never sell anything that is not absolutely perfect.

We have several quilts that I made while I was learning that did not meet her expectations, but my work is much better now after years of practice. Mother helped me understand how to have patience and to sew slowly and carefully. Quilting can be really calming and therapeutic but sometimes, the work can be tedious and aggravating. That's when I have to step away and go do something else for a while.

My favorite quilt that lays atop my bed has beautiful patterns of flowers, such as Lupine, Wildfire Weed, Forget-me-not, which is the Alaska state flower, Bunchberry, Douglas Aster, Salmonberry and Monkshood. Monkshood is a tall plant with slim stems and beautiful blue blossoms, but is extremely poisonous. It has been used throughout history to poison wolves or enemies in earlier times. I can't help but wonder if it could be used to defend ourselves from the criminals who we are dealing with currently. I suddenly felt devious and my eyes narrowed as I pictured myself taking the criminals down singlehandedly. The neurotoxins, aconitine and mesaconitine can be absorbed through the skin causing severe respiratory and cardiac concerns. If I see the plant, I don't dare touch it with bare hands, but I have studied the flower thoroughly, describing it in my journals. The flower print on fabric is gorgeous, so I also included it in my quilt.

I began to daydream about my desired study of botany when Papa knocked on my bedroom door. "Anji?

I'd like to prepare you for our trip tomorrow to speak with the government officials." I opened the door and went out to the living room with him where we sat down to discuss what was on his mind.

"Oh, I'm so happy that you are letting me go with you. I'm not a naïve little girl anymore, you know."

"I do realize that, but I still have concerns about your getting involved. Kaya is also coming and I want you both to stay quiet and listen to what is discussed without interrupting until the end of the meeting. Then you can ask questions, but try to stay calm and speak with confidence so that the representatives will believe that you are capable of helping without putting yourselves in harm's way. They will most likely want you to work with others to help train young people to be aware and alert to suspicious behavior, especially since teenagers often plan field trips to Anchorage." Feelings of apprehension returned.

"Papa, have you observed strange men engaged in suspicious, criminal behavior causing you to be so concerned?"

"No, but after receiving such a puzzling message from spirits in the northern lights, I was prompted to research what has been going on lately and have been disturbed to find out about the growing sex trafficking problem in our state. I have not seen or heard any reports of missing girls here in Miki Tarniq nor in the Inupiat villages, but I want to help keep the people of Alaska safe from these heinous criminals. We cannot allow them to destroy our lives and families resulting in an unsafe environment. I plan to help arrange a watch program including our dogs, which will patrol as much of our

29

territory as possible. We will organize hunting expeditions where our hunters will also be scouting for undesirable people who may be surveying our territory with malicious intentions. If we encounter such criminals, it could be very dangerous for everyone involved. The watch program is one of the main topics we will be discussing."

I pondered what he said. "Are the women of the lower forty-eight states and Canada facing problems with traffickers as well?"

He looked distraught and his charcoal brows lifted. "Yes, people from all villages and territories are in danger of these despicable predators causing harm but for now, we will be focusing on the safety of the people here in Alaska. We will however, be communicating with the governments of all U.S. cities as well as those in Canadian territories."

I wanted to reduce the tension Papa was unintentionally causing, so I reached over and hugged him which immediately softened his exasperated demeanor. "Papa, your fierce dedication to the well-being of our Alaskan people is encouraging and your unwavering faith that the people can work together as a team to protect each other is truly remarkable. I have faith in you to help organize and work through this monumental task."

He breathed in deeply and his warm, earthy eyes lingered on mine. "Thank you, Anji. This is merely the beginning of a long but significant, arduous journey. No Alaskan family can throw caution to the wind. The dark, heartless, soulless beings in this world are too numerous to count, although we can surely send them a message."

I smiled enthusiastically. "Yes, we certainly can."

We talked a bit more and then he left me to think about what we discussed. I was eager to assist in protecting the young people of Alaska and yet, appalled at the same time. How should I feel? I mean Alaska is the last U.S. Great Frontier. Why would anyone want to disturb such a beautiful, pristine environment and the people here? And why are criminals targeting the Native people? I am, if I'm being honest, afraid, not only of these horrible men abducting girls, but also of the possible destruction of our lovely, unspoiled environment. I don't want to have to walk around looking over my shoulder, living with the fear that some shady person might grab me from behind and toss me into his vehicle, never to be seen again. I just cannot allow myself to live with such miserable anxiety and stress.

I thought of Anya, roaming around the wilderness alone while her father hunted. I wander around exploring often, so I guess it's not much different for her, but I think it's strange that she is always there unaccompanied. I have never seen or heard anyone else near-by when we are hiking together. Why does her papa go so far away, leaving her by herself for many long hours? I just cannot understand this. Doesn't he get worried about her? There are hungry wolves and bears out there that might see that she is alone and vulnerable. I suddenly agreed with Papa and Grandma about the concerns of wandering around alone.

I realized I was daydreaming, but then I recalled the seriousness in Papa's face. I will consider what he said earnestly. My thoughts have been all over the board lately, mostly challenged with concerns of living safely when I leave, without the added stress of some creep robbing me of my freedom and well-being.

Maybe I am letting fear take over my normally confident state of mind, but it is concerning that according to Papa, sex crimes occur everywhere. Oh, balderdash! This is horrible. Why can't the governments of our country stop this malevolence from occurring? I guess I have been sheltered from the harsh realities of the world for too long. I just want to pretend that these types of problems don't exist like many other people do, which is probably why sex crimes are rampant. People aren't dealing with the issue at all it seems.

Well, I do feel safe here at home. Miki Tarniq has a small airplane landing strip, which is the only way to get here other than by snowmobiles or ATVs from other remote cities or by river vessels, therefore it's fairly difficult to get to. However, many people fly into Kotzebue, then arrange travel by wilderness planes which might be why Papa is concerned.

Miki Tarniq and some of the Inupiat villages such as Noatak have become quite popular for outdoor enthusiasts, who come to the area to enjoy back-country experiences. Alaska Airlines stops in Kotzebue bringing in tourists from all over the world who then travel to the remote places of northwest Alaska for outdoor sport activities. Many people who visit remote villages enjoy learning about the Native Alaskans and how they live. I enjoyed reading a book called, *What The Elders Have Taught Us, Alaska Native Ways*, written by Natives of Alaska, which describes various native tribes and how they lived in Alaska's magnificent, yet harsh and often frigid, unforgiving environment.[1] Our Inupiat friends taught us their compassionate ways of showing respect to others, honoring our elders, accepting what life brings and sharing what we have. But accepting what life brings couldn't possibly mean that we shouldn't figure out how to prevent malicious criminals from harming us.

Anyway, I'm going to have to learn how to deal with a new life in a raucous, disorderly environment when I go away to school. Knowing my family will continue to reside in Miki Tarniq gives me some comfort and I appreciate that I can always go home if things don't work out as I hope.

5

Anji

I love Papa dearly even though he is stubbornly planted with steadfast convictions which is admirable, but I sometimes worry about him. He has the courage of a lion and never hesitates to handle dangerous situations by himself, if protecting his family and friends is his major concern. He does ask for help from friends and neighbors if the problem is too challenging for him to handle alone, thankfully.

When he senses something like he did while connecting with the spirits of the northern lights, he continues to stay focused on the problem until he finds his resolve. Papa likes the same everyday routines, chores, taking care of the dogs and respecting each other no matter what happens. He worries about our safety around unknown people. We are at one with the wildlife and coexist in harmony with them but tourists, whom we rely on to some extent each year, may be a different story if there really are some who are up to no good. I hope his apprehensions turn out to be unfounded, but only time will tell.

Tourists contract bush pilots, rent boats, pay for fish filleting and icing services, buy fish and wild game permits, rent storage, contract tanning services and they purchase other necessities, souvenirs and memoirs. I personally really like the tourists, because I like to observe them and analyze their behaviors and notice what they find interesting and exciting. I suspect they do the same when they meet people living in remote environments, since we are quite different than they are in so many ways.

I have found that most of the visitors who come here for remote adventures, expect to see us living like the people did in the old days of yesteryear, toiling with fishing seines, skinning and tanning hides, running dog sleds, living in igloos and wearing mukluks and parkas with a piece of raw fish in our hands. Much of that still does describe people here, but we also wear blue jeans, tee shirts, ball caps and colorful jackets just like they do and we live in houses similar to their own. Even though our diet consists mainly of fish, wild game and natural vegetation, we also enjoy eating foods from other cultures, such as Russian cuisine, East Asian and foods from many other countries, just like others do.

I prefer the company of people who just enjoy taking in the natural beauty of Alaska's Wilderness, the fresh air and luxuriant serenity that many don't usually experience in their everyday lives. I've noticed that some folks are in such a hurry to reach their destinations, they forget to experience the invaluable journey. I find that sad and quite pathetic, even though I admit that I sometimes hurry through a project or a chore without attempting to gain something from the task.

Papa has made it quite known that he wants to help the Alaskan government deal with the sex trafficking dilemma and they seem to be receptive to his dedicated interest in assisting them. Papa showed me a report from Adrienne Tucker, a case manager at Priceless Alaska, a non-profit organization which has assisted about 140 women and girls after being trafficked.

I was shocked and appalled to see the numbers and wondered how many more victims there may be, cases that have not been reported. Papa observed my startled expression and looked away with a scowl on his solemn, weathered face, appearing so troubled that he seemed to have aged another ten years within a few seconds. And then I recalled the way he kneeled down, praying to the spirits of the northern lights, begging for clarity. Now that Papa has expressed his concerns, I'm worried as well. Maybe it's true that since the northern lights displayed such an enigmatic demonstration as they did earlier this morning, there may be trouble ahead. Is there some truth in that or was it merely a mysterious coincidence that the animated lights seized our attention with such intensity? Papa said that the spirits didn't reveal exactly what the concern was and never did and yet, he absolutely believed he was receiving a significant message and that it was his task to find out what the concern is and what he must do.

He explained that in the report, Tucker stated that Alaska's main industries, tourism, fishing, hunting, mining and oil drilling make Alaska particularly vulnerable to sex trafficking. She said that trafficking is a growing problem throughout the state, but it's especially a problem for women and girls from rural communities. "Alaska Native women and girls make up the biggest client population at Priceless."[2] Priceless Alaska is an organization set up to help trafficked victims.

Papa said that specifically there had been reports of traffickers lurking around in Anchorage, abducting young women and forcing them to work on the streets. He said one of their techniques is to keep the girls drugged until they are hooked so that they continue to sell their bodies in exchange for more drugs to feed their habits. I shivered at the thought. I have never tried drugs and have absolutely no interest in them, since they have the ability to cloud the mind and suppress one's ability to think rationally. Many people have allowed themselves to fall victim to drugs and alcohol which destroyed their lives, but Papa is extremely strict with us. No drugs or alcohol are allowed in our home at any time.

Papa is the type of man who contemplates for hours, considering every angle, every possibility and means for something to take place. "You must protect your sisters and stay together. If you need something from the market, either we all go or I go alone and you must always keep Kodiak and Nukalik nearby." I understood his rage and disgust.

Kodiak and Nukalik are our lead Malamutes on our dog teams. They are very loyal, protective dogs. We have a wood fence surrounding the area where we keep them, which also surrounds the front and back doors of our home. In this way, the dogs can defend us if a wrongdoer or a wild animal tries to get too close to the house. The dogs stay in a heated barn where we also keep our dog food storage and water troughs so that they stay warm and always have what they need. Papa and Kaya run the dogs every day to keep them fit and like I mentioned earlier, I often run them as well, especially if I'm headed to the market for goods.

There are so many things that I have planned to do this winter, but the first thing on my list is to attend the meeting with Papa and Kaya. To prepare myself, I read several articles online about the sex trafficking of American Natives and about VAWA tribal grant program statutes. Basically, I read that Tribal organization leaders and the federal government have identified the importance of addressing human trafficking, including sex trafficking, and highlighting measures such as providing victim services and training law enforcement and other professionals on identifying and responding properly to victims.

After reading the articles, I have to admit I'm terrified even though I am not a First Nations Native Alaskan. I suddenly realized that since I am a young woman, it's possible that I might find myself exposed to dangerous criminals and should be just as careful as other girls have to be. I snarled in disgust. I just can't believe that we are having to deal with this atrocious sex trafficking issue at all. I felt my eyes well up as I thought about my friends who live in various villages. I prayed for their safety as well as my own, especially while visiting crowded public places in the larger cities.

I know we will need the help of many people who are devoted to the cause and I began to wonder who they might be. We flew to Kotzebue this morning and I have been searching online for information at an internet café, while Papa and Kaya pick up supplies. I researched the sex trafficking dilemma, organizations who help girls who were abducted, training information and editorials about people who have been helping in various ways. I found an interesting article about a woman named Grace Nadeau, who takes in young women at her safe haven ranch in the Yukon Territory, Canada. I couldn't take victims in, but I thought maybe I could at least help some of the girls who have been abducted find assistance, hopefully before it's too late.

I'm not wasting any time. Papa taught me to take action if I am really determined to do something. To offer encouragement, Papa often says, "Those who think they can, will accomplish something," a valued notion that he learned from a wise Inupiat friend. I immediately started typing an email to her.

Dear Miss Nadeau,

My name is Anji Sauveur and I live in Miki Tarniq, Alaska. My family and I are joining in the fight against sex trafficking, but I'm not quite sure how to get involved yet. My Papa, Ethan is taking my brother, Kaya and me to meet with some representatives of the Alaskan government, where there will be in-depth discussions concerning the safety of the young women of our state. He would like for me to help train young people to be alert and observant to malicious, criminal behavior and how to protect each other, but I want to help much more.

I plan to attend college next year, but I'm concerned

about leaving while our people are facing such a dangerous predicament. I also have two sisters, Alina, sixteen and Joie, fifteen years young, that I'm very concerned about. I have always looked after them and of course, my mother, Hana and Papa will continue to take care of them as they always have. But what I'm asking you for is advice on other ways to help and also, to find out how I might find people to assist us in locating and arresting these criminals. Do you know professional people who might be able to come to Alaska to lend us a hand before it's too late?

With a grateful heart,
Anji Sauveur

I tried to occupy my time by doing more research while impatiently waiting for a response. I was sure she was a very busy woman, but I was very hopeful and for some reason, I felt positive about her even though I had never met her. Just a feeling.

6

Grace Nadeau was sitting by the wood stove enjoying a hot cup of orange spice tea while reading news articles on her laptop. Hope Ranch, a warm, compassionate home for women in need, in Whitehorse, Yukon Territory was receiving a deluge of snow, which was piling up around the lodge and ranch cabins. Icy winds were propelling through the evergreens and out onto the open spaces of the ranch creating a whiteout condition. Whitehorse, sitting on the edge of the Yukon River and located at the base of three nearby mountains; Grey Mountain to the east, Mount Sumanik to the northwest and Golden Horn Mountain to the south, sometimes receives gusty, winter Chinook winds and frigid temperatures. Normally, the weather in

Whitehorse is moderate and Grace loves the mountain views never taking for granted how lucky she was to have been able to design and build the ranch on such beautiful, sought-after land. But today, she could barely see the mountain tops through the swirling, blinding snow.

An email alert popped up on her screen. The email was titled, a letter from Anji. "Hmmm", she said to herself. Intrigued, Grace opened the email and began reading. As she read, her heart began pounding furiously as she recollected her past experience with the malicious sex traffickers who cheated her out of ten years of her life. She sprung from her cozy lounge chair, trembling and suddenly feeling enraged. Grace had been involved with helping young women recover from tragic situations for many years without their horrifying stories affecting her personally, but it was just the way Anji worded the letter that reached deeply into her heart and soul. She was asking for help to protect her family, friends and the young women of Alaska and to take down despicable, loathsome criminals before it's too late for too many.

She briskly walked up to Sarah's lodge room and knocked on the door. Sarah Beaulieu, a dear friend of Grace had been staying at the ranch since the end of December last year to recuperate from an emotionally, strenuous year of driving around the U.S., bravely rescuing young women who had been abducted and trafficked. Grace herself was abducted from a nightclub in Edmonton, Alberta, Canada, separating the two women for thirty-nine years. Finally reunited, the two have been enjoying each other's company and getting reacquainted. Sarah loves the ranch and has been relishing the feeling of having a beautiful, tranquil place to call home after being relatively homeless for most of her adult life, preferring to live in her RV in order to be ready to go at a moment's notice. When Grace was kidnapped, Sarah decided to make it her life's work to search for her and to rescue as many unfortunate victims of traffickers as possible.

"Sarah? I'd like to speak with you right away. I'm afraid it's an urgent matter."

"Oh, yeah, sure. I was just finishing up with some research. Come in."

"I just received a letter from a young girl, who lives in Miki Tarniq, Alaska." She showed Sarah the letter.

Sarah gasped, "Oh, no! I've been following the news about the absolutely, heinous sex trafficking dilemma concerning Canadian and Alaskan Natives and I've also been trying to plan how I might begin to help. So now, it looks like maybe I have a place to start."

"I want to go with you to help in any way possible. Lorraine, Claire and Jasmine will be able to take care of things around here until I return." Lorraine Dubois is a French-Canadian woman, who is a partner with Grace at Hope Ranch and Claire LaFlore is an assistant to Grace and Lorraine, helping with just about everything at the ranch. Jasmine was one of the girls who was abducted, rescued and brought to Hope Ranch by Sarah last year. Jasmine helps the girls who come to the ranch, adjust to their new home environment. The girls stay at the ranch as long as they need to, usually until they feel safe enough to return to public life. Some of the women have preferred to stay and work at the ranch, at least for a while as Jasmine has. Jasmine was abducted from the Philippines, along with a group of girls who hoped to find the U.S. a new exciting country to live and work in. None of them even considered that their safety would be compromised as soon as they boarded the ship. They all believed the devious men who promised they would find good jobs and homes and would have never imagined that the terrifying, abusive lives they were forced into was a possibility. When Sarah rescued her and eleven others, Jasmine decided she wanted to stay and help other young women, who regrettably fall victim to such violent, malicious criminals and who do not wish to return to their home countries.

Sarah said with heartfelt concern, "Oh, Grace, I don't know. You remember how I explained that I get directly involved, sometimes in dangerous situations when I find these criminals, don't you? Well, I believe if I let you come with me, I would be putting you in harm's way."

"Sarah, you are so protective of me but really, you don't need to worry to such an extent. Look around. I have endured many hardships and challenges including building this ranch, caring for the girls and keeping them and the ranch safe for many years. I want to help Anji and the people of Alaska. Anyway, it's high time you stopped working alone."

"Well, Anji did find you and probably wants to meet you." She hesitated. "Okay, maybe we could fly to Anchorage, get a feel for the current criminal climate and work out the travel details from there. We'll figure out how to assist Anji and her family as we go along. Write her back, introduce me and tell her that we want to help. Find out when they will be back from the meeting and how they are planning to get involved. Let her know that we would like to sit down with Ethan and strategize."

"Yes! I hoped you'd come around. I have wanted to travel to Northwest Alaska for years. I planned at one time to take some girls on a rafting trip down the Noatak River, but had to cancel to help some girls who were brought to me by a woman who works with PACT-Ottawa. Okay, I'll write to her now and let you know what her response is." PACT-Ottawa, Persons Against the Crime of Trafficking in Humans is the Canadian organization which helps to prevent human trafficking and protects trafficked persons.

Sarah said, "I'm going to call Dakota and talk with him about this. If the Alaskan authorities are just in the planning stages of a new mission, maybe that would give us a few months for the darkness and severe winter weather to change. I remember Dakota mentioning that FBI Agent Dirk Hays wanted the team to work mainly in the north-western states for a few months and that he had also been researching the trafficking problem in Alaska."

Private Detective Dakota Hunt and his trucker task force team, comprising mainly of veteran military and retired police officers, have been working with the FBI, hunting and tracking sex traffickers all over the U.S. quite successfully in the past few years. Grace's fiancé, Jake Losato, who works with Dakota and the team, also has a cabin in the Yukon Territory not far from Hope Ranch. Jake had visited and helped out at the ranch for a couple of weeks in the beginning of January before returning to work. Dakota and the team have plans to work in both Canada and Alaska in late spring when trucks can more easily traverse the Alcan and other highways into mainland Alaska. Dakota has been extremely concerned with the specific targeting of Native Americans by sex traffickers and has studied reports which state that the crimes have escalated in the past decade to a crisis state of affairs.

Knowing that Dakota was planning to help, Sarah wanted to inform him about the letter from Anji as soon as possible.

She looked up his cell number and called him. After a few rings, he answered. "Dakota Hunt."

"Hey, Dakota. This is Sarah. How are you?"

"Well, hello Sarah. It's so good to hear from you, although I'll have to call you back later. We've been up to our eyeballs in criminal tracking work lately and we're currently pursuing a gang of traffickers who were observed lurking around the Colorado college areas. We discovered that they picked up some girls from one of the local bars near one of the universities. Reports have been flooding in about the missing girls and a description of the vehicle was reported by some of the bar patrons. The Colorado highway patrol has several roadblocks in place and we're planning to take them down any minute now. I'll ring you after this plays out."

"Oh, good luck and be careful." They ended the call and Sarah repeated what he said to Grace.

Grace frowned. "No kidding. I sure hope they catch them. Sarah, I just received an email back from Anji. She's excited that we want to help. She said that she will talk with Ethan and get back to me when they return from the meetings."

Sarah gasped. "Alaska currently has the help of the FBI, who is working to identify traffickers and victims and hopefully will make an impact, but I'm furious. I have to figure out how to help as usual, without being detected. The authorities don't tolerate private citizens being directly involved other than to help the victims once they are rescued but you know me, I seem to figure out how to take the varmints down myself when I have to. I'm going to do some more research on the situation in Anchorage and will come up with a plan."

Sarah prefers to work incognito rather than signing on with the authorities. She is considered a vigilante, flying just below the radar and is a master of disguises in order to rescue the girls to get them to safe havens and to avoid deportation for the women who have been abducted and trafficked from other countries. She sometimes does things that are not quite lawful. On several occasions, she injected the criminals with Ketamine, an animal tranquilizer, in order to render the perverts helpless until the authorities arrived to take them into custody, which allowed her to escape with the girls.

Two hours later, Dakota called Sarah back. "Got 'em! Two of our truckers and four police cars pinned the perps in so that they couldn't escape. They arrested the perps and found four teenage girls in the vehicle. The girls were drugged and bruised probably from resisting their captors. I'm furious but once again, I'm pleased that we were able to help round up traffickers and prevent the young women from experiencing a devastating fate."

"Dakota, you and your team are exactly what both the U.S. and Canada needs, courageous, determined people all working together to take as many sex traffickers down as possible." She told him about the letter that Grace received and asked him if they could talk with Dirk about having the team work in the Alaska mainland soon.

"I think the best way to find these criminals is to have more people out scouting, driving around day and night to see what lurks in the shadows. Since you guys have to be out at all times of the day and night with your deliveries, I'm sure you see things that most people don't."

"I have mentioned to Dirk that we want to be able to help in Alaska as early as spring. He has several of our teams working near the Canadian border crossings now. Two of my team members, Mack and Chris, have been staking out an area in Montana and two others, Jake and Zach, are working in Seattle and Vancouver. As I'm sure you are aware, the State of Washington has 13 drivable border crossings across the 427-mile border with British Columbia, Canada. The busiest crossings are the four that serve the Seattle -Vancouver area. There are about 32,000 vehicles that cross the Washington border every day, which pass through the Peace Arch, Blaine Surrey, Lynden or Sumas ports. The ports are usually very congested, making it difficult to recognize suspicious vehicles. I recall you telling me that Grace and the other women who were abducted at the same time from Edmonton, were transported in an RV. I can see that RV's might be difficult to detain if all of the people in the vehicles have passports and since so many people tour both countries via RV travel." Dakota paused and cleared his throat, feeling disgusted.

"Jake and Zach have been busy picking up and delivering loads locally within those areas, because unfortunately, there have been more reports of missing women in both Seattle and Vancouver. While passing an SUV, Jake saw a woman put her hand flat up on the window and looked right at him with wide, frightened eyes. He said he felt the hairs stand up on his neck and called the authorities immediately, giving them a description of the vehicle. He couldn't track them because he had to exit I -5 right at that moment. He's waiting to hear if they caught the driver and so on."

Sarah was exasperated. "I sure hope they caught up to them and were able to help the woman. God, that makes me angry. Well, let me know what Dirk says and please don't tell him that I'm going to be involved in helping Anji and her family, at least not yet. I plan to fly into Anchorage, scout around a bit, then on to Kotzebue and a bush plane from there. I hope to discuss a plan with Ethan as soon as they return from the meeting. Oh, and Grace wants to go. I don't know how Jake will feel about that since he's as protective of her as I am, but I don't see a problem at this time. This is just a preliminary meeting. We will tour around the area, meet the family and other locals if possible and find out what information they may have."

Dakota asked, "Did Grace talk with Jake about this? I mean as you said, her going now may not be concerning but when you get more involved, he might strongly object."

Sarah sighed. "My feelings exactly. I don't have a death wish, but I'm quite fearless as you know and I plan to the tee. I could use the help if something goes awry, but I'm not so sure that it should be Grace. I'm sure she will talk with Jake about it if she hasn't already."

"Well, call me back when you know more and I'll talk with Dirk." They ended the call.

Sarah called Trevor, her computer expert cohort and asked him to do some research on all of the abductions and stories that have been published about women who have gone missing in Alaska as well as where the abductions occurred. Trevor assists Sarah with all sorts of things such as navigation, providing the locations of perpetrators, sometimes planting tracking devices when they locate the offenders and researching the backgrounds of known criminals while she is out on the road. They work as a team also locating safe homes for the women Sarah rescues.

She thought of Anji which instantly triggered her memory of Grace's disappearance so many years ago. She sat still with watery eyes transfixed on a scenic screensaver on her computer.. She wanted to take down as many traffickers as possible and knew she would have to stay focused in order to strategize efficiently. She dried her tears with her sleeve and began planning.

7

Anji

I realize I have been thrust into circumstances in life that I cannot control. I don't know how to feel about having to deal with an evil social problem such as sex trafficking, which seems to have just crashed into my perfect, comfortable world of love, peace and harmony. Endless concerning thoughts have been spinning around in my head like a record set on repeat. My stomach was completely tied in knots as we prepared for the meeting.

Papa, Kaya and I boarded our plane and flew to Kotzebue. When we arrived at the meeting hall, the representatives were quietly getting settled around a conference table. The mood in the room was sullen with grim expressions displayed and boy did I understand their sentiments.

A state official stood, introduced himself and began the discussion. "We are here today to deliberate on a heinous issue that requires immediate action. We have the support of the U.S. government and as you are all aware, the FBI currently has several task force teams working to help the people of Alaska track these sex criminals that intend on harming our children. However, we must act fearlessly and aggressively to end this odious targeting of our native people. I have come up with a plan to recruit as many men as possible in all authoritative sectors to be alert to the movements of hunters, fisherman, shipping port workers and other tourists who arrive and depart our cities and villages. Every plane, ship and boat will be searched upon arrival and departure to make sure there are no possible victims being held and transported against their will.

I realize that this a colossal task, but we must be relentless with our dedication to this heinous dilemma. The second plan is to have our hunters out there hunting for the criminals. All of our local pilots, who normally fly sportsmen out to remote areas and especially on to Anchorage, should be interviewed and educated on what to look out for. If any of these pilots seem to express odd or suspicious behaviors, they should be reported and they and their criminal cohorts should be restricted from flying until thorough investigations determine whether they are guilty of such crimes. I'd like to get all pilots flying in and out of our cities to agree to assist us, especially if they suspect other pilots of such mannerisms." Nods of approval and words of agreement filled the room.

The representative continued. "Of course, educating

our families is first and foremost. Our children, teens and young women could end up falling victim to these criminals who may pose as someone who, for instance needs help, asks for directions, invites one of our young ones to accompany him or her to some location for money, drugs and so on." He sat down so that others could speak.

Papa stood, introduced himself and nodded to the others. I am Ethan Sauveur and as most of you know, my family and I have resided peacefully and respectfully in Miki Tarniq for generations. My family and I owe everything to the Native Alaskans, who for almost a hundred years have shared their knowledge, experiences and necessary skills with us so that we could learn to survive in such a wild, harsh environment. We have been accepted and respected and we, likewise. For these reasons, we want to help in every way possible. I have been sharing information with my teens concerning the atrocious sex trafficking dilemma the people of our state are facing. I have instructed my family to stay together in public areas, specifically during crowded functions and events. They are being educated on what to look out for, especially in Anchorage where corrupt, criminal activity is rampant." He nodded again to the group, receiving smiles and nods in return.

The representatives from Kotzebue each voiced their opinions, ideas and strategies which somewhat comforted the others since they all surmised that Kotzebue could be a major problem, considering airplanes and water vessels containing people and cargo come and go continuously. One of the representatives said, "Reports have proven that young women have been abducted in Anchorage, forced into prostitution and some were found to have been severely abused and even murdered."

Another representative asked, "So how are our children getting there and why are they left alone, providing a means to their vulnerability? These are the questions we must consider and discuss. Are there unsuspected people assisting the criminals? Are there pilots, shipping and tour companies who may be receiving money to be a part of this monstrous activity? We all know that drugs and alcohol play a role in corrupt activity. We must all look inward as well, see and understand our families, especially our teens, to make sure that they do not fall for the lure of drugs or promises of a good job from people they don't know and so forth. We must always accompany our children when in populated public places, protect them and never leave them unattended. I realize that isn't always easy, especially with our teenagers who want to spend time with their friends unchaperoned, but until we make a positive impact on the crisis at hand, this is what is required."

Others agreed and spoke with concern, all ready to fight back. The discussions continued for several more hours moving to Anchorage as a focal point. I raised my hand to express my concerns about attending the colleges in Alaska. "I want to help in every way that I can, but I can't help feeling concerned about the amount of trafficking going on in Anchorage. Should I attend another university in the lower forty-eight states, at least until sex trafficking declines in Anchorage?"

Papa observed me with a concerned expression. "Anji makes a good point, but we should not have to live our lives in fear. We must also understand that people are being targeted in every state in our country. As much as I would like for my children to attend schools near-by, I am open to the discussion about other options. Anji, we will talk about this when we return to Miki Tarniq."

A woman from another small city spoke. "My son and daughter also express interests in attending other universities in the lower forty-eight states. I think that they will receive a broader education if they attend a major university elsewhere, mainly because they have not experienced other environments. They have already compiled research on other schools, so I'd be happy to suggest that they forward their findings to you, if you approve."

Papa smiled and regarded her appreciatively, "That would be helpful, thank you."

I had not mentioned my interest in attending other schools to Papa yet, but I was delighted that it might now be easier to approach the subject since it was brought up at the meeting.

A woman with a seriously concerned expression asked, "Are our traditional festivals safe to attend? We should take precautions to protect each other during such popular events." Alaska offers several yearly festivals and tourist events celebrating its rich history which include entertainment groups performing songs and dances, often wearing ancient costumes. Our family attends as many as we can, mainly out of respect and as a social means to enjoy the company of our friends. I frowned at the woman's concerning words, realizing that wicked criminals could disrupt our joyous lives in so many ways and I felt more determined than ever to help.

One of the Kotzebue representatives responded with a smile. "I believe that we should honor and attend all of our traditional functions without fear, but we should also take extra precautions such as grouping together, forming strict buddy systems, maybe even arming ourselves and so on. My grandson is racing in the Iditarod this year, which as we are all aware, kicks off in Anchorage. Our family and friends are planning to group together for safety, but I think it's wise to meet with the authorities in Anchorage concerning the safety of our women and children during such an event. Major public events and festivals are most likely prime targets for these traffickers."

A plan was drafted to speak with the representatives of the state, the city of Anchorage, event committee representatives, as well as the security team for the Iditarod. All of the representatives agreed that teams of clandestine spies including local authorities, scouting around on a rotating schedule was crucial. The scouting work would be implemented immediately and would take place in hunting and fishing areas, import-export harbors, tourist areas, shopping malls, bars and popular nightclubs and in the high crime sectors of larger cities.

After the meeting, Papa, Kaya and I headed to a previously booked hotel room to rest for the night. The next day, we scouted around Kotzebue together, keeping our eyes peeled for mischievous behavior while shopping for supplies on our list. We visited with the bush plane and helicopter companies, speaking to as many of the pilots as we could, hoping for some sympathetic resolve.

Ethan again recalled the feeling he had while observing the northern lights display a few days earlier.

He felt certain that he would be led to a suspicious group or person who might be in on corrupt activity, but he also felt deeply within his soul that something else or someone else was calling for his attention. Even though he felt perplexed, he sensed that he would soon discover who needed his assistance.

After visiting with the fourth small air travel company, we spoke with Wily Johns, the owner of a bush flight operation who seemed dreadfully shady. He informed us that he leased tour plane space at his hangar to several customers who were based out of Anchorage. He said he didn't have much information about his clients, only that they would check in several times a year with hunting or fishing parties. Papa explained his concerns and asked the owner to make sure that he observed who boarded and deplaned and to watch out for young girls who may be in their company and who did not arrive with them. The man was not cooperative, explaining that whoever boarded or deplaned a private aircraft was not his concern. Papa stared at him with wild fury and shouted, "It would be your concern if they intended on kidnapping your daughter!" The man just sat there with a scowl on his face, not saying a word.

I whirled around and held the nasty man's eyes with an angry glare, appalled by his genuine lack of concern. The man's teeth were stained brown and the foul stench of his body odor hung in the air. I had never met someone who I felt so completely repulsed by and I couldn't imagine how he stayed in business.

As I turned away from the creep, I noticed Anya outside of the window, appearing as if she was trying to tell me something. I wondered what she was doing there and if maybe she knew this man. I thought it might soon be time to discuss her with Papa. I excused myself and ran outside to talk with her but to my surprise, she was nowhere in sight. She is so mysteriously elusive, I thought and again I wondered why she might have been at the shady bush pilot's office. I decided to make a note every time I saw Anya, when, where and during what events, because it seemed distressingly obvious that she was in some kind of trouble.

I was afraid that if I spoke about Anya, Papa and Kaya would think I was letting my imagination take over my normally sensible mind because no one else had seen her, not yet anyway. I would discuss it with Papa later, maybe when I had a chance to bring her home for a visit and then Anya could explain her situation. I thought maybe she could introduce her family to Papa and they would become friends, go hunting together and she could stay safely with me while they were away.

I moseyed back into the airplane hangar to join Papa. While he was speaking with the strange man, all of a sudden, the hairs stood up on my neck and arms. I noticed the man's shifty eyes and when he spoke, I recoiled from his foul, sour breath. This is not a good man and he is obviously up to something suspicious. I wondered if Papa had the same feeling. Was this disgusting, dubious man the reason Anya was there? She must be keeping an eye on him and delving into his affairs as well but if she wants to help, why does she take off when I try to go to her? I thought about this and realized that so far, Anya has only talked with me in private. Maybe she is afraid of being recognized by someone who might want to harm her, so she has to conceal her identity, but in any case she must need my help. I inhaled deeply and whispered to myself, "What an enigma."

We left the building and drove immediately to the police station. Papa informed the officer on duty about Wily Johns and the disturbing conversation that took place. Papa requested that he and his business be immediately put on a watch list. He also reviewed the highlights of the meeting with officer Nicholas Atka, who has been a friend of Papa's for many years and who also attends government meetings regularly. Papa presented the plan that all tour, import and export crafts at the airports and shipping ports should be under thorough scrutiny. Officer Atka said, "Thanks for checking him out. I will definitely keep an eye on him and will make regular visits. In fact, I think I'll pay him a visit right now while it's fresh in his mind in case he thinks we aren't gravely sincere."

Kaya noticed the fearful, concerned expression on my face, so while walking to the shops for supplies, he put his arm around me and said, "I'll look after you, don't worry. We'll all stick together." Kaya has kind, mocha eyes, shoulder length, straight, black hair and is over six feet tall with a muscular build. He has always protected Alina, Joie and me and I love and respect him for that. He went on to say, "Last year, I led twelve hunting parties with Inuksuk and we did not see or feel any kind of hostile intent from the men. I will be on my guard this year and will make sure that my hunting parties are tracked and observed until they leave." Inuksuk is a sincere, confident young man and has been Kaya's good friend for many years.

"Good idea, Kaya." Papa smiled at him. "Most of

the hunters fly to Kotzebue for their connecting flights and then on to Anchorage, which makes it almost impossible to hide a person, but if they book with a shady bush pilot who flies them on to other remote places, they could easily smuggle someone on board and transfer them to a boat or fly on to another city. We must catch or prevent them from having any success at all."

Papa paused to gather his thoughts. "I have been meaning to discuss something with you for a while and now that you are young adults, the time is right. You both are good kids and so far, I have not observed you having an interest in drinking alcohol, but if you should be tempted, please come to me first to discuss the consequences. You will be exposed to it when you go off to college. When people get drunk, they aren't careful and alert to their surroundings and may not notice suspicious people who may be there to harm them. Possibly one of the main reasons young women and men were abducted was because they were drunk or high on drugs, causing them to be either careless or naïve, going with the criminal con men willingly at first and then realizing their mistake when it's too late. Do you both understand this?"

Kaya and I nodded. I have to admit, I have always wondered what alcohol tastes like and what all of the fuss is about, but I have heard enough horror stories about all sorts of people who have gotten into drunken brawls with friends and foes, so at this point, Papa doesn't have to worry about that. But if I ever do decide to have a drink of some kind of alcohol, I will force myself to remember what he said and will try an alcoholic beverage in good company. I don't consider myself naïve and certainly not weak minded. I believe I can protect myself, but I also understand why much of the state of Alaska has banned the sale and possession of alcohol, particularly in small cities and villages. Alcohol has been involved in an overwhelming amount of crime in Alaska.

We boarded our plane with a cargo hold full of supplies and flew home. On the way back, I continued to think about the substantial alcohol problem in the state of Alaska and how it is linked to sex crimes. I read in a news article that Alaska has one of the highest rates of alcohol abuse and the state leads the country in the rate of sexual assault and other violent crimes. Maybe because it's dark for so many hours in the winter and people are bored, so they hang out in restaurants and bars or maybe they get drunk because they are depressed and have no ambition or will-power to do something about an unfavorable situation. Well, I want to help and I pray that I will never fall victim to alcohol abuse or anything else that might cause me to act inappropriately or naively.

8

Wily Johns had just been interrogated by several police officers, leaving him feeling concerned about his recent corrupt activity. As soon as the police left, he immediately called his customers who were arriving on the third of March. "Mr. Heller, you had better watch your back for a while. People around here, including the police have been stirring things up. The authorities are planning to interrogate all travelers, especially hunters and fishermen and are planning to inspect all cargo on planes, private vessels, fishing boats as well as import and export ships."

"Wily, I have never been deterred before and I don't intend on putting a hold on our operation. We're making money hand over fist with these girls and I will continue as planned. Just don't give them any reason to be alarmed. We will be arriving around noon and we'll need the plane fueled up and ready to go so that we can quickly board and take off. If you act normally, no one will be the wiser. I can count on you, right?"

"Yes, of course. I just thought you might want to know what's going on here in case you want to re-strategize. I'm not going down with you if you get caught transporting girls, guns or any other type of contraband. You aren't paying me enough to cover your back in light of the recent police activity."

"Oh, I see. It always comes down to more money, doesn't it?"

Wily cleared his throat. "I want triple the amount you've been paying me. With more money, I can hire another man to make sure that you pass your cargo inspections. I might not be able to doctor your flight logs anymore. The authorities will be monitoring the flight paths and destinations much more carefully. They are also planning to employ more people to inspect hunting and fishing permits and will be carefully inspecting what you are removing from your excursions. Those girls you hid in your cargo hold last year were transported successfully, but if you try to get away with girls now, they will probably be discovered and you, my friend, will find yourself in prison and most likely on death row. And like I said, I'm not going down with you."

"Wily, you just said I could count on you so which is it? I'm afraid you are already in too deep. If we go down, you will, too, so I would advise you to make sure that we pass inspection. And don't you worry, I'll make sure you get what you deserve." He chortled in such a sinister way that the hairs on Wily's neck stood upright. "I'll be seeing you soon."

Wily hung up feeling like his days were numbered. He wanted out, but he was not sure how to go about it. He thought, if he triples my take, I could make enough to move my business out of Kotzebue and relocate to a warmer place without being trapped into working with such dangerous criminals. He thought about Hawaii and how he could make plenty of money flying tourists back and forth to the various islands. He always wanted to live in Hawaii to join his brother in his lucrative venture there. He really began to be concerned after Heller said, "I'll make sure you get what you deserve."

Wily decided it might be best to leave immediately. He said to himself, "As soon as these gangsters leave next week, I'm making my move." He shivered as he envisioned Heller's chilling black eyes, windows to his sinister, dark soul.

Axle Heller planned and charted his coastal tour for the upcoming year, which would include flying to each of the northwest Alaskan coastal cities, scoping out Red Dog Mine and scrutinizing port activity up the coast from Kotzebue to Pt. Hope. After returning to Kotzebue, he planned to fly south, across the Seward Peninsula to Nome, Unalakleet, Hooper Bay, King Salmon and finally terminating in Anchorage. He has two large yachts that he sails around the coast of Alaska several times a year. His main guests include several business partners who are all part of his criminal organization and wealthy business prospects who they pick up along the way. For the pleasure of his guests, Heller lures unsuspecting girls aboard, some boarding willingly with promises of good employment opportunities and others who are coerced by vicious threats to themselves and their families. Most of the girls are then forced to work in one of Heller's night clubs, hotels, massage parlors or cathouses in Anchorage without the ability to leave on their own or contact anyone outside of the organization. The girls are guarded and observed and are not allowed to have or use phones or computers. If they cause problems or try to escape, they are eliminated, no questions asked and no excuses tolerated.

After Heller hung up, he called his right-hand man, Lex Scorpo. "Lex, we have a problem. It seems that Wily is having second thoughts about making sure that our northwest Alaskan operation goes smoothly. Get rid of him. I need his services for our March expedition, but after that, we'll replace him with one of our own."

"You've got it boss. I'll handle it myself."

"Good. How is it going in Anchorage?"

"We're all set. We have several new houses that are full of good girls bringing in thousands a day at each house and we have men working all over the city, picking up more girls every week."

"You're my man, Lex. I expect you to bring in at least ten more from the Iditarod race. There will be so many people there that it will be easy to slip away unnoticed."

"On it. I have six men and three vans planned for the festival."

"Keep me informed." The sinister man sat back, grinning as he lit a cigar, feeling confident that no amount of FBI or police activity would thwart his profitable operation.

Axle Heller manages corrupt activity including

money laundering, assault weapons, drug and sex trafficking in almost every major city in the Alaska mainland with the largest division in Anchorage. He is considered the principal crime lord in the state. Most criminals working in Alaska know him and are aware of his corrupt activities, would never interfere with his operations and would never try to compete with him on such an enormous level. No criminal is more powerful and vicious than Axle Heller. He has managed to repeatedly elude the authorities as his criminal operations continue to grow exponentially, especially his sex trafficking division in which he personally partakes in. He makes sure that the girls he brings in are fed as much alcohol and drugs as they desire and he force feeds the ones who don't accept it willingly.

Heller personally selects the most unusual, exquisite looking girls to work in his night clubs, Sea Maiden and Sweet Gems, which are strip clubs in Anchorage. The clubs offer surf and turf dining, strip tease dancing and gambling, including high stakes poker games which he operates in hidden back rooms and are fronts for his money laundering operation. The top floors of both buildings serve as his offices for business deals and negotiations. One-sided mirrored walls provide views down to the main floors, so that Heller can monitor what goes on at all times.

Authorities frequently inspect his clubs but have never been able to locate him. His clubs and hotels have video monitoring systems which Heller personally keeps an eye on while at the establishments. On several occasions, Heller was able to somehow escape from his night clubs, evading the authorities with no one the wiser.

The hotels are luxurious resorts which include public spaces for gambling and conferences and private rooms for his massage business. He figured that if he kept his known businesses functioning lawfully, his criminal organization would be difficult to gain access to or even locate. He was right, so far. The FBI believed however, that someone would eventually leak information which would help them connect the dots. The clubs and hotels are owned by trusts using fictitious names of various men from other states and countries, but are all actually Axle Heller. The FBI recently planted several spies in his nightclubs, but are not yet aware that Heller also owns the hotels next to each club and have not yet figured out how he escapes or where he goes undetected.

The FBI has been on to Heller for some time, tracking what they know of his operation and movements. The problem has been that the organization is so colossal, linking criminal activity to Heller has been difficult even though it is probable that much of it is associated somehow to his organization. They have arrested many sex criminals, drug lords and other deviants, subjecting them to hours of interrogation expecting to find some connection to Heller, so that they would have a reason to take him down. Since the businesses are managed by other men, most of the employees don't even know who Heller is and that he owns the establishments.

Heller had been arrested in the past on three occasions for minor offenses, once for the possession of a small quantity of marijuana which was more like a slap on the wrist, once for petty theft and a third time for aggravated assault, which his lawyer was able to get dismissed based on a technicality during the time of the arrest. He was much younger at the time and a small player in a shady criminal organization in Washington state. Eighteen years ago, he separated from the outfit in Washington with a colleague who also wanted to build an organization in Anchorage trafficking drugs and girls.

The operation was small time for many years until Heller opened up his first night club. With the money he earned at the club, he was able to build the second club and hired several managers, all deviants with criminal pasts, who were hungry for power and money. His employees were all malicious deviants who were dangerously and often fatally abusive to women. Heller believed the men possessed the exact qualities he desired to help him create a massive criminal, trafficking organization. No one brings drugs, women, weapons or any other contraband into mainland Alaska without his knowing. His devious eyes and ears are everywhere. If anyone working for Heller shows any sign of disloyalty, he or she would soon cease to exist. Wily Johns was correct in thinking his days were numbered.

9

Anji

It is now Saturday, March 2nd, 2019. Papa, Kaya and I are in Anchorage near fourth street enjoying the exciting ceremonial events at the beginning of the forty-seventh Iditarod Trail Sled Dog Race. We are grouped together for safety reasons and so far, we are having an absolute blast. I can't even imagine running in such a long, unforgiving race so I have tremendous admiration for the athletic, dedicated, but entirely fanatical competitors who attempt such a feat. We've been observing the contestants with Umiaktorvik and cheering on his grandson, Toklo, who is near the front of the pack of racers with his excited sled dogs, all of them barking and howling along with the spectators. Toklo is a handsome, robust young man and I hope he wins. I say a silent prayer for him, to stay safe and strong and to bravely endure the harsh environment that he prepares to traverse.

The trail runs from Willow, up the Rainy Pass of the Alaska Range, into mostly desolate wildernesses, then along the shore of the Bering Sea, finally reaching Nome in Western Alaska. The mushers have to endure a harsh, unforgiving environment of tundra and spruce forests, over steep hills and treacherous mountain passes and across frozen rivers. I cannot even imagine how they can complete even one full day, which is usually about 100 miles, let alone ten or more days.

Papa had previously spoken with Sarah and Grace, arranging to meet them at the Iditarod festival in Anchorage. After the festivities, the plan is to travel together to Kotzebue and then on to Miki Tarniq. I was super excited and couldn't wait to meet them. I felt proud of myself for reaching out to them and believed they could help, although I wasn't sure how yet. I made some flags attached to long sticks with their names on them so that we could be easily spotted. "Papa, it's so crowded here, so I can't imagine how Grace and Sarah will find us even with our flags. Should we move toward the outskirts of the mass of people?" Just then, I noticed Anya. I called out and ran toward her. "Anya."

Papa yelled, "Anji, stop! Where are you going and who is Anya?"

While Papa and Kaya ran after me, I heard Kaya shout over the noise of the crowd, "Anya is a mysterious girl who Anji has seen in the forest near a hunting camp several times. I have never seen her, but Anji talks about her often."

I lost sight of Anya when she disappeared behind two women walking toward me. They were Grace and Sarah. Grace spotted my flag with my name on it. "Anji? I'm Grace Nadeau. That flag was a great idea." To my surprise, she hugged me. "This is Sarah Beaulieu, the friend I mentioned." Sarah shook my hand as Kaya and Papa caught up to us.

"Anji, you know we talked about staying together." Papa was irritated and winded as he put his arms around me.

"Grace and Sarah, meet my Papa, Ethan and my brother, Kaya." Grace had a lovely, kind face with hazel eyes and wavy, auburn hair. Sarah smiled while shaking Papa's hand. She flipped her long, chestnut hair away from her face and I observed compassion in her warm, caramel eyes. First impressions are important to me and I perceived that Grace and Sarah were respectful, trustworthy people.

Sarah spoke loudly over the noisy crowd, marching bands with blaring horns and loud, drubbing drums. "I'm absolutely thrilled to meet you. We arrived yesterday and have been scouting around the area and talking with authorities and various organizations. I have a plan, but should we have a little fun watching the start of the race and talk later when we can hear each other better?"

Papa said, "Yes, I think so. We plan to stay here in Anchorage until tomorrow morning, so we can talk over dinner later if that works for you."

Sarah said excitedly, "Sounds good. Let's try to make our way toward the starting line. I have always wanted to see the race or at least the beginning of it." We walked

71

together moving slowly through the crowd of spectators while Sarah spoke with me. "Who were you calling out for when we saw you?"

"Anya. She is my friend from my exploration trips in the preserve. She sometimes picks berries with me while her papa hunts. She was right in front of you, but then I lost sight of her when I saw you." The hairs stood up on Sarah's neck. She did not see a girl in front of them when Anji approached them, although she couldn't be sure with the massive crowd of people, all heading toward the starting line. Sarah glanced at Grace who was listening to the conversation. She shrugged and seemed to dismiss it for now.

Fervently, I yelled, "Come on! You'll love watching the mushers start out." I pointed out Toklo as we made it to a spot where we could see better. A few minutes later, the gun fired and off the contestants sprinted, shouting with excitement as the crowd cheered and the band played on in celebration.

As the group made their way toward the starting line, Ethan was distracted by an unruly commotion in the crowd. He slipped away to see what was going on and observed two men scuffling with a couple of girls. The men had their arms around their torsos, forcing them toward an unmarked van which was parked on a side street near the main crowd of people. The girls were screaming and struggling, obviously trying desperately to get away from the men. The band and crowd commotion were so loud that others did not hear their cries. Ethan caught up to the men and forcefully grabbed one man in each arm and hurled them both to the side of the crowd. "Let go of the girls, now!" Both men released their grips while shouting obscene protests. Ethan shoved the men to the ground and twisted their arms back in debilitating strongholds. He whistled loudly several times in an attempt to alert others to the situation. Another man leapt onto the back of one of the culprits so that Ethan could release his hold and concentrate on the other. The crowd gathered around the men on the ground, mostly in shock as they witnessed the raucous scuffle. The two terrified girls ran off disappearing into the crowd. Ethan shouted above the noisy crowd, "Find security, now!" A couple of minutes later, three Anchorage policemen arrived at the scene. "I caught these two men trying to get away with two young girls." Unbeknownst to Ethan nor the police, the two men worked for Axle Heller.

One of the policemen shouted over the noisy crowd, "We've got them. Are the girls alright?"

"I'm not sure. They ran off to the left of the crowd when I grabbed the men, but I can describe them." He drew in a deep breath of air, then exhaled slowly with his eyes closed in order to recall as much detail as he possibly could. "They were both wearing green Iditarod shirts, one with a blue, short jacket and a colorful knitted hat and the other was wearing an orange parka with a fur lined hood. They both had long, black hair, one with braids. I'd say they were maybe thirteen or fourteen years old."

"Did you see which way the girls ran?" Ethan pointed to the east of the crowd and two of the policemen took off to try to find the girls.

Ethan said to the third policeman, "I'll help you find the girls."

"Okay, but come into the station today to write down every detail you can. I don't intend on allowing those two perverts to slip away. We also need a full report from the victims describing what happened."

Ethan sprinted through the crowd and caught up to the other policemen. "Look, over there." The two girls were in utter hysterics sitting by several women who were trying to console them as they described what they had just experienced. The girls glanced at Ethan with trembling, grim smiles.

The girl in the orange parka said, "Thank you, thank you." She turned to the policeman, "He saved us. We were watching the mushers when those nasty men grabbed us. We tried to get away, but they gripped our necks and pointed knives into our sides." She showed them a torn place on the side of her coat, not realizing that she had been cut with the knife. Blood was seeping through her t-shirt.

The policeman said with concern, "You're injured. I'm taking you to the hospital." He then checked out the other girl, who didn't seem to have any injuries, but he said, "I'd like for you to come with us as well, just to make sure you aren't hurt and then we'll take your statements. It's very important that you give us as much detail as possible, so that those men will not be able to harm others."

She sniffled and dried her tears with the sleeve of her jacket. "Okay, but I want to find my parents first. They are here, somewhere near the starting line. My uncle is one of the contestants."

The policeman shook Ethan's hand and nodded to him. "We'll see you at the station. Thanks for being alert to the situation." With exasperation, he nodded back.

Sarah noticed several policemen and people gathered

around them. She spotted Ethan with his hands in his pockets and his head bowed toward the ground. Observing his forbidding expression, she asked, "Hey, what happened?"

Ethan choked on his words as he described the scene. "Damn it! Evil creatures seem to be crawling up out of the depths of hell. How has crime in this city progressed to this extent?" He shook his head in disgust. "No one is safe anymore. We must act aggressively to hunt for these offenders and the public needs to be educated to be more aware and alert. Those girls were not with their parents. Sex offenders have probably been getting away with abducting young people because their victims were not protected. These kids are walking around, completely unaware that they look like candy to perverse villains."

Sara placed her hand compassionately on his arm. "Yes, that's why many more people should get involved. There are so many people in our country that don't understand how enormous the problem is. It makes me feel ill as well, which is why I do what I do. I'd like to see many more books, magazine and news articles published, not only outlining sex trafficking as a major social concern, but which also include information about how people can join the fight. Until everyone steps up to the plate, involuntary sex slavery will continue to plague our countries. I'm pleased that you are one of the few who care enough to get directly involved, even though you just put your own life in danger."

Ethan reflected on his experience during the mysterious northern light display and believed that he now understood what he must do. "As I'm sure you have noticed, I'm a man of substantial size which gives me an advantage and I have no fear of these degenerates. I have daughters who I will protect over my own life if it comes down to it, no problem." He thought back to the moments just prior to meeting with Sarah and Grace, when Anji ran off to find her friend. He shivered at the thought that those men could have tried to abduct her. He would describe the dangerous event that had just occurred to her with hope that from now on, she will stay with her group when in public. Ethan and Sarah made their way to the others who were excitedly cheering on the contestants as they sprinted down the trail.

After the mushers were out of sight, we made our way to The Historic Anchorage Hotel on fourth street, where we would be staying for the night. Papa suggested a spectacular restaurant for dinner and with growling stomachs, we were on our way. The menu had some delectable choices of seafood, salads and luscious sweets. We ordered delicious Alaskan cuisine including Halibut, wild caught Sockeye Salmon and Dungeness crab legs with soups and salads.

While waiting for scrumptious desserts including Agutuk, which is Eskimo Ice Cream made by mixing seal oil, reindeer fat, snow, and berries, and also Rhubarb pie and mixed berry crumble, Sarah began the dreaded conversation that everyone wished we didn't have to think about. "That was delicious." She flashed a wide toothy smile, then turned toward me and held my eyes with her own, suddenly very serious. "While you were watching the race, your father took down two criminals who tried abduct two young girls. The men were arrested and the girls were taken to the hospital." I stared at Papa in silence and my face flushed as an icy chill crept up my spine.

Papa reached toward me and held my hand. "You cannot run off like you did earlier. I realize that you are now a young adult, but you must take this seriously. I witnessed the men clutching those girls and I was able to wrestle them down before they escaped, but many girls may not be not so lucky." He glared at me with anger and yet teary-eyed love in his eyes."

"Oh, I had no idea. We were engaged in the race and not even aware that you walked away. I thought you were right behind us."

In all of my years so far, I have perceived life as beautiful with most people expressing compassion toward each other. I am not naïve and have read about and studied historical wars, crime and slavery in the world but overall, I figured that most people were inherently good natured and merely struggling to survive. I thought about Grace and Sarah, two examples of good-natured people who traveled a fairly long distance to help others whom they had never met. But now I am seeing for myself that not all people are inherently good. In fact, some should not even be allowed to live among the rest of us. I scowled and clenched my fists, more determined than ever to help take sinister criminals down.

I remembered reading about Sodom and Gomorrah in the book of Genesis, where God turned Lot's wife into a pillar of salt for looking back at the sinful burning city of Sodom, disobeying God's order. Why doesn't God turn all of the malicious, harmful criminals into pillars of salt, which could then just blow away in the wind? It seems to me that the world would be a much safer, harmonious place if he did.

Sarah's voice shook me out of my vengeful thoughts

which until recently, I didn't know I possessed. "Well, we are lucky that Ethan was alert to his surroundings. After scouting around yesterday, Grace and I discovered a few areas that we want to check out tonight and maybe again when we return from Miki Tarniq. We spoke with several college and university officials and toured the campuses. I feel that the schools are probably fairly safe from predators on campus, so I wouldn't think you'd have to worry about your safety there, however, off campus is another story." She held my eyes steadily with her own. "If you choose to attend school in Anchorage, you should stay on campus as much as possible and travel in groups when you want to journey off site. Just like any other large city, there are safe areas and also dangerous areas, so you just have to stay alert to your surroundings."

I felt like I had been knocked off my axis, understanding that I cannot control all situations, since there are so many unknown factors that might disrupt my courageous journey. I guess I'll have to learn to deal with the unexpected and somehow be prepared for the worst, which will be difficult because I have always prepared myself for the most pleasant and adventurous. I understand that I also must learn to trust others outside of my family. I think I'm on the right track at least on that point, by trusting completely in Grace and Sarah.

Sarah sipped her coffee and continued. "I am interested in walking around at night on the streets of Anchorage to see what goes on and what shady figures may be lurking in the shadows." We all stared at her with stunned, concerned eyes. "I have the police department on speed dial, don't worry. There are local police and undercover agents, who have been working in specific areas in Anchorage, particularly at night, hoping to catch these villains. I'd like to scout out local parks, popular bars, movie theaters, shopping malls and large entertainment centers to see what crawls out." She glanced at Grace. They had decided earlier that Grace would reveal part of her story, so that Anji could understand how important it is to stay alert and make good decisions.

Grace gulped as she tried to summon the courage to speak about her past. She at least wanted to express a brief summary of her story. After many years of healing, she could tolerate talking about it and often did, to the girls who were brought to her at Hope Ranch. She began. "Local bars and dance clubs are target venues for sex predators to frequent. I was abducted a long time ago from right inside a crowded dance club, thrown into a van with other girls who were also kidnapped from various clubs in the area and transported to an X-rated night club in Seattle, Washington. I was forced to stay there and dance for obnoxious men with no way to escape for many years. Other uncomfortable and abusive things occurred which I'm not prepared to talk about, but I'm sure you could imagine. The reason I'm telling you this is because I'm hoping you will choose to stay away from crowded bars and raucous parties."

Tears threatened to spill over and my lips trembled as I struggled to suppress my feelings. I had never known anyone who experienced such suffering. Grace continued. "I eventually escaped with another girl and met some people along the way who helped us find a safe place to go to. That is why I decided to build Hope Ranch, to help other girls who need safe places to go, to heal and rebuild their lives. After sharing my story, I don't wish for you to feel frightened. I only hope that you will make intelligent decisions and that you will be very careful in public. You may have friends who want to dress in skimpy clothing and go out to a dance club and may even want to attract attention to themselves, maybe hoping a cute boy will notice them. If you make the decision to go with them, just remember my story and dress appropriately. Ask yourself, what kind of person you want to attract. There are nice men of course, but you now see that there are also malicious men who have harmful intentions."

Sarah put her hand on Grace's, nodding warmly. She understood that speaking about her terrifying past was difficult. "Since there are so many dark hours for half of the year here in Alaska, attending another university in the lower forty-eight states might prove to be a safer option, if you plan to journey off campus for research and other activities, just a thought."

Papa caught Sarah's eyes which seemed to be waiting for a like-minded response. "I have been pondering similar thoughts as well." He smiled at Kaya and me. "These two are strong, confident individuals who I believe will make good decisions however, none of us have toured the lower forty-eight states and we are not at all familiar with large, populated cities other than Anchorage. My children, hmmm, excuse me, my grown-up teens," he cleared his throat and smiled, not wanting to offend us, "have been raised in a quiet, pristine, remote atmosphere that is quite different from other more populated, crime infested environments and where there will be an enormous culture shock. This, I am certain of."

Sarah grinned with a sly, previously planned retort, something she had thought about after reading Anji's letter. "I have an idea about that which I think you might be partial to and may ease your apprehensions. Grace and I have some really good friends who I want you to meet as soon as we can devise a plan. Private Detective Dakota Hunt and his family live in Evergreen, Colorado. They are extraordinarily caring, compassionate people including Dakota's niece, Autumn, who will be attending Colorado State University in September. Autumn is a kind, responsible girl who would probably be thrilled to have a school companion. She lives in Missoula, Montana with her mother and father, Jillian and Liam McKinney, until school starts. If you think you might be interested in the idea, I would like to fly Autumn to your home to meet with you and maybe if it's possible, she could stay with you for a few weeks this summer to get to know you."

Sarah paused to sip some water. "Dakota and his trucking team are a significant part of an FBI task force who will be working in and out of Alaska and Canada soon. I have discussed the current sex trafficking dilemma here in Alaska with them and they are preparing to work here specifically to take down traffickers, which the team has been doing successfully across the lower forty-eight states in the past few years. Dakota will want to meet you all as soon as he can arrange it and when your schedule permits."

"Well now," Papa said, "that sounds like a positive idea and a good potential plan. I'd love to have Autumn and Dakota here and I'm sure Anji will be excited to make a new friend, who might very well turn out to be a splendid school companion."

"Oh, yes." I clapped my hands displaying an enormous smile. "When can she come? I'll show her around our little town and we'll hike in the Preserve. Colorado State is one of the schools that I applied to." I glanced prudently up at Papa, wondering if he would react, since I hadn't yet discussed studying out of state with him.

Sarah answered thoughtfully, "I think Autumn graduates this spring, hmmm, let's see, I believe in mid-May. I'll discuss the possible plan with Dakota right away so that both of your families will have a chance to make arrangements on time for the upcoming semester. I have a feeling that Autumn will jump at the chance to have the opportunity to spend a few weeks of her summer in Alaska. She is planning to study Psychology and Sociology with emphasis on helping girls and young women in need, who have been through abductions and other abusive situations. She is planning to work at Brooke Macfie's Harmony Ranch in Grand County, Colorado for part of the summer, but I bet she could spare a few weeks for such a wonderful opportunity."

Grace added, "Harmony Ranch is a lot like mine in Whitehorse, which I would love for you to visit sometime. We take care of many young women who have unfortunately endured horrible, abusive experiences and who work conscientiously to overcome sorrow and suffering. The girls seem to really love working in the greenhouses. We grow as many of our own vegetables, fruits, berries and herbs as possible in large Quonset huts. There are many therapeutic programs which have proven to be effective such as taking care of and riding horses, milking cows, feeding chickens, gathering eggs and involvement in all sorts of other chores and activities. Educational programs are also available to them. Brooke is planning the same type of education and activities, so I bet if you are interested, you could work for a few weeks during the summers with Autumn at Harmony Ranch which could be a rewarding experience." She turned to Papa. "I'm sure the Hunt family would welcome you and your family with open arms whenever you want to visit."

"Oh, that sounds so awesome." I got up and hugged Grace and Sarah and then hugged Papa displaying a pouty pleading smile.

"How could I refuse such a face. But let's take one step at a time. I like what you are proposing, so let's work on getting Dakota and Autumn home for a visit. If it all works out, Autumn will be absolutely welcomed. Hana, my wife, and Alina and Joie, my two younger daughters will be delighted to have her around."

Kaya teased, "Are you sure Anya won't mind another friend occupying your time?"

Everyone stared at me quietly, all with concerned faces. Papa said, "Kaya, don't tease her. We'll all meet Anya when the time is right."

I defended myself, "You will like her. She likes to hike around and explore like I do. She can visit at the same time, you'll see," I promised with utter sincerity.

Papa's eyes lingered on mine, silently searching for the truth in my earnestness. When we finished our delicious desserts, Papa said, "Well let's all retire and meet up for breakfast but Sarah, I would like to join you in your hunting party tonight. It sounds dangerous, so I would feel more comfortable being around and lending a hand if needed." Sarah escorted Papa away from the rest of us to discuss a few details of her strategy while walking back to the hotel.

Grace accompanied me to my hotel room, hoping to get to the bottom of what was going on with Anya, I felt sure of that. I described my encounters with Anya. "I just don't understand why Kaya didn't see her when we were out by the hunting camp. Anya was standing right in plain sight at the edge of the trees. And I don't understand why you and Sarah didn't see her when we met up earlier at the race."

"Grace asked thoughtfully, "Anji, do you have many other friends at your school?"

"Not really. Since we study at home, we are not around other kids very often, but I do have a few friends that I visit in the villages from time to time. None of them like to go hike in the preserve like I do but honestly, I'm not making her up like Kaya thinks I am. I don't have any problem being alone out there, because there are so many things to do and experience. Anya seems to be in trouble and I haven't figured out why yet. She behaves mysteriously, but I think that is because she might be hiding from someone sinister." I mentioned observing Anya at Wily's airplane hangar. I shivered as I thought about how I had seen Anya right in front of Sarah and Grace, minutes before two girls were almost abducted by nasty thugs. It's as though Anya knew something dangerous might happen. I wondered if Anya saw the men prowling around in the crowd, hunting for their prey like vultures. Maybe she tried to get my attention to warn me, but when she saw Grace and Sarah, she got spooked and ran off. I really think that maybe she doesn't want to be recognized by someone harmful who might be trying to track her down.

Grace smiled concerningly. "It's okay. Like you

mentioned earlier, try to have her visit with you at your home. A young girl off by herself in the wilderness while her father hunts doesn't sound safe. Next time you see her, ask what her story is and try to get her to open up to you. Who knows, maybe she found you because she needs a reliable person such as yourself to confide in."

"Okay, I'll do that."

10

Sarah and Ethan met in the hotel lobby prepared to scout around to find out what goes on in Anchorage during the dark hours. Sarah whispered, "Let's check out a subdivision called Forget-Me-Not Valley, which has the highest crime in the city. We'll take my Jeep and drive around the area. I thought we could start there and then drive south to the university to check out city parks along the way."

The hairs stood up on Ethan's arms. "I want to see something and yet I don't. I'm not sure I trust myself to remain detached or even calm if we witness a young girl in trouble."

"I know what you mean. I feel the same, but if this city is as corrupt as reports have shown, we just might spot something suspicious. We'll call the police if we do. I'm only interested in finding out where traffickers are working and if we are lucky, where they take the girls." She glanced at Ethan, "I'm always confident that I will find someone or something that will lead me to girls in desperate need of rescue."

The two brave souls ventured down the road staying alert to any late-night suspicious activity. As they got closer to the subdivision, they noticed an elementary school and decided to drive around the school and through the neighborhood. A gang of rowdy teenagers were gathered around a house where hard rock music was blaring. The kids were noticeably drunk and shouting, basically an unruly bunch surely up to no good. One of the young men pointed at the Jeep causing some of the teens to run away and others to run toward it. Sarah turned the corner and sped down the road. "Whew! We don't want to hang around there. We are possible disrupters to them which would only cause unnecessary excitement."

They passed a trailer park and decided to drive down the streets checking out trailers. Sarah slowed down when she noticed some women being hastily herded from two cars into a trailer by several rough looking men. She stopped far enough away to spy on the group without the men noticing them. She zoomed in with her phone camera and snapped a few photos. "I don't want to go there now, but I'll be back. That doesn't look right to me." There was no way Sarah could have known, but several homes in that particular trailer park were owned by Axle Heller and the men Sarah observed, worked for him. "I have a really bad feeling about that place. I am going to forward these photos along with the address to the police and the FBI." She typed a message, attached the photos and sent it to her contacts. "Let's hope they act immediately so that the girls will have a chance to get rescued before their lives are destroyed."

They continued down the road toward a local park which was shadowy from large evergreen trees which swayed in the gusty winds. Sarah drove slowly around the park alert to any possible movement in the shadows. "Watch out!" Ethan pointed to a crazed dog which bolted into the street, barking madly. "What is it running from? Look! Two girls were running vigorously as if someone was chasing them."

A large, sinister looking man caught up to one of the girls and clutched her jacket as she screamed in horror. The dog turned on its heels and as fast as lightening, sprinted toward the man who was wrestling with the girl and pounced on him, snapping its jowls at his throat. The man swung something at the dog knocking him off for a second, but it seemed that the dog wasn't about to give up just yet. He pounced again, growling and tugging the man's shirt collar by its teeth. A gun was fired and the dog went down, yelping and whining. He seemed to be hurt, but the bullet must not have hit him fatally, because he got back to his feet just as Sarah pulled in front of them and turned on her high beams. She hastily pulled out her phone and called the police as Ethan jumped out of the Jeep and ran toward the man. The man fired at him wildly, barely missing him as Ethan vaulted onto him, pinning him to the ground. The girl ran toward the Jeep screaming and waving her arms.

Sarah opened the door. "Get in. We saw your friend

as well, but did you see where she went?"

"Na, no, but there is another man." She said, trembling, "Oh no, I hope he didn't catch her."

Sarah quickly described the situation to the police, where they were and hung up. "Stay here." She grabbed a can of mace and a large, heavy flashlight that she had picked up at a hardware store earlier and ran toward Ethan, who had the man pinned to the ground. When the police arrived, Sarah described the other girl and the second perpetrator. One police officer relieved Ethan of his burden as the other two dashed into the park. Ethan told the officer that they could drive around to the other side of the park to try to trap him.

The policeman yelled, "Okay, good. Backup is on the way."

As they quickly drove to the other side of the park, Sarah asked the girl what her name was. "Alasie. My friend is Nikki. We were walking my dog when those men started chasing us. They got out of a gray SUV over there." She pointed to the north side of the park. Sarah sped up to block the vehicle, just as the policemen reached it with guns raised.

"Get out of the vehicle with your arms raised!" The criminals did not respond.

Gun shots rang out into the darkness. "Duck down!" They all ducked down toward the floor of the Jeep.

Alasie screamed, "I just saw Nikki in the back seat of the SUV." Another police car pulled up behind the culprit's vehicle.

Sarah shouted to the nearest policeman, "The girl is in the back seat of the SUV!"

One of the officers who was either wearing a bullet

proof vest or was completely crazy sprinted toward the vehicle, gun at the ready. "Get out, now. I have no problem killing you, swine. Get out with your arms raised." The man fired at the officer who backed away from the window just in the nick of time and fired back into the front of the vehicle hoping the girl was laying low in the back seat.

The man cried out in agony, "Okay, I'm getting out. Don't shoot." They watched as he raised one arm in surrender and the other tucked to his side where he had been hit. The officer questioned him, trying to get him to reveal where they were going. "None of your business." The officer cuffed him and shoved him into his car while another officer helped Nikki out of the back seat.

"Are you okay?" She was shaking violently and tears streamed down her face.

She said, trembling, "Yes."

An officer walked over toward Sarah's Jeep. "Looks like you were at the right place at the right time. You two are brave souls. What are your names?"

"Sarah Beaulieu and this is Ethan Sauveur. We just happened to be driving by when we saw the dog run into the road and then witnessed the man grab Alasie. Is the dog with you?"

"Yes, he is in the front passenger seat. He's a good dog. He's panting heavily, but he must know instinctively that we're here to help the girls and is fairly calm now."

Alasie cried out, "Kallik, oh Kallik. Is he okay? He tried to save us but then when I heard the shots, I thought he might have been hit."

"He's okay. He has an injured leg, so we'll take him to an emergency veterinarian." The officer turned to

Sarah again, "Can you follow us to the station with the girls, so that we can take these two asses in the cars? I need your statements anyway."

"Yes, of course."

"By the way, about a half hour ago, we received a call from the FBI asking us to check out an address just down the road. They said it was urgent and that a woman called it in with photos. Was that you?"

"Yes." She gulped, because her story that she just happened to be driving by was sounding not so believable. She had to think quickly to come up with a story that was more plausible.

"So, were you really just driving by?"

"Yes. I've been thinking about buying a home here in Anchorage and just thought I would drive around during the night, so that I could chose neighborhoods that are, should I say fairly crime free? But this area is not so great, is it?"

"No, Ma'am. You really don't want to live in this area. I would hire a Realtor if I were you. They'll be able to show you homes in more desirable locations."

"Yes, thank you. I'll follow you with the girls." Nikki climbed into the Jeep with Alasie and hugged her friend and both girls began sobbing hysterically. "Shhhh." Sarah whispered. "It's all okay now. You're safe. We'll get you home after we talk with the police unless you have someone who can pick you up."

Alasie said with a quivering voice, "That would be nice. We are attending the university and we plan on staying in student housing on campus next fall, which wasn't available this semester. We want to get out of this area as soon as possible."

"Yes, that is a very good idea and maybe I could help. I'm very resourceful." Sarah smiled compassionately.

Exhausted and disturbed, Ethan glanced at Sarah gratefully. "I've seen enough to understand. I think our ideas for Anji might be good plans, so let's get Dakota out here as soon as possible. I don't want Anji here until Anchorage figures out how to clean this mess up. You're some woman. I don't think I've ever known a more courageous lady. I'm very grateful that you are willing to help, but you are surely putting yourself in harm's way."

"Yes, I seem to do that but Ethan, this is my work. I usually work under cover, because my efforts often include detaining the perverts until I extract information out of them and taking the girls to safe homes. I don't want the authorities knowing who I am. Oh, when we talk with the police, please don't mention that. My story is that we just happened to be driving by. Officials don't like vigilantes and I have many times been labeled as such. Obviously, the local officers who helped us tonight have seen me, but I don't want my identity in the mainstream. The police criminal investigators have been coordinating with the FBI task force here in Anchorage and aren't interested in the public getting directly involved with dangerous criminals, so I definitely have to try harder to keep a low profile."

"I understand." They arrived at the police station and made sure that Alasie, Nikki and Kallik were checked in and being taken care of. Sarah told the police that they would be happy to take the girls home if they were okay with that, but she was informed that the police would take the girls home to make sure it was safe to leave them there. Sarah exchanged information with the girls and headed back to her Jeep with Ethan.

Sarah was independently wealthy, something she kept to herself. Her father passed away when she was very young and her mother was murdered during a burglary at their home when she was a teenager. Her parents left a small fortune to her, which has provided all the funds needed to drive around the country in her decked-out RV, rescuing girls who were trafficked. She planned on helping Alasie and Nikki find a nice, safe home near the university which she would pay for. She liked using her money to help others in need and knowing the girls would be safer, made her happy.

Sarah and Ethan headed back to their hotel rooms to rest for the night. She sent a text to the police to find out if they had arrested the men who forced the girls into the trailer earlier. She knew that she would not be able to sleep until she heard whether or not the girls were safe, so she paced around until she received a reply. Thirty-six minutes later, a text popped up. It read, "Yes. Thank you for the tip. The girls are being held in a safe place until tomorrow morning." She blew out a lengthy breath of relief.

Sarah began to wonder if she should come back to Anchorage to work for a while, but shivered at the thought. She said to herself, "I don't think I could handle being involved with this much vile, criminal behavior on a daily basis. The corruption here seems to be crawling out of the depths of hell at an alarming rate. My luck could run out sooner than I anticipate. Phew!" She went to bed, tossing and turning for most of the night.

After a delicious breakfast which included crab and halibut crepes, fresh berries and freshly brewed coffee, the Sauveurs, Sarah and Grace headed to the airport, flew to Kotzebue, then on to Miki Tarniq in Ethan's plane. Sarah and Ethan decided not to tell Anji and Kaya about the night's events to avoid instilling unnecessary fear and concern, at least not until later. The kids were already concerned about the incident at the Iditarod earlier. Sarah did however, reveal the details of the incident to Grace who was grateful to hear that Sarah once again rescued girls in need before their lives were dreadfully altered.

Sarah was seriously dedicated to her work and couldn't imagine quitting no matter how dangerous the work was at times, and certainly not while sex predators were running rampant. She thought many times that her mother would be proud of her and her accomplishments. She had an idea that might help catch more traffickers in Anchorage and hoped Dakota and his team would be arriving soon.

11

Anji

When we arrived in Kotzebue, we decided to scout around before heading to Miki Tarniq. We walked a short distance to the market to pick up a few things and then to Wily John's shady bush flight business to find out how Grace and Sarah felt about his operation and his demeanor. Papa stopped, turning to them, "I'm interested in what you think about this suspicious little man. Last time we were here, I had a talk with him about the possibility of traffickers booking flights with his outfit. I was not pleased to say the least. He is an extremely shady character with a severely bad attitude. I don't like him and I don't trust him."

I was concerned and not at all feeling comfortable

about going there again, but Kaya assured me that everything would be okay. We walked into the office and looked around, but no one was inside. Papa and I noticed Wily leading a group of men to their plane.

While waiting for Wily to return, Sarah glanced at the flight manifest on the desk and snapped a photo of the names and flight plans. Since Wily was outside, I decided to look around the office to see if I could find anything incriminating. I felt like Nancy Drew searching for clues on a mysterious case. I hesitated at his desk and shuffled through his papers, although I wasn't really sure what I was looking for. I picked up his cup, which was still warm with coffee and swirled it around. I admit, I did have sinister thoughts, but whether or not I would act on them was another question. I wondered what I was capable of if threatened? I noticed that Sarah was occupied with her own agenda and not concerned with me or my actions.

A minute later, Wily entered the office. "Oh, it's you again," He scoffed. He seemed shaken, sweating profusely, ghostly white and seemed seriously disturbed about something. "I told you that I don't get involved with the private business of my customers and you sent that cop over here, didn't you?"

"Nope." Papa answered. "He must have checked you out on his own, but I'm sure glad he did."

"Dude, what do you have against me? I haven't done anything to you and I don't assist criminals." His eyes darted around when he spoke. He was lying and Papa knew it.

"But you would if they paid you enough, right?"

Wily scoffed again. "Whatever. What do you want now?"

Sarah sauntered toward him. "He brought me here to check out your business. I plan on flying here several times in the near future and I asked him to show me several bush plane companies. Is that okay with you?"

"Take the brochure and book well ahead if you are planning to fly this summer. I'm already almost fully booked until next spring."

"I'll do that." She nodded to him as they sauntered out. "He's a real piece of work. I don't trust him either."

Papa said, "My sentiments exactly. Anji gets really nervous around that guy."

"Well, I'm thankful that you are on to him. I also believe that it's possible that some pilots may be helping traffickers and could actually be working for criminal organizations. Abducting and trafficking people on any significant scale is a group effort."

We briskly walked down the road to Papa's hangar, boarded our plane and were on our way home. Grace said loudly over the roar of the engine, "The meandering river and icy tundra is absolutely beautiful. I'd really like to come back here and raft on the Noatak sometime. I'm sure it's an exciting, adventurous trip. When does the ice melt?"

"Usually the second or third week of June, but most rafters arrive in July. The mosquitoes die out a bit by then. I hope you do come back. I'd love to float down the river with you. Even if I go to school in the lower forty-eight states, I'll still be back here during the summer months."

I thought for a moment. "You can raft on the Yukon right where you live, right? I mean, this is really a remote, wilderness environment which I'm sure is a little bit different than the Yukon near Whitehorse. I'd love to go there sometime, just to raft on the great Yukon River."

Grace laughed. "Sounds like we both think alike. I'd like to raft on the Noatak River just because it's different."

"I think we are going to be good friends. Maybe next summer you could meet me in Kotzebue and we could fly home together. Then I'll take you to The Noatak Wildlife Preserve. We'll pick berries for Mother and Grandma and I'll show you the beautiful wildflowers. After being away at college for nine months, I'm sure I'll be missing my home."

Papa said, "You better come back every summer. You know I will miss you and I'll miss your help around the shop. Hana will be beside herself worrying about you and also missing your help with the quilts and jackets."

I was elated to hear that Papa was speaking as if he had already decided that I could go to Colorado for school. "Yes, I know. I'll miss everyone terribly. I guess it will take some time to get used to a new environment and other people." I sat quietly, thinking about my upcoming journey to Colorado. I was excited, but a tiny bit nervous and started wondering if I will be completely miserable without my family around.

Papa noticed my eyes welling up. "I plan on visiting you, maybe several times a year, just to make sure you are not getting into too much trouble." He snickered, knowingly. "I will have a talk with Dakota and will find out how he and his folks feel about my visiting every now and then. I'm really looking forward to meeting the Hunt family and touring around Colorado and I will be going with you on your flight this fall."

"Oh, brilliant, Papa. Can the whole family come with us?"

"I don't think Hana will feel right about leaving everything for Tulugaak to handle alone. So maybe Kaya will have to stay behind on the first trip, but he could join us the next time we visit." Grandma and Grandpapa live with us and help with sewing quilts, leather clothing, cooking and other chores around our home.

Kaya said, "I'd like to check the schools out as well, but I don't mind taking care of things while you and Mother go in August. I will be attending school in Anchorage for the first two years at least, so I will have time to arrange it."

Papa smiled. "Sounds like we have a plan. I'll speak with Hana about it when we get home."

We landed at the air strip, loaded up Papa's Bronco and headed home. Grace was gasping in awe at the scenery around us. "This little town is lovely. I certainly understand why you all love it here so much and your log home is magnificent. I like the heavy timber and stone columns. I constructed my ranch buildings with similar materials and design."

Sarah, interested in the dogs, said, "Your Malamutes are beautiful. I have thought many times about having a Malamute or Husky buddy to tour around with me. They are such intelligent, protective, loyal dogs." The dogs were all barking and whimpering, welcoming us home. Kaya and I jumped out of the Bronco and hugged the dogs as Mother opened the door to greet us with Joie and Alina at her side.

Papa kissed her rosy cheek. "Hana, Joie and Alina, meet Miss Sarah Beaulieu and Miss Grace Nadeau."

Hana beamed, "I'm so thrilled to meet you. Come in and warm up by the fire. I have dinner all prepared, so

I hope you are hungry."

Sarah said, "I'm famished and it smells delicious."

I grinned, throwing my arms around Mother. "She is an amazing cook."

She smiled. "I have your rooms all made up. Kaya, please help the ladies carry their luggage to their rooms."

"Sure, Mother." He led them to their rooms, each decorated with exquisite, colorful homemade quilts depicting Alaskan flora and fauna atop comfy beds. Skillfully crafted night tables and wardrobes were made from Sitka Spruce logs each detailed with intricate carvings of mountain scenes and wild animals on the tops and drawer fronts. We have one guest room and Alina was sweet enough to tidy up her room and share Joie's room for a few nights.

Mother said, "You ladies can freshen up while I get dinner ready to serve." I sauntered into the dining room to help her set the table. "Well, how did it go?"

"We had a fantastic time in Anchorage watching the start of the race and afterwards we enjoyed a delicious dinner. Grace and Sarah are absolutely lovely, women and I'm so happy that they are here to help. They have been working for years rescuing girls from horrible situations and I truly believe that they can help us. Sarah is really brave to do what she does and Grace owns a safe haven home called Hope Ranch, in Whitehorse, Yukon Territory. I would love to go visit her there sometime. She grows her own vegetables and herbs, has horses and there are all sorts of other activities to do at the ranch." I gulped down a glass of water.

"Grace said that a woman named Brooke owns a ranch that is similar to hers in Colorado. She thinks that if I go to the university there, I might be able to work on the weekends at the ranch."

Mother eyed me intently. "What does Papa think about that?"

"He thinks it's a grand idea. Of course, he wants to meet with Mr. Hunt, I mean, Private Detective Dakota Hunt, first. It makes me comfortable knowing he is a detective and that he is working with the FBI to take down nasty criminals that abduct girls. He must be a very honorable, caring man. And his niece, Autumn, hopefully is coming out here to visit us after she graduates from high school in May. She will be attending Colorado State University and might want to be my roommate and friend while I'm there. I haven't had a chance to speak with her yet, but Sarah talked with Dakota about it this morning and he will be suggesting the idea to Autumn and her parents, that is, if you are okay with this plan."

Papa was standing in the doorway listening to the conversation. He watched Mother closely to perceive her reaction to all of the news. "Ahem. Hana, I wanted to talk with you first about this, but it seems Anji beat me to it. We will take one step at a time. First we will meet with Dakota and Autumn, then we'll spend some time here with them in May or June when they visit and see how everything goes at that time. After what I saw and experienced while in Anchorage, I think it might be a good plan if it all works out. Anji could come home every summer to help you fill your orders."

Mother looked sad, but at the same time she seemed to be prepared for the day when we would go off to college and find the world. She has always treated me as her special girl, sometimes reliving her youth vicariously through me and I have always loved that about her. I understand that she adores my courageous, adventurous nature and that I am accomplished with many things at such a young age, so my excitement about my plans didn't really surprise her. "We will see." She smiled at me with a loving twinkle in her eye. She glanced at Papa with a questioning look. I perceived that she wondered what he meant when he said, "After what I saw in Anchorage." I'm sure she will get him to elaborate on that later.

Papa introduced Grandma and Grandpapa as we all sat down to dinner. We enjoyed a delicious meal of caribou pot roast with savory herbed red potatoes, carrots, tomatoes and green beans with freshly baked rosemary sourdough bread. Sarah said, "I have never eaten such delicious pot roast. It's one of my favorites, but I have never tried it before with caribou. What a treat."

Kaya said, "This is my favorite dinner. Mother is the master of creating delicious meals with caribou."

Mother grinned, "It's all about the right spices and herbs and of course you have to add a pinch of love."

"Yes, indeed." Papa got up to refill everyone's glasses with a special carbonated water infused with mint and berries.

Alina said excitedly, "Just wait until you taste Grandma's salmonberry rhubarb pie. Mmmm."

Alina is a tall, slight, feminine girl with long, silky, sable hair that she often wears in a single braid. She smiles a lot and her coffee brown eyes glisten when she talks about things that interest her.

Sarah grinned at Alina and Joie, "What types of things do you girls like to do here?"

Alina said, "I like to design and sew long, drapey

dresses and skirts, so I'm thinking about studying fashion design. I also like to make silver and semi-precious stone jewelry and caribou leather handbags with colorful stones and fringe. Beautiful minerals are mined in Alaska like amethyst, jade, serpentine and tremolite, so I have plenty of resources available."

"Oh, I would love to buy one of your handbags, and I love long, drapey dresses. Let's talk about that after dinner. Maybe you could show me a sample of what you make."

Joie announced, "I like carving bowls and boxes out of birch, poplar and aspen. I'm working on a large popcorn bowl using birch wood that has rich, defined grain. I'm in the sanding phase where the grains look like watery, wavelike designs. The birch wood grain sometimes has a moiré effect which is really beautiful. Every piece of wood is unique with its own special characteristics. Papa lets me sell my carved pieces in his shop, but sometimes I'm selfish and I want to keep them all here for us to enjoy." She giggled.

Joie is 5'-4" tall, with a sporty, slim build and intriguing dark umber eyes. She often wears her shoulder length, black hair in pigtail braids, which accentuates her delightful, cheery disposition. She beamed at Kaya.

"Kaya wants to be an architect. He likes to build things and is really creative. He is helping me build some small birch wood tables."

Kaya grinned at Joie sheepishly. "Thank you Joie, for your vote of confidence. I appreciate that. I actually think I am quite good at designing and building. It's all I seem to think about lately, but the trick is to get into a good school. I helped Papa and Grandpapa build this house and all of the furniture and some of the ideas came from this goofy noggin up here." He chuckled as he pointed to his head.

Papa said, "Kaya came up with many structurally sound and attractive features for our cozy home. He might think he's goofy, but he's just being humble. He does very good work and I'm proud of him. I'm proud of all of you." He smiled widely, nodding to each one of us. I'm also saddened that some of you will move away someday, maybe too soon. I am so used to all of you being around that I suppose it's just beginning to affect me. I hope you all come home after your studies at least for long visits and surely for the winter holidays."

"I don't want to live somewhere else," Joie stated. "I can make my wood creations right here. I'll look after you, Papa. And anyway, you will always need help at the shop and Mother will always need help with her leather clothing and pottery. Consider me a permanent fixture." She grinned.

Tulugaak smiled affectionately. "This is love. I agree with Ethan. All of our children are gifted, skilled and also grateful, compassionate people. You and Hana have done well in raising them."

"Thank you, Papa." He smiled reflectively. "Well, how about we clear the table and bring out that luscious berry pie."

I asked, "Who wants spiced tea with dessert?" Everyone said yes, so I got up to brew a pot and clear the dishes with Alina and Joie while Mother brought the warm fruit pie to the table. We all enjoyed the delicious dessert and good conversation.

After almost an hour of light chatting and laughter,

Papa stood and glanced at Sarah and Grace. "We'll show you around tomorrow after breakfast. I'm sure you are exhausted from the travel and today's events, I know I am. But feel free to stay up as long as you like. I'm hitting the bed. See you all in the morning."

12

Sarah awoke at six in the morning, to the delightful aroma of a rich coffee brew and the sounds of someone bustling around in the kitchen. The sun would not rise for another couple of hours but she had been stirring for the past hour, so she dressed and tiptoed down the stairs. "Good morning. I smell the most delicious coffee."

Sniffing the air, Ethan said, "Ah, yes. That would be our special blueberry chocolate dark roast." He poured a cup for her. "There is plenty, so help yourself if you want more. I'm headed out to feed the dogs and bring in firewood."

"Wow. This is the most delicious coffee I've tasted in a long time." She sipped her coffee with her eyes closed for a moment. "Do you mind if I help you? I need to wake up the old bones and I would also like to talk with you."

"Sure. Grab your coat and gloves. How did you sleep?"

"When I first hit the bed, I slept like a baby. After yesterday's events and travel, I was utterly exhausted however, I've been feeling a bit anxious for the past few hours."

"I bet you aren't used to such peaceful silence, no traffic, car horns, sirens."

"You're spot-on. Hope Ranch is also quiet and tranquil, but I'm used to being out on the road, waking early to the unpleasant sounds of engines and traffic. I surely could get used to the peacefulness of an environment like this. I'm surprised that I didn't hear the dogs barking this morning."

"Oh, no. They don't usually start moving around until Kaya and I go out each morning to feed them. Actually, Kaya might already be out there. He is an early riser and loves to take care of the dogs. We usually feed them early and after their stomachs settle, Kaya and Anji run them for a couple of hours. If I have orders to be delivered, they will run the dogs into town, pack the boxes on the sleds and deliver them."

"Oh, what a fantastic service. What types of products do they deliver?"

"It's often animal feed, firewood and other supplies and goods that are flown in from Anchorage to Kotzebue and then bush pilots fly the goods to our airstrip. I have regular shipments of products that come in each week and I run out to meet the plane, load it all up and bring it to the shop. The kids meet me at the shop to unpack and either shelve the products or they take them directly to our customers. It's a great way for the kids and the dogs to get their daily exercise."

Ethan sipped his coffee. "Kaya and I also take the dogs out to the wooded areas several times a month and bring back fallen trees to cut for firewood. Right now, I have roughly 1,300 cubic feet or ten cords of wood in a covered area behind the shop. I'll only have a couple of cords left by mid-June. There are many people living within thirty square miles who all need firewood at least three fourths of the year. It's either a challenge for some people to haul firewood out of the woods or they are working long hours, so they appreciate having the wood available to pick up or be delivered."

Sarah said, "Well, it looks like you have a terrific business here."

"I have to say, I feel grateful to finally have the business operating successfully. I worked for many back-breaking years to get it to this point with the help of Tulugaak, Hana and all of my kids. Kaya has been my right-hand man for years now and I've been wondering what I will do when he goes off to school. I'll have to hire someone else, but I believe he may not be easy to replace. He does a lot around here and has still managed to keep his grades up. I really don't know how he accomplishes everything with energy to spare."

"Well, maybe he will come back here every summer to help you. I read that a few more people move to northwest Alaska every year and will all need well built homes. You never know, maybe when he graduates and completes his architectural testing, he could specialize in building homes out here and he'll be around more often."

"That would please me more than anything. I love that boy and will miss him tremendously. I have talked with him about living here permanently many times before. He does love it here and seems to be very interested in learning the structural engineering necessary to build homes and commercial buildings in an environment such as we have here. He has to learn wind and snow loads, occasional seismic activity, roof and beam loads and so on. He thinks that The University of Alaska Anchorage will be a good school for that type of study."

"That all sounds really interesting." Sarah savored her delicious coffee. "Have you felt any seismic activity here?"

"Not recently, but in April and again in June 2014, we felt a swarm of earthquakes, two having a magnitude of 5.7 and many others measuring 4 or more. If I remember correctly, the epicenter of the strongest one was about twelve miles northeast of Noatak and approximately twenty-five miles south of Red Dog Mine. Scientists went to the mine to see if the mining activity caused the quakes, but they found no evidence to support that."

Sarah's eyebrows raised. "Please, tell me more about Red Dog Mine. What is mined there?"

"Zinc, lead and silver. It's an open-pit surface mine providing about 10% of the world's zinc production. A Canadian based company, Teck Resources owns the mine and Northwest Arctic Native Association owns the land. In 1986, residents of the eleven native villages voted to form the Northwest Arctic Borough, to be economically based on taxing the Red Dog Mine, which began operating in December of 1989. By 2008, the mine had produced over 500,000 metric tons of zinc, almost 121 metric tons of lead and something like 280 metric tons of silver. That equates to a total metal value of over $1,000,000,000. NANA has about 55% shareholding."

"Oh, wow. I wasn't aware that the mine was so enormous." Sarah sipped her coffee, then changed the subject. "Have you been able to find out if any of the villages have experienced someone being abducted directly from a village or is it all happening in the large cities?"

"There have been no reports of abductions here or in any of the villages, but what disturbs me is that there are over 140 cases of girls who were trafficked and no one is reporting exactly where they were abducted from. This is why it is crucial that we have as many people as possible on the lookout for these criminals. They must also be ready to act defensively which could be dangerous, though necessary. Apparently, from the information I have gathered in my research, most of the victims were picked up in Anchorage. I was so angry at Anji for running off at the Iditarod like she did. Even though she didn't run far, it's painfully obvious that a girl or boy could be snatched so quickly from a congested public event that no one would notice. It was so crowded at the Iditarod and the bands were playing so loudly, that no one else observed those girls being grabbed. I just happened to turn around at the right time."

They walked around to the dog gate and Ethan turned to Sarah, giving her a box of peanut butter oat biscuits that Hana and Sophia made. "When we walk into the barn, with your gloves on, hand one to each dog. They are used to people, so they won't bite you and we have trained them ever since they were small pups to never jump up on you unless you pose a threat to us or them, but since they don't know you, the treats will make them happy. Kodiak and Nukilik will be the first to come up to you because they are our team Malamute leaders. Kodiak has light copper and grey on his ears and above his eyes and Nukilik has charcoal grey surrounding his face with a star shaped white patch between his ears. Call them by their names, talk to them and give them the biscuits and you'll be just fine." He studied her face to see if there was any sign of fear or discomfort. He saw none, so they entered the barn.

"No worries. I love dogs and they seem to know that." Kaya had just finished feeding twenty-four dogs, eight Malamutes and sixteen Siberian Huskies. The two lead dogs noticed Sarah and cautiously approached her. "Hi, Kodiak. Oh, look how beautiful and healthy you are." She scratched between his ears. "And Nukilik, you are such a sweet dog." She talked with them in a syrupy voice as she gave them the biscuits. They allowed her to pet them as they nuzzled up to her legs. She ran her hands along their backs, giving them welcomed massages. She took off her winter gloves to feel their silky fur. Once the other dogs saw that she had the approval of Kodiak and Nukilik, they all began approaching her for the delicious peanut butter treats.

"You've done it now. They'll all want massages." Kaya and Ethan both kneeled down by Sarah to rub and brush the dogs so that she wouldn't feel overwhelmed.

Sarah laughed when Kodiak licked her face and sniffed her hair. "I want to take you all home. So the

Malamutes are usually the bigger dogs, right?"

Kaya was happy to describe the differences to her. "Yes. Malamutes are bigger, heavier dogs and are extremely loyal to their owners. They can pull more weight, but we need more Huskies because they are lighter weight and run faster. Huskies are more loyal to the rest of the pack, which is helpful. I think of them as good team players. Huskies are also usually more intelligent, although Kodiak and Nukilik are our leaders because they have been around the longest and know our routines. You are looking at two teams, twelve dogs per team."

Two Huskies approached Sarah, wanting in on the love. Kaya laughed. "The one on the left with the bright, blue eyes and a pointy white streak on his nose is Zoey. He is usually feisty, playful and has more energy than any of the others, so he leads second behind Kodiak. Zoey can get the others moving in a hurry. They all seem to want to compete with each other when pulling a sled, which is super good. The other is Piper, a sweetie female Husky. She is Mama to four of our Huskies and she is one of my favorites because she likes mothering the other dogs, when and if they let her."

"Aw, I can see why you prefer sled dogs rather than snowmobiles. They are part of the family and probably provide protection, right?"

Ethan said, "We have two snowmobiles, but they are so darn noisy. I grew up with sled dogs and can't imagine living out here without them. If we have to be out making deliveries in a snowstorm, the dogs are a much better choice. They can see, smell and sense what we can't. I have been caught in blinding blizzards many times and if I hadn't had my dog team leading me, I would have been lost until the storms passed and when it's below zero, that could mean freezing to death. They do provide protection especially since there are twenty-four dogs, but many of them are not very vocal. If they all sense an unwelcomed animal or person, they will immediately be on guard and they often take on some of the characteristics of wolves such as quietly observing, circling and grouping together, which can be unnerving to a predatory animal or a wrongdoer. They also howl and talk in their own language. Kaya talks to them all the time and I've witnessed Anji and Joie having delightful, long conversations with them. It's quite funny." Piper began talking, murmuring right on que as if she was participating in the conversation. Sarah laughed and talked back to her.

"Did I hear someone say my name?" Joie was standing by the door observing. She went over to the group and began petting Piper. "She is one of my favorites. She's a good Mama. When we are out picking berries, she's the first one to growl if an animal gets too close to us. Once a Mama, always a Mama even though her pups are fully grown. I think our dogs will protect us if a bad person comes around."

They all observed her and Ethan walked to her. "Do you want to discuss something, Joie?"

"Well, I've heard you talking about girls being abducted by criminals. They better not come here or they will get attacked by our dogs, I'm sure of it."

"Well, I hope so. That's why I would like for you, Alina and Anji to stay together when you have to go out somewhere and bring the dogs when you can but Joie, I believe that we are safe here in Miki Tarniq. I don't want you to be afraid, just alert to your surroundings when the tourists begin arriving. You should be able to continue to live and do things as you normally do." He paused. "So what will you do and say if a stranger comes up to you and asks you to show them where the shop is, for instance?"

"I would not go with them, but I would explain where to go and I wouldn't let them get too close. And if I felt the need to, I would take off running toward home or if I was in town, I would run to your shop."

"Good, and you would be with one of us. You, Alina and Anji should just make a habit of running errands together."

Joie had been concerned about the news and was frightened during the mysterious, dynamic northern lights. When she observed Ethan kneeling and praying, she knew something wasn't right. "Yes, I understand." She searched Sarah's eyes. "You are here to help us find these criminals, aren't you?"

Sarah forced a slight smile. "Yes. I will come up with a way to find them like I always do. I have ways of locating and tracking wicked criminals. I think that most of my work will be in Anchorage, but I really wanted to meet you all and let you know that there are others such as myself who care and who really want to help. If I'm welcome, I'd like to come back and visit again. Anji suggested to Grace and me that we all go on a float trip."

"Oh, that would be so much fun. I have rafted down the river many times, but not for a while. We usually just play around in our kayaks near home."

"Well, let's plan it. I thought we might come back in June or July. Dakota and Autumn will be here by then."

"Anji told me about Autumn. She just received an

email letter from her which made her smile. I don't want Anji to go away to school. I mean, I understand but with all of this talk about wicked men skulking around, I would rather she stay here."

Sarah gave Joie a hug. "We'll find the wicked men and your Papa makes a lot of sense when he tells you and Alina to stay together. You have school and plenty of things to do here at home as well as helping your papa at the shop, right?"

"Yes." Joie reached down and hugged Zoey and Nukilik. "You'll protect us, won't you?" The dogs whimpered and murmured.

Ethan got up with a scowl on his face, realizing that his girls were feeling more uncomfortable than he intended. "We will do everything we can to protect our family and everyone here in our town. Well, I have to get to the shop soon." He turned to Sarah. "Would you and Grace like to go with Kaya and Anji on a sled ride?"

"Oh yes, that would be really fun. I'll go ask Grace if she wants to go."

"Joie, you and Alina could go, too. Two on each sled. Let's go inside and have breakfast and then you guys have some fun. The weather is cold, but it's supposed to be only partly cloudy today, just a bit of light snow until later this afternoon. A blustery snow storm will be moving in later, so it would be best to head out right after breakfast."

"Yes!" Joie jumped up and down. "I'll go tell Alina."

13

Anji

Hana and Sophia were in the kitchen cooking up a storm. The delicious aroma of caribou sausage and freshly made buttermilk biscuits wafted through the house. Tulugaak was sipping coffee at the table. "Good morning. I thought I'd be one of the first ones up, but you all look as if you've been up for hours. What's going on this morning?"

Ethan rubbed his growling belly and sniffed the delicious aroma of buttery biscuits. "We've been introducing Sarah to the dogs. After breakfast they are going on a sled ride."

Tulugaak said, "Oh, that sounds like fun." He sipped his hot coffee and smiled at Ethan. "I'd like to go to the shop with you, Ethan. I am meeting Ujurak for a game of Nunami."

Sarah looked puzzled. "What is Nunami?"

Tulugaak explained, "Nunami is a tabletop card game that promotes healthy cohabitation with natural elements and it encourages people to collaborate. Each fifteen minute game is an enriching experience that requires critical thinking. Like life, it starts out simple but becomes more challenging as you develop your Nunami skills such as managing your place of living."

Alina said, "Grandpapa is very good at that game. He says it is not meant to control the land or beat your opponent. It's meant to learn how to live together and you can play the role of either human or nature."

Tulugaak grinned. "Your cousin, Philip sent it to me on my birthday to try it out. He met the creator of the game who lives in Quebec, Canada.

Most of the Sauveurs' relatives have remained in Canada and work for commercial fishing companies. They have stayed in contact with each other, often reporting on the health and economic stability of various small cities and villages. Ethan stood to help Hana bring breakfast platters to the table. "Smells delicious, Hana." He kissed her on the cheek and she grinned lovingly at him.

I moseyed out to the kitchen, still feeling tired from the previous day's events. Grandma brought salmonberry jam and one of Mother's special omelets to the table to go with the caribou sausage. "Mother made the omelets with dandelion, fireweed shoots, devil's club and ricotta cheese with baked Eskimo potatoes. I highly recommend trying the salmonberry jam with it."

Intrigued, Sarah asked, "What are devil's club and

fireweed shoots?"

I was delighted to explain, "Devil's club is a plant which grows soft leaf buds that are delicious when sautéed in olive oil and garlic and fireweed shoots taste kind of like asparagus."

"Oh, this is delicious." Grace beamed. "You are an amazing cook. I would love to write down some of your recipes, only I'm not sure I could make them taste this good."

"Well, you're in luck because I published a northwest Alaskan cookbook called, Savory Delectables of the Wildlife Preserve. I have them at the shop. I'm sure Ethan could bring one back for you."

"Well, I would really like to visit the shop and could buy one there while I look around and see what other treasures you have, maybe after the sled ride if that's okay."

Kaya chugged some orange juice and turned to Grace. "I have a box of jackets and quilts that I'll be taking to the shop later. Maybe after we run the dogs, we could add that box to the load and take you on to the shop in the sled."

Sarah chimed in. "I'm really getting the feel of what your life is like here. I can see why you love it. This is turning into an interesting and entertaining visit rather than just a disturbing work-related trip."

Grandpapa said, "To experience is to know. Your stay here will help you understand the people here and our appreciation for such a precious environment."

She regarded Tulugaak's words. "I understand and that's why I have made it my life's work to help purge the country of criminals who want to harm respectable, peaceful people such as yourselves." She smiled warmly at him.

Ethan decided to reveal the details of the incident that occurred while he and Sarah were in Anchorage. "I'm grateful to have Grace and Sarah here as well. Sarah has already helped capture a couple criminals who tried to abduct two young girls who were just walking their dog in the park. She saved the girls and is helping them find a better place to live while they attend the university."

"He is being too humble. I could not have helped them without Ethan." She raised a glass to him. "And we'll continue to do everything we can."

Mother stared at him with concern. "Ethan, you involved yourself with dangerous criminals?"

He looked at her boldly. "Yes, and I will continue to do so, if I catch them trying to abduct young women. What would you rather me do, stand by and watch them abduct our children? Whether the girls who find themselves victims of these criminals are known to us or not, they are vulnerable and need protection or at least education. And we all must be prepared to act with the courage of the fiercest bears if we are called to the task."

I could sense Mother considering his convictions. "No, I wouldn't want you to stand by and watch, but I worry about you. These criminals are dangerous and I don't think they would hesitate to kill you."

Papa softened his demeanor just a bit as he held Mother's eyes with his own. "I know you worry, but now is the time to act if we want to prevent more abductions. We will be hunting for these predators all over Alaska if that's what it takes. It's time to clean this mess up."

Mother smiled at him adoringly, even though she

recognized as I did, that he might find himself in a grave situation that could be much more perilous than he bargained for, but she understood that he had to do what he could or he would not rest well. "Enjoy your breakfast for now. You all have a big day ahead of you." She kissed his cheek and smiled affectionately.

I had been sitting silently, poking at my breakfast while listening to the conversation. I thought, I must take more aggressive action myself, only I just have to figure out how. I surprised myself because I didn't realize that I had it in me to take on such a feat, but Papa said that we all must act now. The knife that I use to cut florals and herbs when I'm out on the tundra is quite small and I don't really want to carry a larger knife. I shivered thinking about stabbing a person with a knife even if he was attacking me, but I know I would defend myself even if I paid for it with my life. I thought about Monkshood, Aconitum napellus, and how I could prepare a tincture to use for protection. Maybe if I get close enough to a malicious person, I could toss it in his eyes. I shivered again. I'm sure I could never kill a person, but I know I would fight back even if it meant wounding the pervert fatally. I wished again, that the criminals would just turn into pillars of salt and blow away in the wind.

I wondered if I would use Monkshood on someone like Wily Johns. He is a pervert and I believe that Anya knows he is as well. I remembered his cup of coffee when we were in his office. Would I put poison in his coffee? Maybe I would if he tried to harm me. I shook off the sinister thoughts and tried to figure out a way to help.

I took a bite of my honey biscuit and chewed it slowly while still debating whether or not I should carry around

Monkshood. I will have to find a small bottle with a tight cap, so that it won't leak out. I thought about Grandma's tinctures and the bottles she uses. She has a large box of assorted sizes. She keeps a collection of various herbal blends for injuries and medicinal purposes, so she might have Monkshood left from last spring. It can be used for muscle and joint pain, but only after boiling it down to reduce the toxicity. The plant should never be swallowed in spite of the information out there claiming that the leaves and roots can treat all sorts of illnesses. If swallowed, the poisonous effects are instantaneous, slowing the heart rate down to extreme measures, swollen throat, violent vomiting and diarrhea, sweating profusely as the body tries to purge itself of the poison and if enough was ingested, the heart would cease to function causing immediate death.

I noticed Grandma observing me while I pushed my food around on my plate with my eyes downcast, absorbed in intense concentration. She squinted at me, probably wondering what kind of thoughts were churning in my head. I recalled that Grandma rarely uses the tincture, preferring to use other herbal treatments that are not toxic to humans but back in her youth, her mother made preparations of the plant to use specifically as a method to kill a harmful enemy or an animal that had been threatening people. The poison has been used throughout history on the tips of arrows to rapidly bring down an enemy in war.

"Anji, are you not hungry this morning?" Grandma asked.

"Oh, not really but the omelet is delicious and I want to boost my strength to run the dogs." I hastily shoveled a few more large bites of food into my mouth, took my dishes to the sink and left the room.

I heard Mother whisper, "I wonder what that was about?"

Sophia said, "I'll give her a few minutes and then I'll go talk with her. I'm sure she has a lot on her mind with school studies and all of this talk about missing girls. I think maybe she is overwhelmed." She stared at Ethan and shook her head with a hint of agitation. "You've certainly stirred up a hornet's nest."

Ethan bowed his head and nodded.

Sarah caught Ethan's concerned eyes. "Maybe we should discuss our plans in private for now. Anji wants to help, but it might be best to try to get her to let us handle the matter for now."

"Yes, I agree. I will not discuss our plans with the family any more. I think I have made it clear to all of you that you should go on with your lives as usual, but just stay together in public. The last thing I want is for you all to feel frightened and anxious about the unknown. Please forgive me for speaking my thoughts out loud and for sharing a few too many details. Okay, let's go on with our daily activities. Papa, let me know when you are ready to go. I'll have the Bronco warmed up."

I was getting dressed when Grandma knocked on my door, "Anji, can I come in?"

"Sure. What's up?" I realized that Grandma was observing me at the breakfast table and figured she would come speak with me. I wasn't sure that I should share my thoughts about Monkshood. For now, I will keep that to myself.

"What's troubling you?"

"Oh, I was just thinking about safety. Grace and Sarah are here to help us because of my letter and I just think there is something I could do to help find these wicked men before another girl falls victim to their clutches. I was also thinking about Anya. I want to find her and talk with her, but she probably won't be around again until sometime in April or May when her papa hunts caribou."

"Anji, I think you should leave the human predator hunting to your papa and the other men in the villages. Listen to what he tells you. You can help most by protecting Alina and Joie and being alert to your surroundings when the tourists arrive. You have a lot on your plate now with your high school graduation approaching and your plans for college. If you are too distracted with these other things, you will berate yourself later if you end up with low grades and work that is not up to your normal high standards."

"Yes, you're right. I will try to stay focused on my work. I trust Papa and I know he will do what he can to help protect the people here."

"Why don't you plan to go to the preserve with Kaya and your papa, the first week of April. Maybe you can scout around and search for Anya together while they hunt for caribou. You said you wanted Ethan to meet Anya's papa anyway, right?"

"That's a good idea. I'll talk with them and come up with a plan to go on a weekend in April, if Papa can get away from the shop for a day."

Grandma's warm, concerned eyes stayed fixed on mine. "Is there anything else you want to discuss?"

I was aware that Grandma sensed that I had other

secret thoughts and she would pry them out of me in time. "No. I'm fine. I do need to get going, though. Grace and Sarah will be waiting to go on the sled ride and may already be bundled up in warm winter gear."

"Well, alright. Make sure you come back by the house to pick up the box for the shop. Your mother wants the two quilts to be draped over the high rods. Maybe you could ask Grace and Sarah to help you rearrange the quilts to show the newest ones in front. Also, it's time to do an inventory of jackets, hats and gloves, to make sure that we have plenty available."

"Okay, sure. Thank you, Grandma. We'll talk again later." I finished dressing and crept as quietly as a cat downstairs and opened the cellar door. I quickly began rummaging through Grandma's bottles and found a small four-inch bottle with a cork which should do just fine, I thought. I searched through the dried herbs and found a shelf labeled medicinal. The herbs were listed in alphabetical order, Lavender, Lemon Balm, Milk Thistle, Mint, Monkshood. "There you are." I whispered to myself. I pulled on a pair of gardening gloves, quickly opened the jar and pinched off a small stem with several leaves and a piece of the root. I then slipped it into the small bottle and pushed the cork on tightly.

"Anji, can I help you with something?" As Grandma was walking down the steps, I quickly slid the bottle into my pocket and put the jar of Monkshood back on the shelf, then pretended to look for another herb.

"I found it. I took off the gloves, stuffed them into my pocket and took the jar of peppermint leaves off the shelf, removing the lid as she approached me. "My stomach has been bothering me, so I wanted to make a little peppermint tea. The jar in the kitchen is almost empty, so I'll bring some up." I started to put some of the leaves into a plastic baggy but she put her hand on mine, preventing me from doing so.

"I'll take care of it. You go on out to the barn and help with the dogs. I'll brew a pot and bring some out to you." She searched for the truth in my eyes, a look I knew very well. "Are you sure you feel well enough to run the dogs? If your stomach is bothering you, maybe you should go lie down. Joie can take the other sled."

"Ah, na, no, I'll be fine. Just a little indigestion." I smiled in a crooked way and hugged her. "Thank you." As I trudged up the stairs, I wondered if Grandma had spotted me putting the Monkshood back on the shelf. I should have just confided in her because I hated lying to her, but she would never approve. I'll just put the bottle in a safe place until I need it. I opened the bottom drawer of my dresser and shoved the bottle carefully into a thick wool sock. When I stood, I caught a glimpse of myself in the mirror and hardly recognized the reflection staring back at me. I observed a frightened, confused young girl tangled in a sticky web of deception and disrespect. I quickly braided my hair while examining my guilt-ridden eyes. I would resolve my predicament soon, once again earning Grandma's respect.

Sophia started to take the peppermint jar up to the kitchen when she noticed two of the jars on the shelf out of place and one of them had the label turned backwards. She turned the jar around and stood, momentarily frozen in her stance as she read the label, Monkshood, pondering the meaning of this. She whispered, "What is Anji up to?" Then she figured at least one possibility. She wanted to use it for protection. She supposed Anji was afraid of the unknown because of all of the talk about wicked men. She hissed with exasperation believing that Ethan had stirred up more than he understood. She would speak with him, but she would not tell him about Anji's mysterious actions until she had a chance to discuss it with her. She had never known Anji to lie to her. It was just not in her nature. She whispered, "Anji must be up to something that she may not even be able to discuss with me. Another secret of many."

Deep in thought, Sophia trudged up the stairs and into the kitchen to replenish the peppermint tea, noticing the jar was almost completely full, another fib. Disappointed and concerned, she sighed and brewed a pot of tea.

14

Anji

I was almost to the barn door, when a magnificent raven flew onto the roof and kraad loudly as it perched and began observing me. I recalled the raven who visited us the other night and wondered if it was the same perplexing creature. Kaya opened the barn door just as the raven vocalized and noticed my intense focus on the peculiar bird. "It looks like we have a friendly visitor."

I immediately thought of Anya, though I wasn't sure why. "It has something in its beak, something long and drapey." It appeared to be a scarf with a design and color that seemed familiar. I searched my memory, focusing on the crimson scarf. The raven abruptly lifted off the ridge and glided with air currents in wide circles above the barn, displaying its magnificent long-feathered wings. Then it swiftly swooped down toward me and dropped the scarf at my feet. My eyes widened in surprise. "Okay, that's extraordinarily bizarre." I picked up the scarf and noticed the raven, perched on a tree branch by the barn. Its striking bronze eyes were keenly fixed on us in an obvious scrutinizing manner. I stood there gazing back at the raven with my mouth still agape feeling absolute bewilderment.

"That is really weird and mysterious if you ask me." Kaya studied the scarf. "Is that yours?"

"No, it's Anya's." I remembered seeing Anya wearing that long, red wool scarf. I felt sure that it was the same one, because it had beaded fringe identical to this one.

"Are you sure because if so, I apologize for not believing you about Anya."

"Yes, I'm sure and thank you for finally believing me. I want to go with you and Papa when you go hunting in a few weeks so that I can look for Anya, and if we find her, I'll give her the scarf. And of course it's important that you both meet her and her papa. Anya probably dropped her scarf by the hunting camp where I saw her last, then the raven must have picked it up and maybe it has been flying around with it. What a peculiar bird."

With a pot of tea and cups in her hands, Sophia stepped outside walking slowly toward the barn, then stopped motionless in her tracks. She witnessed the raven circling above Anji as it dropped a red scarf, then soared up to a tree branch where it perched gravely still and continued to observe her. With seemingly deliberate communication, it said with a deep throaty voice, "Kraa-kraa."

"An omen." Sophia whispered. She stood still for a

few minutes listening to the conversation. She finally understood that there was a mysterious connection between the raven and Anji's enigmatic behavior. She sensed that it also had something to do with Anya, but she could not yet grasp the significance of the connection.

Sophia had also been mesmerized and strangely affected by the mystifying, animated purple and green northern lights which had become more and more intense in the past week. She and Tulugaak watched the extraordinary light demonstration from the window and also observed Ethan kneeling in a trance-like state, absorbing its surreal energy.

Tulugaak has a quiet, contemplative demeanor that Sophia has always found comforting. She absolutely believed that he and the raven were linked, giving him the power to see beyond the depths of the darkness and into the light both physically and metaphorically. She never disturbed Tulugaak while he focused meditatively. She believed that he could communicate with the spirits of his ancestors but he never revealed their secrets, because to do so would be interfering with fate and the destiny of others. However, he has often suggested alternative solutions to many problems and concerns so that one might choose a more suitable path.

Ethan has the gift as well, although the spirits only offer him fore-warnings of potential threats which infuriates him, because he at first doesn't understand how to help not knowing any specifics. Ethan will meditate for hours after a spiritual vision, which helps him concentrate his mental energy on being open and alert to concerns or challenges. His intense focus has always helped him put plans into action.

Grandma handed me a cup of peppermint tea. "Drink up, sweetheart. I added a pinch of tulsi." She gave me a tender squeeze on my arm. Tulsi is holy basil, Ocimum tenuiflorum, one of the most valued medicinal herbs on earth and is widely used by people in both the east and west. Holy basil is not only used in cooking and in fresh foods, but is also used to treat the negative effects of stress in the body, maintain stable blood sugar levels, headaches, stomach disorders and promotes alertness and clarity. Grandma looked intently into my eyes. "The raven speaks to you. You must seek to understand, Anji." She set the pot of tea down on the bench by the barn and returned to the house.

I sipped my tea. "I wonder what made the raven bring the scarf here?"

"I don't know. That is really uncanny." Kaya still held a questioning expression after Grandma's words, but he dropped it. "Let's go prepare the sleds."

I wanted to hang onto the scarf just in case Anya was out hiking or if she showed up in Miki Tarniq later, so I shoved it into my coat pocket. Then I remembered the ancient totem legend that ravens have the ability to be shapeshifters. I wondered if the raven was representing Anya. Was it possible? I certainly did not know enough about Anya to surmise that she might have some spiritual ability to connect with wildlife, and yet the raven is a mysterious creature. My scientific side would say that the legends are nothing more than myths that some people actually believed in. But I had a strong suspicion that the raven might be communicating with Anya, once again trying to tell me something extremely significant. I felt confused again, as if mystery was to blame for blurring the lines of truth and reality by interacting with a spiritual, mystical phenomenon. I want to believe in magic, because sometimes it's easier to believe that something mystical is the answer for something that we can't explain, but I guess I'm stubborn. I just can't make sense of it.

I read somewhere that there are spaces in our DNA that scientists can't explain or rather, they don't yet know what they are for. Some scientists believe that humans have more brain function capabilities than we currently utilize and that extra sensory perception and spiritual communication may be functions that are possible. There may actually be an expanded intuitive right brain functionality and only a small percentage of humans have the ability to utilize it. Maybe some people purposely use their intuitive right brain so often that a sixth sense actually exists.

I sighed and shook off my thoughts of scientific conundrums and the mysterious actions of the raven and Anya, when Grace entered the barn. "Sarah is on her way. Is there anything I can help with?"

I glanced around. "Well, you could grab two blankets from the shelf there, one for each sled. You will need the blankets when we gain speed, especially since there is an icy, gusty wind chill today. Kaya and I will be warm while we run, but since it's eighteen degrees, you will need to bundle up."

"Kodiak, Nukilik!" Kaya summoned the dogs excitedly, preparing them for their exercise. Once the lead dogs were up, the rest followed. They scrambled to their feet and a few of them howled and paced in anticipation. Kaya and I led the dogs out to the front of the house, then he attached the harnesses to each dog and glanced at Grace and Sarah. "Okay, hop on the sleds. You will want to sit down and lean against the pillows. The women got settled, one on each sled and Alina and Joie sat in front of them. "Ready?"

"Ready." We all yelled, excitedly.

Kaya whistled and I shouted, "Hike!" The dogs in perfect unison, dashed off moving faster and faster as if they were in a race. We were running fast and furiously at first and then we jumped on the foot boards as the sleds swooshed and glided in the soft snow. Puffs of powdery snow spewed up around us and wafted across the sleds from the dogs' paws.

"Whoop-whooo-hooo!" Grace hooted and laughed and we were all smiling widely, enjoying the extraordinary experience. As we glided across the peaceful tundra, the only sounds heard were the swishing of the sled rails and whistling winds through swaying spruce trees. Running the dogs is truly exhilarating. The dogs ran for almost half an hour, before they were ready to stop for a break. "That was so much fun. The beauty around us is breathtaking." She pointed up into the gray-blue sky. "Look at the raven soaring gracefully with the air currents."

As I marveled at the impressive glider, I sensed that it was the same raven that brought the scarf to me. I observed the raven as it flew toward the edge of the trees in the same area where I often pick berries and near the same place where I met Anya. Just then, Grandma's words came back to me; "Seek to understand." I began to put the pieces of the puzzle in place. I thought of the raven, the scarf, Anya and the hunting camp. I understood that I must go back to that same place if I am going to solve the mystery. I put my hand in my coat pocket and caressed the soft scarf between my fingers while observing the raven. I said quietly to the raven, "What are you trying to tell me? What is your mysterious message and what do you know about Anya?"

Grace asked, "How long do you run the dogs?"

"About an hour or two each day." Kaya bent down to stroke the dogs' fur. "We will only run for an hour this morning, since we'll be running them again later when we go to the shop. I'll miss exercising the dogs when I head off to school. I don't know how Papa is going to be able to do all of the work he does and mine as well. I feel guilty about leaving, but Papa says he'll find someone to help if he needs to. Each summer, I plan on hauling out and chopping as much firewood as I can, so that the shop is fully stocked before I return to school at the end of August."

I said, "Yeah, I have been thinking about all of the work I will be leaving them with as well, but we both must leave to fulfill our dreams and we can always come back. I'm still not sure where I want to live for the rest of my life. I love it here so much that who knows, maybe I'll come back for good but for now, I'm excited to find out where my next journey is. Kaya, you could always build spectacular Alaskan homes so that you won't be so far away. I can see it now, Architect Kaya Sauveur's Alaskan Homes. And you'll have fabulous brochures and a beautiful website displaying your extraordinary work. Soon, you'll be famous."

"Yeah, you never know. I would like that very much. Thanks for your confidence in me."

Sarah said, "If I ever decide to build a home, I'll be contacting you. After seeing how you designed and built your own home, I believe in you. You are already very skilled and you have your first project to display on your website."

"Thanks." He blushed and flashed a self-assured smile. "Well, let's head back. I'll be helping Papa unpack and shelve some products for at least an hour and I still have wood to chop when we return from the shop."

"Yeah, me, too. Mother wants Joie, Alina and me to reorganize a few things and take some inventory so that she can plan how much more of each thing to make. She came up with a new design for some lighter weight, suede leather jackets for both men and women. She and Alina want to complete them before June. She also has a new canvas cloth hat with a drapey edge to Velcro on mosquito netting. I told her that I would help her make as many of those as we can. I think they will sell really well, especially in June. The bottom of the netting will have a drawstring to help seal it above the shoulders."

Grace grinned. "What a good idea. It will be like wearing a little tent around your head, which will keep those pesky gnats and mosquitoes out of our faces. I have seen something similar except the netting was attached and after a while it tears, leaving holes for the mosquitoes to crawl into. I wish I could stay a bit longer to help make those, because I'd like to take a few back with me. We have quite a mosquito problem for about a month in the summer, mostly down near the Yukon River."

"I'll send you a few and you could copy the design and make more. I bet some of the girls at the ranch would like to help you take on the project."

Grace laughed. "You are full of ideas. I like that. You can come visit any time and show us how to make all sorts of things."

We got situated on the sleds. "Kodiak, Nukilik, hike!" And off we glided.

While on the way back to Miki Tarniq, Sarah thought of Dakota and his team, wondering when Dirk Hays would arrange for them to head up to the Alaska mainland. She had a strange feeling that their criminal tracking work in Anchorage would soon become an urgent matter to deal with rather than in June, when they originally planned to work in the area. She understood that planning and ironing out all of the details would take time, but she felt like a good team had to be in place at the right time, or they would miss their opportunity to infiltrate the massive trafficking ring that was no doubt the main reason why trafficking in Alaska has been so prevalent.

Sarah and Grace planned to return to Whitehorse to strategize with Dakota's team. She would call him as soon as they returned to Anchorage.

15

It is mid-March and stormy all across mainland Alaska, western Canada and the northwestern states. Dakota's trucking team had been working nonstop, not only tracking criminals with great success in the northwest part of the country, but also delivering tremendous amounts of food to western distribution centers. Dakota had just requested that his drivers take a break for a few days to rest and regroup after working for the past few weeks in treacherous winter weather conditions. FBI Agent Dirk Hays had the team on a conference call in order to update his plans for their work.

Dirk began, "I have some great news or not so great depending on how you look at it. I have the approval to go ahead with criminal tracking work in mainland Alaska collaborating with Canada, mostly British Columbia, Alberta, Saskatchewan, Northwest Territories and the Yukon. Dakota and I have been working on establishing some trade freight lanes between shippers and receivers of both countries so that you will have predetermined routes and are not held up at the border crossings. You will all have special preapproved permits and letters from the Canadian government which will include the name of your company, Dakota Hunt Trucking, a list of each of your names as a sort of deputized authority, your identification and preapproved passports. You will be scouting out certain rest areas, small off the road motels and truck stops through Canada and on the way to Anchorage or Fairbanks where we have had some trafficking reports.

"The reason for all of this is that we have been investigating a few main trafficking routes including probable destinations in both countries. There have been a couple of arrests on these routes, which I'm excited to say, had everything to do with PACT-Ottawa's Truck Stop Campaign,[3] which is similar to TAT,[4] which led to further investigations. Both Canada and the U.S. are working diligently as you know, to combat sex trafficking by creating aggressive legislation and allocating as many monetary resources as possible to the appropriate organizations. Dakota, you mentioned that you have an additional announcement?"

"Yes. I have received some information from Grace Nadeau who as most of you know, owns and operates Hope Ranch in Whitehorse, Yukon Territory. She has been in contact with a family living in a remote town in northwest Alaska who along with many others are

137

aggressively planning involvement in the hunt for the criminals who have been abducting young women. I surely understand their commitment and determination to join the fight."

Dakota sipped some water then continued. "Since we now have the go ahead from Dirk, I'll be scheduling loads as soon as possible to Anchorage where we'll be meeting Ethan Sauveur of Miki Tarniq, Alaska and hopefully a few government officials. I have a feeling we will be able to track a few wretched criminals to their squalid lairs in Anchorage. Jake, you and Zach and two other teams, Cheynne and I and Mack and Chris will be on the first run with deliveries planned together, so that we can all convoy into Alaska. If there is as much trafficking on our route as the authorities believe there is, we may need to have several of us available to help each other at a moment's notice. Please be on guard for dangerous situations and call the authorities as soon as you encounter criminal activity. Just stay alert and if they are out there, we'll find them skulking around in the shadows."

Jake said, excitedly, "As soon as Grace told me about Anji's letter, I knew she wanted to get involved, so I'm on board and ready to go. I have a few ideas so that she won't be in harm's way but still helping the team. When I went back to Hope Ranch with her after the Christmas holidays, we researched every organization we could find in Canada and Alaska so that when we rescue the girls, we are prepared to immediately find safe places for them to go. Of course, Hope Ranch is at the top of the list for our northwest work. She will be hosting representatives from various organizations in the next few weeks, who will be checking out the ranch, accommodations and social programs for the girls who go there. She is super excited about that, because they will help her find funding through Canadian government support and private donations. I'm thrilled that I will get to pop in and see her and we may get to do a little fishing while we're up there." He threw his arms up with enthusiasm and laughed heartily.

Jake had proposed to Grace during the past Christmas holiday and wanted to spend as much time with her as possible. They planned on getting married in autumn and hoped that Grace's obligations with the girls at the ranch and Jake's work out on the road would not cause delays. He would be understanding if plans changed, because he truly felt that when the time was right everything would fall into place. Thinking about criminal fiends was not exactly conducive to jubilant, loving thoughts and feelings and he knew that Grace felt the same.

Dakota acknowledged Jake's information and enthusiasm. "I'm sure that we can find time to toss a few lines in the water." He grinned appreciating that Jake was reflecting on his tender relationship with Grace. "On another note, I have talked with Sarah, who has a very good idea. Anji mentioned in her letter that she is planning to attend college, possibly at a major university in the lower forty-eight states. Since Autumn will be attending Colorado State University in the Fall, I'm going to invite Anji's family to Colorado to meet our family and hopefully Ethan will give his approval for the two girls to room together at the university. That might be a good plan to keep Autumn and Anji safe and out of Anchorage where trafficking is rampant. The university will have adequate security measures in place to protect the students on campus and maybe Autumn and Anji will end up being great friends who will protect each other. Autumn, Jillian and Liam are driving to Harmony Ranch during Autumn's spring break to help set things up. Also, Brooke plans on opening the ranch on June first, so she took some time off to wrap things up."

Dirk said, "That sounds like a great plan. Well, let me know when you're ready to go. I'll be distributing your border crossing permits, letters and a list of Canadian and Alaskan contacts hopefully by tomorrow. I'm planning for you to start this campaign in May, which will give you time to finalize your work in the U.S. northwest but if we find that you are needed sooner, I'd like for you to be ready to go as soon as you can arrange it. When I'm off duty, my partner, Agent Kate Lindt will be ready and available to help you. She will know what boots on the ground agents are in your area for backup. Be safe out there and I'll be in touch."

The team wrapped up the meeting, then Dakota called Rich at the terminal to fill him in on the details. He thought about Jillian and Brooke and wondered if the ranch construction had progressed according to Brooke's schedule. He would call Jillian soon to discuss a plan for Autumn's trip to Miki Tarniq in June.

16

Brooke and Jillian were at Harmony Ranch finishing the final details in preparation for the grand opening. Brooke believes that a temporary home in a natural, tranquil environment with all sorts of enjoyable and educational things to do, might be a more beneficial way for young women who escaped or were rescued from sex criminals, to recover. She wanted the girls to feel a sense of harmony as soon as they arrive at the ranch. Brooke felt that making every detail lovely and homey was very important because the environment should feel like a friendly, safe, welcoming atmosphere.

The two had been working on landscape plans for the past two weeks and were busy reviewing the final set of permitted documents. Jillian pointed to the landscape plans. "I planned aspens, Douglas Fir, spruce and fruit trees that will show spectacular color at different times of the year."

Brooke deliberately hired Jillian to plan and organize her landscape project hoping she would have further interest in helping at the ranch and was overjoyed to hear her describe her plans. "Oh, that sounds absolutely lovely. What flowers and shrubs are you planning?"

"Oh, you're going to love this." Jillian showed Brooke a colorful sketch and tear sheets of each floral species and pointed to the areas where each plant will be placed. "I love the idea of having an edible garden, so you'll be able to grow all sorts of vegetables in the Quonset hut and I also planned an area in the hut for planting winter squash, sage and rosemary shrubs, all sorts of herbs and an assortment of florals including lilies."

Brooke flashed Jillian an empathetic smile. "I know lilies are an important symbol to you and your family. Could I ask you how you were able to get over what happened to you or if you'd prefer not to talk about it, I surely understand?"

"I'm okay talking about it now." Jillian smiled reflectively. She and her mother planted beautiful lily gardens together every year when she was a young girl. Calla lilies were her favorites which became extremely significant to the Hunt family during the many long years that Jillian was missing. When she escaped from her captors, she began sending calla lilies to her parents to let them know she was still alive. Because of her lily orders, Dakota and their father, Chevyo were finally able to track her down after being missing for over forty grief-stricken years .

"To start with, when I escaped, I left with a young woman named Julia Ivanov which seemed to make things easier, because we were able to share our concerns as well as our new experiences. Working out how to get away was frightening and yet quite adventurous since we had to travel by bus to Missoula, Montana, a place that neither of us knew anything about. I read that Missoula was a lovely mountain city where for some reason, I knew I would feel comfortable and safe."

Jillian swallowed and drew in a deep breath. "We were fortunate to have met Chrys and Nicholas Jensen, who I lived and worked with at their landscaping business for many years. Because of their love and support, they changed my life so miraculously that I was able to move on. And I think you are spot on in planning comfortable, homey, educational and exciting things for the girls to experience. I absolutely feel that being immediately immersed in a healthy, safe environment is a very good idea. If you can provide a harmonious home for them to transition into their new lives, they might feel even happier than they were before they were abducted."

"Yes, that is exactly why I wanted to open this ranch." Brooke reflected. "I think institutional facilities are necessary, but I truly believe that spending time on a ranch such as this is a much healthier, more enjoyable way for young women to get through the nightmares of what they experienced. When I toured Grace's Hope Ranch in Whitehorse, I studied all of the programs that she had set up, including single and group therapy sessions with psychologists and other classes offering all sorts of training in various subjects. She has women who come in to teach accounting, book-keeping, cooking, painting, sculpting, horseback riding and all sorts of ranch duties. I fell in love with the whole idea and thanks to Grace, we will have a terrific safe haven ranch like hers, right here in Grand County, Colorado."

"I agree." Jillian breathed deeply to steady her nerves after thinking about her tragic past. "If I had stumbled on a ranch like this when I was in need of a safe place to go, I would have ended up just fine, just as I was with the Jensens." She was ready to change the subject so she turned back to the plans. "I created as many lovely, tranquil outdoor spaces as possible. Look at this." She pointed to a nicely designed area right in the middle of the property. "I designed a water feature as you requested, which includes a fountain cascading down several boulders and into a small pond which will be surrounded by flowers of different types."

Brooke clapped her hands. "This is so exciting. I'm so happy that you are so good with landscaping. It looks like we will be on track for my opening Gala on June first. I've invited over a hundred people who I thought might have an interest in the Ranch and hopefully will provide ongoing funding, government and private contributions. Sarah donated a generous amount of money to help me complete the ranch and also set up a special account to help me pay for things that the girls might need as soon as they arrive, such as clothing, personal items and books." She took Jillian by the hands. "I thought that since Autumn will be graduating in May, she might like to come help and I'll pay her of course. I'd like to talk with her again about working at the ranch on the weekends, if she thinks she can handle a job with her college studies and also during the summers."

"Thank you for offering her such a terrific opportunity. She has already been planning to work with you and hopes that you will sign off on a journal of her duties at the ranch which will be important to her studies and her resume."

"Oh, absolutely. Hey, have you talked with Dakota about Anji?"

Jillian nodded. "He filled me in on a plan that he has worked out with Sarah and Grace. I'm waiting to find out when Autumn will be flying to Alaska for a visit. I'm really intrigued about the whole thing. Autumn is excited to be able to experience such an unusual adventure and is looking forward to meeting Anji. Dakota will be there at the same time for her safety and I'm going with her. I've never been to Alaska and would love to do a river float trip with them if we can arrange that while we're there. I've been reading about Noatak and the Iñupiat settlements in Alaska. I've also been reading about the horrible sex trafficking problems that Alaska is plagued with. You must know how upset that makes me, since I lost so many years of my life to such a tragic predicament." She met Brooke's eyes. "I really admire you for designing and building Harmony Ranch and I am so very grateful that you hired me to help. I have been yearning to give back, since so many people have helped me. I was one of the lucky ones and I want to lend a hand and my heart to other girls in any way that I can."

"Thank you." Brooke beamed. "I feel very good about the ranch myself. I had been searching for my new life journey for years and now I know that I have chosen the right path. I've been thinking about the work you have accomplished here and I wondered if maybe you and Liam would be interested in living in Colorado for longer than just the summer months? I could use the help around here and I thought maybe you might be interested in teaching the girls how to work with the planting and care of the greenhouse as well as being there for them to talk with. Just an idea."

"I'll give that some thought although I'm not sure that I want to leave my home and move away from Chrys and Nicholas just yet. They are such an important part of my life and will always be family to me. But I'll consider a few months here and a few months in Missoula, alternating. I think Liam will be able to travel with me whenever I want to come back. He can do a lot of his work anywhere online and over conference calls. Speaking of Liam, he and Autumn are on their way here, probably arriving sometime tonight. They'll be here to help for a week during Autumn's spring break."

"Oh, good. I have so much to do and can certainly put them to work."

Jillian's cell phone rang. It was Autumn. "Speak of the angels. Hey, where are you guys?"

Autumn said with excitement, "We are only two hours away. Are you still at the ranch?"

"Yes. The trees arrived and we've been reviewing the plans. Are you planning to come up here?"

"Well, that's why we're calling." Autumn said. "We didn't want to head to Grand's house in Evergreen if you are still at the ranch. Maybe we could stay there for the night if the lodge rooms are set up for sleeping in." Dakota and his folks live in Evergreen, Colorado, not too far from Grand County where the ranch is located.

Jillian smiled. "Oh, yes. The lodge looks charming with each room all made up. Gram and Gramps will be joining us here in the morning, so you'll get to visit with everybody. I guess we'll see you around dinner time. We have a huge pot of green chili cooking on the stove and blueberry pie for dessert."

"Yum! You're making my tummy grumble. While Dad was driving, I wrote Anji a letter to let her know that I would love to visit her. I also told her that I think it would be really fun to have her come here to go to the university with me. The plan makes me feel more comfortable knowing that I will already be familiar with someone at school and that I will have a companion. I've had a little anxiety about going to school in a place that I haven't quite adjusted to yet, so we'll be exploring together. We'll talk about it more when I get there."

"Okay, we'll see you soon."

Brooke thought about Sarah and Grace and figured they were having a good time in Alaska getting to know the Sauveurs. She wished she could go with Jillian and Autumn to meet them and explore The Noatak Wildlife Preserve, but she recognized that her responsibilities at the ranch will be too extensive to go at this time. She was also beginning to realize that she will not be able to continue working with Dakota's company. She felt sad, yet exhilarated at the same time to be finally able to begin her new life journey.

17

Anji

Papa met with several people from other small cities, who were all feeling much more confident about the arrival of tourists in June. They organized a good watch program and worked out a plan to have several locals accompany hunting parties and they will be carefully scrutinizing each party and the pilots who fly them out to various remote locations.

Sarah and Grace had fun touring around our town and the shop and spending time helping me organize the home and gift section of the shop. Kaya completed his work and found us gathered around a lovely quilt, admiring skillfully stitched floral and evergreen patterns surrounding a cluster of bear and caribou prints at the center. The colors were shades of green, purples, wine

148

red and brown shades for the animals, intermingled with the floral patterns. Sarah announced with delight, "I must have this quilt." She got out her purse to pay for it.

"I'll ring you up." I took her by the arm. "Follow me to the register."

Sarah added. "Oh, I'd like to have one of Hana's cookbooks as well. I'm buying it for Grace to enjoy using at Hope Ranch."

I carefully wrapped and placed Sarah's quilt and cookbook into a box to protect them from the snow.

Kaya said, "We have to get back. The dogs are probably stirring outside and ready for lunch. They've been waiting patiently at the back of the shop. Speaking of lunch, I'm starving. Mother will probably have something really tasty ready for us when we get there. See ya later, Papa."

"I'll be right behind you. I'm coming home for lunch and Tulugaak is ready to go home as well."

We were only a half of a mile away from the house when the wind kicked up, fiercely propelling heavily falling snow. The dogs struggled to keep up the pace against the powerful winds and blinding, whirling snow, but they managed to maintain their strength. Kaya and I stepped off the foot boards and ran as fast as we could, to help the dogs pick up the pace. By the time we reached the house, we were engulfed in such a heavy blizzard that we could hardly see in front of us. "Whew! Grace exclaimed. "That wind whipping across the tundra is a mighty force. Can Ethan drive home in this? I can hardly see down the road."

"He's driven this road millions of times. Kaya turned on the front porch lights. "Now you know why the dogs provide such beneficial transportation out here. And of course, they know the way from the shop to the house."

Papa arrived a few minutes later. Kaya was piling up wood to take inside. He handed Papa an armful. "I expected snow today, but I didn't see this coming. The blizzard blew in like a raging bull."

"Yeah, no kidding. Grandfather and I had just closed the door to the shop when a tremendous wind gust just about knocked us both down. I just drove through an absolute whiteout. I'll get the wood stove fired up. I might have to keep the shop closed for the rest of the day, unless this storm settles down after a while."

"Mother called out to them, "Looks like you made it here just in time. The storm is supposed to last all day and maybe into tomorrow. I have elk red chili on the stove and freshly baked poblano pepper cornbread keeping warm in the oven."

Sarah removed her coat and boots and sauntered into the kitchen. "Well, if these strong wind gusts continue through tomorrow, we may have to stay a little longer." She smiled conspiratorially.

"Oh, good." Alina grinned as she warmed her frozen fingers in front of the wood stove. "We would love for you to stay as long as you want to."

Papa said, "I can't fly in this weather that's for sure and you are welcome to stay as long as you like. We don't have many visitors here and it's been good to get to know you." Papa removed his hat and combed his tousled hair with his fingers.

I pulled out a puzzle that I'd been wanting to start. "We have puzzles and games that are perfect for a stormy day."

After lunch, Grace walked over to a sunken living area where several instruments were propped on their stands, waiting to be played. "Who are the musicians?"

Kaya skipped down the steps to the keyboards and began skillfully tapping the keys, transitioning into a jazzy, lively tune. I picked up my violin, joining him with a New Age bowing technique, Jean Luc Ponty style. "Come on Alina, we need some base tones." Kaya laughed as he slid his fingers across the keys.

Alina sat down behind her cello and plucked the deep, resonating strings with her fingers, creating deep rhythmic sounds and vibrations that were more like a base than a cello. Kaya sat back allowing me to play an exquisite lively solo. After a moment, Alina joined us drawing her bow slowly across the strings, then faster and faster, rising to a crescendo, then continued to play a rapidly paced rhythm. Kaya joined in on the low keys, walking his nimble fingers up toward the higher scales as I slowed the pace with long, melodious bowing. We skillfully created a remarkable harmony with a mysterious undertone.

When Joie joined us with her wood flutes, we shifted to an almost surreal melody which sounded like howling wind and raindrops tapping on the keys, the violin sweet and mellow like a soaring eagle. Alina nodded to Papa, who until then was happy to sit and listen. He grinned as he picked up his tumbadora drum beating and popping the sides alternately creating such an inviting danceable rhythm that Mother and Grandma got up and began swaying, twirling and popping their hips to the drum beats. Everyone laughed and hooted. Sarah took Grace's hands and twirled her around while Mother began to wiggle her hips and move her arms and hands, portraying a graceful poetic story.

Grace stood next to Mother and tried to imitate her movements unsuccessfully, but she was having fun anyway. Sarah joined them while laughing hysterically. "Hey, I think I'm getting the hang of this." She wiggled her hips struggling to keep up with Mother. After a few minutes of continuous energetic hip wiggling, Sarah and Grace both dropped to the floor, one after the other, breathing heavily and still giggling.

"I haven't had this much fun in a long time." Sarah said, gasping for breath. "Phew! You guys are remarkable. I bet you all have been playing for years. What a magnificent ensemble. Do you ever play in public?"

Kaya said, "We have played many times in school concerts and several times a year we play at festivals, pot luck dinners and sometimes at the Nalukataq, which is the Whaling festival. Hey, you should come back for that, June 14th through the 30th. We will most likely be celebrating the festival at Pt. Hope this year with some friends from Noatak."

Sarah thought for a minute. She was planning to come back, but hadn't decided when. "Okay, I think I will. You know, maybe we can arrange for Dakota and Autumn to arrive then as well. They might enjoy the festival and we could do the float trip afterwards. Grace, could you arrange to come back with me?"

"Absolutely. I'm not letting you guys have all of the fun without me. I love it here."

The crackle and flicker of the flames in the wood stove kept us warm and toasty, while we enjoyed each other's company, music and games for the rest of the unforgettable day.

18

Anji

The next day, the storm had moved on, so Sarah and Grace decided that they should head out before another spring storm threatened their travel home. I accompanied Papa on the plane with Grace and Sarah to Kotzebue, where they would board their flight back to Anchorage and then on to Whitehorse. I was unhappy that they were leaving, but I would write to them often and knew I'd be seeing them again in a couple of months.

Papa turned to Sarah, "You have about an hour before your flight leaves, so I'd like to check in on our shady little friend, Wily." I instantly felt a sour expression cross my face which reflected how repulsed I felt at the thought of seeing that creep again.

Sarah said, "Yes, I actually would. I had an unsettling nightmare about that strange little man last night." We walked over to the small building and entered, but there was no one around. Papa peered out of the hanger windows and noticed Wily in the company of a group of men appearing as if they were quarreling about something. There were angry facial expressions and pointing fingers. Since he was outside, I walked around his office looking at things. I hoped once again that I would find something that proved his perverted guilt. Sarah joined me, "Are you thinking what I'm thinking?"

I glanced at his messy desk. "His computer is turned on. Should we look at his photos. I wonder if he is the pervert that I believe he is."

"Let's do it." We found several files on his desktop screen. Sarah clicked on the first one. Nothing but fishing photos. She tried the second one and to our disgust, photos of naked girls in nasty poses were too numerous and too revolting to look at. Sarah shook her head. "Let's get out of here before he comes back. She wiped her prints off the keyboard and walked out to join Papa.

I lingered a little longer with sinister thoughts, wondering again what I was capable of. A few minutes later, I scurried out to join the others. "Let's go, please. I don't want to come back here ever again. That man is a twisted pervert."

Papa led us out and we headed toward the airport while Sarah described to him what we saw on Wily's computer. "I knew it, the snake. Well, sorry to involve you in a distasteful visit after all of the fun you've had. Just forget that unpleasant little visit. I'd prefer for you to have a more enjoyable mental picture on your flight home. I also hope you aren't planning to spend more time in Anchorage when you get there. That city has many beautiful areas, views and terrific restaurants, but during the dark, shadowy hours as you are well aware, corruption and perversion smolder under the rocks. It's just not safe for you at this time."

"No. I'm planning to go back when Dakota and his team arrive, but not now. Grace needs to get back and I have a lot of planning and research to do. How about this; I'll think about Hana and her energetic story dancing. She sure has some moves. I'm going to practice when I get home." She laughed and we all joined in.

"Now that's a wonderful mental picture." He chuckled. "I'll tell her what you said."

After we made sure Sarah and Grace boarded the plane safely, Papa and I were walking to our plane when we ran into Nicholas Atka. "Hey, how are you?"

"Oh, we're doing just fine. We just dropped off our guests at the airport to catch their flight back to Anchorage. What are you up to?"

"Have you heard that Wily Johns was found dead about a half hour ago in his office?"

"No kidding. We were there almost an hour ago and I saw him outside arguing with several other men. We were waiting to talk with him, but he took too long and we had to get our friends to the airport. Do you know what happened?"

"Well at first we thought he may have had a heart attack, but evidence might prove that he was murdered. His lips were blue and he had vomit on his shirt, so we think he was poisoned. He also had some kind of rash on his throat, arms and hands. My forensics team is there now. They'll take samples of things he may have touched and swallowed such as his coffee and water glass and will check him out to find out what poison was used. I hope he has the names of the men he was arguing with on his flight manifest. A plane was seen flying off to the south just before he was discovered. A customer found him in his office chair and called us."

"Well, I can't say that I'm sorry he's dead, but I hope you find out who killed him in any case."

"I'm curious about those other men he was with. Maybe they had something to do with it. Let me know if you recall anything that might help and have a safe flight home. That storm yesterday was a doozy!"

"Thanks, Nicholas. I'll be back next week and I'll pop in."

I was pleased to know that Wily was dead and relieved that Papa had witnessed him arguing with the other men. During our flight home, I sat quietly contemplating. One pervert down and many more to go. I wished that all abusive, nasty criminals would fall victim to such poetic justice.

When we walked into the house, Mother, Grandma and Grandpapa were sitting at the kitchen table drinking jasmine tea. Grandfather glanced up and noticed Papa's disturbed expression. "What news do you have, Ethan?"

"Do you recall my mentioning Wily Johns, who owns the suspicious bush flight company?" Grandpapa nodded. "He was found dead in his office this morning, possibly murdered. Nicholas Atka thinks he may have been poisoned. They are waiting for the forensics team to complete their investigation. I can't say that I'm sorry, but it's still shocking."

I said in disgust, "He was a pervert. Sarah and I saw nasty photos on his computer and we could all perceive that he was lying to us. I say good riddance and one less vile criminal to be concerned with."

Sophia scrutinized her, remembering the Monkshood that Anji had secretly removed from the jar and her mysterious behavior. She said a silent prayer that Anji had nothing to do with the murder. It just wasn't like her to possess such hatred. "Anji, I've never heard you speak that way. He might have been a horrible man, but be careful not to hold hatred in your heart."

"I won't and it's not that I really wished death upon him, but I did wish he would be arrested. I mean, nobody needs that kind of dreadful, deceitful man around. He could have been in on some of the abductions and possibly working with some other corrupt men, like the ones we saw him with at his hangar"

"She does have a point," Papa considered. "I witnessed Wily out by a plane with several men apparently in a heated argument and an hour later he was found dead. Maybe he was mixed up with some criminals. Someone saw a plane take off from there after we left and the other men who were with him were suddenly nowhere in sight. There was no flight plan recorded for the group either."

Sophia closed her eyes releasing a subtle breath. She thought, I hope Anji is innocent but I'll keep what I know a secret which I will take to my grave. She glanced up at Anji with teary eyes hoping that she could never do such a thing. If the poison turns out to be Monkshood, Anji could be guilty. She excused herself and left the room to go pray by her bed.

In the morning, Ethan left early to meet a bush plane

carrying supplies and a few customer orders. The pilot, Ujurak Moon, a good friend of Ethan, had just opened the cargo door of his DHC-6 Twin Otter 19 passenger plane as Ethan drove up. "Hey, brother. How's it going?"

Ethan shook his hand. "Glad you're back from the lower forty-eight. I had to fly with Jay Hawkins yesterday. I haven't trusted his ability to stay alert lately. He seemed preoccupied."

Ujurak shook his head. "Yeah, I think we've spooked some of these guys with our watch program. They're getting nervous, but I wouldn't think Hawkins would have anything to do with criminal activity. He has had enough trouble with his own boys, especially Ben who has been getting into trouble lately in one form or another."

"Last time I heard, the two boys were hanging out in Kotzebue at a motel and working in a bar where they had plenty of opportunities to get inebriated and apparently did on several occasions."

"I think Jim still works at the bar, but Ben got fired for drinking on the job and was also caught in the company of a suspicious man who owns a yacht. After the yacht departed, Ben seemed to have just disappeared. It's my suspicion that he hired on with the owner of the yacht. Hawkins has been trying to find out more about the man, with no luck so far. I don't think the guy comes around more than a few times a year."

Ujurak chugged some water, then raised his eyebrows. "Hey, did you hear about Wily Johns? They figured out that he was poisoned with some local plant called Monkshood. They discovered the poison in his coffee cup and his blood work showed the same poison. I heard you were at his hangar the day he was killed. Did you see anything?"

"Yes. He was outside with two men engaged in some kind of heated argument and I spoke with Nicholas Atka who informed me that Wily may have been murdered."

"Wow, it looks like whoever he was arguing with may have taken him down. Did you happen to get a description of the plane? Since I'm there often, I could keep an eye out for it. And since Wily is gone, those guys may be looking for another company to contract airfare with, which we should be very leery of."

Ethan thought for a moment. "Come to think of it, I believe it was a DHC-6, like yours only mostly white with a black killer whale on the side. One guy was a huge man, who kind of looked like a Sumo wrestler and the other was wearing a black tourist style hat and a black leather knee length coat, but I didn't see either of their faces. Too far away."

"I'll keep an eye out for it and I'll spread the word to other pilots. Someone will probably be buying Wily's operation. That's a good hangar, maybe large enough for at least four bush planes, but I think it's shut down until the investigation is over."

Ethan scrunched his face, looking like he had a sour taste in his mouth. "Wily was a shady character. Anji and my friend Sarah saw some disturbing photos on his computer. He was a pervert as Anji put it. I spoke with him on several occasions, hoping to find out if he was involved with smuggling or criminal activity of any sort. If those men were working with Wily, they were probably involved in some kind of crime, maybe even trafficking. Keep an eye out and call me if you find out more. I want to look into this further."

"Yeah, me too." Ethan and Ujurak transferred the cargo into Ethan's Bronco.

"Hey, come by the shop next time you're in the area. We have a hunting trip to plan and you know how much Hana likes to cook for you. She has been wondering why you haven't been around lately. I told her you were in the lower forty-eight picking up her fabric order. She wants to know if you were able to pick up her hides from Takumi. He wasn't quite finished with them a few weeks ago and she is ready to start making jackets."

"Yep. They're in those large boxes. How about I come by Friday night when I bring out your next order."

"Why don't you plan on staying with us. That way, you can enjoy dinner and you won't have to fly back at night."

"I'll plan on that. See ya then."

Ethan headed home arriving on time to eat breakfast with the kids before they began their school studies. He kissed Hana on her cheek. "Ujurak picked up your hides."

"Oh, good. I want to have the jackets completed sometime next week. And the quilt materials?"

"Yes. Kaya will help me unload your boxes before I head to the shop." He smiled at Kaya.

"Sure. I'd like to have one of your new jackets, Mother. My jacket is too small. I guess my muscles are getting too big." He raised his arms flexing his bulging muscles.

Alina snickered. "Jessica has noticed those bulging muscles. I saw her staring at you after we tested last week. Are you sweet on her, too?"

"Maybe. She's cute. She is in my monthly shop class. I showed her how to use the mitering tool for a cedar chest that she's making. I kind of like girls who like to build things, rather than sitting around acting helpless, giggling and saying stupid things. She's different."

Alina said teasingly, "And her curvy figure has nothing to do with it, right."

"Shut up, Alina."

Hana snickered. "Okay, you two clowns, eat up. We'll begin your studies in ten minutes."

Kaya stood, acknowledging Ethan's presence. "I had an assignment to finish, so I didn't have time to run the dogs. I'll do it as soon as school is over."

"Come by the shop. I have a delivery for you, two stops. If I can get away, I'll go with you."

Hana closed the door of the study so that the kids could focus on their school assignments without being disturbed by the discussion she perceived would be brewing shortly. Sophia drowsily moseyed into the kitchen. "Good morning, Hana. I overheard the conversation about Wily. Does it sound to you like they might know who the killer was?"

"Well the authorities are still investigating, but Ethan witnessed two men arguing as I'm sure you heard. They think that Wily was poisoned with Monkshood. I wonder where the men got that idea from." She shook her head and sighed heavily. "What concerns me is that the criminals may have heard that the people from rural communities have been hunting for traffickers, so what if they were trying to make it look like we are to blame? If that is the case, then we must prove it otherwise and make sure the criminals responsible are arrested. Oh, and one of Jay Hawkins' boys, Ben was recently fired from his job, then was later seen in the company of a few men

161

on a large yacht which is no longer anchored at the marina. That boy has been troubled for over a year now and he knows plenty about medicinal herbs since Jay owns the pharmacy. What if he has been working for whoever owns the yacht? And before you berate me for suggesting that Ben is guilty of anything sinister, I'm simply trying to figure out what Ben's association with the men in question might be."

Sophia sat immobile, contemplating. She thought to herself, I think Anji may not have had anything to do with it after all. She felt relief, but she still wondered what in the world she was planning to do with the Monkshood. She also pondered on the possibility that Ben Hawkins could be a spying on a criminal organization. Ben used to be a respectful, hardworking young man and it troubled her that he suddenly changed his demeanor and began drinking and fighting.

"Are you okay, Sophia? You look tired. Have you not been sleeping well?"

"I'll be fine. Maybe I'll take a nap later." She had been so worried about Anji, that she was not sleeping well at all, but now she felt somewhat liberated from her secret burden. "Do you remember a year ago, Jay Hawkins was talking about how Ben was involved with a girl from one of the northwest cities and traveled often to see her? I can't remember what her name was. Something like Dalianya maybe? Yes, I think that was her name."

Hana thought for a minute. "Yes, that name does sound familiar. I think you are right, but what does that mean to you?"

"I'm not sure, but Ben was on top of the world for a while and all of a sudden, a year ago he began engaging in deviant behavior. He would not say what was troubling him, but I think it must have had something to do with Dalianya because he no longer went to visit her. I wonder what happened to make him so angry? I'm going to speak with Ethan about it and ask him to meet with Jay. Maybe he can shed some light on the mystery. It's just that I know a good character when I meet one and Ben is a good man. He obviously has been experiencing some difficult times and I think we should stand by him. I don't believe that he is involved in any criminal activity. That kind of behavior is just not in his nature. To act in a villainous manner, a person has to possess extreme hatred, anger, vengefulness and so on. Ben was always treated with love and compassion by Jay and Elisapee and he has always reflected those qualities in his personality until last year, so he must be very upset by something that happened."

"Sophia, you might be right, but you must take care of yourself. You seem to be so deeply immersed in troubling events lately, that you are not well. I'll make some peppermint chamomile tea for you. Just sit right there. Are you hungry? You missed breakfast. I'll make some oatmeal with salmon berries for you."

"That sounds good, dear. Thank you. I'll go check on Tulugaak. He'll be awake by now."

"Did I hear my name?" Tulugaak made his way into the kitchen and poured himself a cup of coffee.

Hana said, "I'll have your breakfast ready in fifteen minutes. There are some biscuits and honey on the table. Ethan picked up my hides this morning from Takumi. I'd appreciate help with cutting the patterns if you aren't busy with other things."

"I'd be happy to help. I'll be smoking some caribou

163

today for Ethan's hunting trip, but I surely don't need to just sit and watch it." He chuckled. They filled him in on the discussion earlier about Wily. He caught the attention of Sophia's eyes. "Oh, Monkshood, you say? I haven't heard of anyone using the herb for many years although, I know Anji brings it to you to keep in your medicinal inventory." He grinned at her devilishly. Sophia narrowed her eyes as she squirmed in her chair. He went on. "Not a good way to die. He suffered greatly."

After breakfast, Hana, Sophia and Tulugaak worked on the leather jackets quietly, each deeply absorbed in their own thoughts. Tulugaak had overheard the conversation about Ben Hawkins before he walked into the kitchen. As he worked on the hides, he shook his head in disgust, contemplating. He had heard some talk about the possibility that a major crime syndicate may be responsible for the abductions in Anchorage. He thought it could be possible that someone who knows about the activities of the criminals could be acting alone albeit heroically, but is most likely in danger. He would meet with Jay Hawkins later to try to locate Ben. He has known the Hawkins family for generations and really wanted to rule Ben out as any sort of guilty party, but things that have occurred recently were surely not in his favor. He instinctively decided that if Ben was in trouble, he must have some help as soon as possible.

He recalled that at one time, Ben wanted to work as a detective with the police department. When he was younger, he was always reading detective stories and he visited the Kotzebue Sheriff often to ask about the latest crimes and how they were solving the cases. Unfortunately, when his mother, Elisapee passed away after suffering from cancer for almost a year, Ben was horribly affected and became severely depressed. He blamed his father for not taking care of her well enough which was way off base, but Ben began drinking, fighting and gambling away any money he had earned. And then he met a young woman from Kobuk who seemed to turn him around. He talked about her, but Tulugaak couldn't recall Ben ever bringing her home. He wondered if Jay had met her at some point. Tulugaak wasn't sure when Ben stopped seeing the girl, but he remembered seeing him in Kotzebue a year ago in another drunken rage.

What was bothering Tulugaak was that even though Ben seemed to be lost, he continued to respect and love his family and friends and it seemed unthinkable that he would do anything to harm the people of Alaska. When he overheard Sophia talking about Ben's girlfriend, Dalianya and that something could have happened to her to cause him to act so mysteriously, Tulugaak decided that there was only one conclusion; that Ben was finally playing the role of a detective by working undercover to get to the heart of the mighty corruption that has plagued Alaska for far, too long. Maybe Dalianya was the connection. The more Tulugaak contemplated this scenario, the more he believed it might be the case. If so, how could they find him, help him and join him in his efforts?

Everything began to make sense. If Wily was working with a criminal organization involved in trafficking Alaskan girls and Ben discovered it, he might have figured out how to be at the right place at the right time to take him out, therefore earning his right to work for the organization. He would not do such a thing to be a part of a criminal organization, but he could be working for them to try to infiltrate the corrupt syndicate in order to demolish the head of the beast and destroy the organization from the top down to the lowest ranks. Tulugaak wondered if Ben was the source of the Monkshood for that reason.

Sophia noticed Tulugaak's intense concentration. "What's going on in that handsome head of yours? I can see smoke pouring out of your ears."

"Oh, it's nothing. I just have some things to discuss with Jay and Ethan concerning Ben."

"Oh? Anything you'd like to share?"

"No, but didn't Ben take sailing lessons and didn't he have a tattoo of a yacht on his forearm that he walked around showing everyone, bragging about how he was going to own a yacht someday and sail around solving land and sea crimes? I mean he used to tell the most elaborate stories, one more magnificent than the last." He donned a conspiratorial grin that made Hana and Sophia clap and laugh. They understood immediately what Tulugaak was alluding to. "Anji used to spend time with Ben when they were younger. What ever happened to their friendship?"

Hana said, "High school happened. I think Anji began studying so intently that she stopped doing things with the others. Not only that, she has been working hard, helping with Ethan's deliveries and her explorations in the preserve. Ever since she began studying botany, she has spent almost all of her extra time out there taking photos and picking floral samples to study. She has become somewhat of an expert on every plant species that grows in Alaska."

"Including Monkshood." Tulugaak eyed Sophia with suspicion. He had studied her reactions every time the subject of Monkshood arose in connection with Anji. He wondered as well if Anji had something to do with Wily's demise, especially since she acted so strangely during the conversation at the dinner table and right after her trip to Kotzebue. He noticed Hana's stunned eyes and shook his head. "No. I don't believe our girl had anything to do with it. I would sense it if she had." Sophia searched his eyes and smiled with relief.

Hana gasped in horror. "No, she would never. I don't blame her for hating criminals who abduct our girls, but she would never conspire to kill another. No, not Anji. Someone will shed light on this soon enough. I think Anji has worked so hard and has been so certain of her future endeavors that she seems to be willing to do whatever it takes to prevent anything from hindering her plans, but she would never cross that line."

"I agree." Tulugaak hugged Hana. "Anji is realizing that the world is not safe and she knows she must do what she can to protect herself. She has never trusted anyone outside of our family until now, with Grace and Sarah. These are big steps for her and I believe she will figure things out soon enough. She is a good girl and she knows the difference between right and wrong." He paused in a knowing way as he has always done when he senses something that others don't. "A storm is brewing and soon we will discover a favorable resolve for all of us."

19

Anji

It's May 18th and dark skies have given way to longer spring days with the sun setting at one in the morning and rising at four-thirty, over twenty hours of daylight. The plants and wildflowers have been showing off beautiful displays of color and emitting lovely scents which drift through the air while they bask in the sunshine along with various animals roaming around the area.

I have been having a glorious time finding and charting the flowers that bloom in the spring so far. I'm thrilled with an unusual, but beautiful flower called Woolly Lousewort, Pedicularis dasyantha, which I discovered in a stony tundra area. The flower is protected by a layer of fuzzy wool which wraps around the stem of the plant, shielding it from wind and cold temperatures.

It grows well in arctic conditions because the wool traps solar energy, retaining warm air around the plant. The plant grows about six inches tall and has pink or purple flowers that bloom in a cluster. What is really interesting is that when the weather warms, the flowers break through the wool, showing off gorgeous clusters of color. The entire lousewort plant is edible. The blossoms can be eaten raw and taste sweet or they can be covered with water and left to ferment into a dish similar to sauerkraut. Grandma makes scrumptious dishes with steamed leaves and stems added to soups and casseroles. The root, called taproot is thick and fleshy and tastes like a baby carrot. I like those raw in a salad.

Another blooming treasure that I discovered this year near the Woolly Lousewort, is the bright and cheerful yellow flower called One-flowered Cinquefoil, Potentilla uniflora, which is in the rose family, showing off five petals with an orange spot near the base of the bloom. I noticed the flowers peeking out from between rocks and boulders. I've been searching for Mountain Harebell, Campanula lasiocarpa, a violet blue trumpet shaped flower that I see sometimes in the same rocky tundra, but I haven't located it yet this year.

While relaxing in my room, I gazed at the colorful floral covered tundra as I thought about the upcoming tourist season. Numerous outdoor enthusiasts will begin arriving to enjoy the Noatak Wildlife Preserve and the Noatak River in another month and a half. The mosquitoes are terrible in June and the river can still be quite icy until July, so most river floaters and fishing enthusiasts will visit between July and September. Tourist season is always an exciting time of the year and Papa's shop is quite popular during the summer months. I suddenly shivered and frowned when I thought about the non-resident hunters who will arrive in September. I whispered to myself, "Will we run across a suspicious group of men with malicious intentions lurking in the shadows?" I had been trying to stay busy so that I wouldn't dwell in the frightening, disconcerting corners of my mind.

In preparation for the tourist season, we've been helping Mother complete several large quilts, leather jackets and hats, mukluks and pottery. Joie has been scrambling to complete a few exquisite wooden bowls and two small birch wood side tables. She has been arranging some colorful tiles that she broke into small pieces so that they are all different shapes. She will then place the tiles in thin set and mortar resulting in exquisite, colorful mosaic top tables.

Alina has been working on about a dozen colorful, skirts and dresses, one of which I might buy from her. The one that I like is a beautiful, drapey, soft blue-gray, cotton skirt with a scarf-like cut at the bottom and a wide beaded suede leather belt. She said she will give it to me, but I like to support her efforts by paying for her lovely creations. Joie and I are happy to be her models at different stages of her work which is really fun sometimes, as we pretend to strut and saunter down a runway, taunting and seducing the attention of glamorous fashion consultants.

I have been working diligently on my senior high studies and will be graduating soon. I received another letter from Grace who informed me that Autumn will definitely be attending Colorado State University. I've been feeling more confident about going to a strange place in the lower forty-eight states for the first time because of Autumn. Planning is overwhelming, but I've been trying to take one step at a time to lessen a bit of anxiety. I'm so excited that I will already have a friend when I arrive. I realize that I'm jumping the gun, but I will not let this extraordinary opportunity pass me by.

I also received a letter from Autumn letting me know how excited she is about meeting me and coming here to visit. I'm planning lots of activities for her vacation, including a river float trip, which she inquired about. She said that her mother, Jillian may be coming with her. I think it would be terrific if our families become good friends.

I had been thinking about the more populated cities such as Denver, Steamboat Springs, Boulder and Fort Collins which is where Colorado State University is located. I'm definitely considering CSU, especially if I like Autumn's and Dakota Hunt's demeanors and personalities. That is super important to me. I want to be certain that we feel comfortable with each other.

I'm proud of myself for trusting Grace and Sarah and I sense that they both have my well-being and best interests at heart. I'm so happy that I received such a positive response from my letter to Grace and I was so delighted that they were able to come out for such a fun visit and to strategize with Papa.

I was thinking about what I wanted to write in a return letter to Autumn when the dogs started barking uncontrollably. I peered out of my window, noticing the daylight had faded and dark clouds had moved in. I stared into the shadowy gray sky and suddenly, something caught my eye startling me, but I couldn't make out what I was seeing. The trees were swaying in the whistling wind and sleety rain was tapping on the windows. I saw Papa step out from the front door of the house to find out what all of the commotion was about. He scouted around and then checked on the dogs as he did every night. It was probably an animal of some sort, maybe trying to find shelter from the spring storm.

I continued to watch out of the window as Papa went back inside, oddly frozen in my stance as I tried to figure out what I had seen. It wasn't an animal, but more like a shadowy, flowing figure, moving swiftly across the yard. "Hmmm," I voiced out loud nervously. "I wonder if the mysterious raven was visiting again." You never know what you will see out here in the wilderness. I tried to think about what I wanted to say to Autumn, but I kept envisioning the shadowy figure.

The sight reminded me about a time when I was picking berries in the wilderness and I thought I saw something peculiar in a dense area of trees, a dark figure crouching by a rock outcropping. Kodiak and Nukilik were with me and were barking and growling aggressively which they rarely ever did to that extent. The dogs wanted to go discover what or who it was and were tugging relentlessly on their leashes. I quickly gathered my things and hiked away in the opposite direction, not wanting to encounter a pack of wolves or perhaps a grizzly bear who may have been after my berries. I shivered at the memory because not knowing what was lurking in the shadows was more unnerving than seeing a wild animal close by. As we hurriedly walked away, the dogs continued barking and howling while whatever it was, rustled in the shadowy

172

forest. I thought it would be best to head home as quickly as we could. I didn't tell anyone about it, but maybe I should have. The experience occurred during hunting season in September last year, so I just figured I was too close to a hunting party. But what if it was something more sinister. Maybe my imagination was once again conjuring up something that really wasn't anything at all.

I have always been unwavering in my beliefs about reality and what is factual compared to what is fantasy or mysticism, but lately everything seems to be challenging what I have always accepted as true. Heightened spirituality has always been a part of the Alaskan culture, but I have chosen to believe that there could only be one or the other and I have chosen science. Am I wrong? Does the material world and the immaterial, spiritual world coincide and do we have to rely on faith that this is true? If not, then why are the hairs standing up on my neck and arms as I gaze out of my window at the mysterious, shadowy figure soaring with the wind? And why did I see the mysterious image in the northern lights?

I feel like I have grown up quite a bit in the past year and I feel more responsible and maybe not so naïve now. I have been harboring a secret that I have not yet revealed to Papa and I decided I had better discuss it with him soon. I want to do some research first about that disturbing day last year, while we were shopping in Anchorage. My mind was too preoccupied to write to Autumn so I decided to reply to her in the morning.

Before I retired for the night, I opened up my laptop and connected to the internet. I looked up missing persons in the year 2018 in Anchorage and found several reports of girls who were abducted, but I was not sure if any of them was the I girl I witnessed being plucked from the world like a vulture snagging its prey. I decided to talk with Grandma about it in the morning.

I tossed and turned all night, hardly sleeping at all. I felt frustrated and my head was throbbing. I drew in several deep breaths, exhaling slowly to calm my nerves. I glanced at the clock, seeing four in the morning, then peeked out of my window and noticed that the cloudy gray sky had given way to the soft glow of a lovely tangerine and crimson dawn. I heard slight clatters in the kitchen, so I put on my slippers and a warm, cozy robe and ambled downstairs to see who was up so early.

Grandma was kneading dough, so I assumed that Papa would be showing up soon, relishing the scent of freshly baked biscuits wafting through the house as he did every morning. "Good morning, Grandma." She noticed the apprehensive look on my face and asked me what I was troubled with so early in the morning. I'm always amazed at how easily she senses something bothering me. I decided to unleash my unsettling secret that I have preferred to keep to myself, not only to ease my guilt, but so that I could relieve my mind from the escalating, disturbing turmoil churning within my subconscious. She looked at me perceptively with raised eyebrows, but how could she possibly know what was on my mind?

Sophia prayed that Anji was not going to tell her that she poisoned Wily Johns. She desperately wanted to be relieved of her morose concerns and had been suppressing the urge to ask Anji to explain herself.

I could almost see smoke pouring out of Grandma's ears as she attempted to discover my mysterious burden. "Last summer, Papa, Kaya and I were shopping in

Anchorage and I witnessed a disturbing incident that I have kept to myself for a year. I didn't really understand at the time what was going on, but I recognized that something wasn't right. I'm ashamed because I could have helped and I didn't."

Grandma studied my eyes and urged me to elaborate. "You are troubled with your Papa's concerns about the disappearances of young women, aren't you?"

"Yes, but there is a reason why I am particularly concerned. A girl about my age was putting her groceries in her car and a man grabbed her from behind and forced her into a van and drove off. What disturbs me the most is that when the man was maliciously shoving her toward the van, she turned her head and stared right at me with terror in her eyes. I stood there stunned with my mouth open, but no sound escaped. I feel certain now that she was kidnapped. I didn't say anything to Papa and I should have. She obviously wanted my help, but I just turned and ran to catch up to Papa and went on about my business." My voice was quivering and tears filled my eyes as I confessed my shameful ineptitude. "I could have saved her if I wasn't so naïve, so unaware and ignorant."

"You couldn't have known what the situation was. When we first settled here, we were pleased with the plentiful environment and everything Miki Tarniq and the Noatak River Valley had to offer us. We worked very hard to build our home and our new way of life with everything we needed, with no outsiders who could have caused harm as they may have in other cities. The women of our town and family have always been confident and capable of defending ourselves and the men have been kind, compassionate, caring men, but I have heard of families who had to deal with the shame of alcoholism and family violence. As far as I know, our community is a respectful one and I hope the day never arrives when I hear differently, although I am not naïve." She stood there quietly for a moment, contemplating her next question. "Anji, tell me more about Anya."

I sat there stunned, utterly speechless. I had already talked with her about Anya, but did she find out that I saw her in Anchorage at the Iditarod and again in Kotzebue? I wondered if Kaya mentioned that. "I see her here and there, but when I notice her in public places, she becomes mysteriously elusive." I had a strange feeling about Anya in connection with Anchorage, as if there was something not quite right about her time there. I haven't been able to understand why I felt strange about it and Anya hasn't elaborated on her stay there. I have been meaning to ask her about it and will if she returns to the hunting camp this year.

Grandma narrowed her eyes. "Does she look familiar to you? Search your soul, Anji."

I drew in a deep breath and closed my eyes, relaxing my mind while I pictured Anya. Suddenly, the hairs on my arms stood upright as if a cold blast of wind whirled around me. With my eyes still closed, I had a feeling of extreme discomfort as my memory of that strange day came flooding back to me as clearly as if it was happening all over again. I stood up on rubbery legs and spoke with a shaky voice. "Anya is the girl that I saw being shoved into the van. I remember the way she looked, with long black hair in braids and she wore a red coat and a long, drapey red scarf with colorful beads. It's the same scarf that she was wearing one day at the hunting camp and the

176

same scarf that the raven flew here with and dropped for me. But why didn't she say anything to me when we were picking berries in the preserve? She must be outraged that I didn't help her, but she isn't and she seems to need my help now. I saw her when we were at the Iditarod in Anchorage, but just for a few seconds while we were waiting for Grace and Sarah to meet us. I was concerned that they wouldn't find us in the crowd of people and then right after I saw Anya, Grace and Sarah showed up. She must have been spooked by someone there who frightened her causing her to flee. She was also peering at me through the window at Wily John's airplane hangar. I think she might know something disturbing about him and was trying to give me a message."

"Anji, you need to speak with her. You must find out what happened to her. She is finding you for a reason and it's vital that you figure out what that reason is." Sophia stood transfixed with her thoughts, now wondering if Anya could have poisoned Wily since she was seen there. Maybe she had experienced some distressing situation with Wily in the past and wanted to make sure he was punished for his offenses.

"Oh, I feel terrible. What if she suffered a terrifying, dreadful ordeal? I want to help her, but how can I when I don't know where to find her? Should I discuss her with Papa?"

"If you need to unburden yourself, go ahead, but you needn't feel shame. You now understand more than you did before and what you do with this new information is more important. I also want to discuss a few things with you, concerning social activities while you are away at school. Anji, I know you will be attending a university away from Alaska. You will learn about and be exposed to many things, including alcohol and drugs. You must stay clear of these bad spirits or they will take you down."

"Yes, Grandma. I understand. Papa is worried about that as well, but I'd like to believe that I am strong minded and will be able to choose a healthier beverage that doesn't cloud my judgment." Papa moseyed into the kitchen and poured himself a cup of coffee.

"Good morning." He smiled, glancing at my bewildered face revealing obvious ambiguity as I sat hunched over in my chair. "What are you pondering over so early in the morning?"

"Oh, I didn't sleep well last night and Grandma's baking lured me into the kitchen for a cup of jasmine tea and a chat."

"Oh? What's on your mind?"

I set my burdening conundrum aside, stood up and hugged him. "Thank you for being a respectful, honorable man and a kind, caring Papa." With that, I sauntered out of the room with a forced grin. I was not ready to discuss Anya with him, because I didn't think he would understand and might possibly prevent me from conducting investigative work concerning her situation for safety reasons. We'll soon be able to work it all out together on our next hunting trip.

I thought about Private Detective Dakota Hunt and wondered when he and his team would be arriving to help us. I think I will sleep easier knowing that skilled professionals are doing everything they can to help us protect the peaceful people of our exquisite state. I wondered if Anya had managed to escape and has been hiding out, desperate for help. While Papa, Sarah and

Detective Hunt are hunting for traffickers in Anchorage, maybe they can help me find out who kidnapped her that fateful day and what happened to her.

20

Dakota and Cheynne Demarka, his companion and co-driver, were making their way into the Yukon Territory, preparing to exchange a trailer load of freight for a shipment headed to Anchorage. They would be arriving in Whitehorse soon and had plans to enjoy the day with Micco and Sylvia, Cheynne's brother, sister-in-law and their kids. The following day, they planned to visit with Grace which would include a fun filled day at Hope Ranch. Cheynne was looking forward to a nice hot soak in the Takhini Hot Pools and Dakota had an interest in riding horses with the kids and doing a bit of touring historic sites in the area.

Cheynne broke the silence they had been enjoying for the past half hour, while marveling at the serene remote environment. "Hey, I just received a text from Micco. He is excited that we will be visiting, but he's disappointed that we will only be there for one day. Do you think we might be able to arrange another visit and stay longer on our way back?"

Cheynne had managed to visit with Micco and Sylvia at least once a year for the past four years. Micco owns a fishing tour company and Sylvia is a renowned chef who owns her own restaurant, Sylvia's Bistro, specializing in delectable dishes of freshwater fish, wild game and delectable pastries.

Dakota smiled, appreciating the idea that they could spend some quality time together off work. "I'm sure we can arrange that especially if we accomplish what I hope to while in Anchorage and as long as we stay in contact with Dirk. I just have a feeling that we will be there at a significant time, particularly since Sarah has already been scouting around. I think I'm beginning to understand how the woman thinks. I'm sure she has a plan developing as we speak."

"Yes, I bet she does and I'm sure we'll find out at the Ranch. On another note, I'll be excited to introduce Micco and Sylvia to Grace. It's possible that they have already met her and aren't aware of our connection. Silvia's Bistro is quite popular with the locals."

They arrived at a rest area to stop for a quick break. Dakota got out of the truck to stretch his legs and noticed an abandoned car with the rear doors opened wide. Something did not feel right to him, so he cautiously ambled over to investigate and to his dismay, he spotted a woman's hiking boot on the ground by the car door. He also noticed two backpacks on the back seat, but no one was in sight. "Cheynne, come check this out." She jogged to the car, immediately understanding Dakota's concerns. "Please search the car for identification, but try not to touch anything with bare hands. I'll scout around down by the river."

Dakota carefully searched the surrounding area in the grass and shrubs on the way down to the riverbank. He noticed some footprints and kneeled down to examine the tread pattern to see if they matched the hiking boot by the car. There were several different prints and the grass around the area had been matted down. Some of the shrub branches surrounding the area were broken. He wondered if there had been a struggle there. And then he saw something that sent a chill up his spine. He noticed human hair and blood streaks on a torn piece of clothing, possibly a t-shirt. He snapped photos of everything he was seeing to give to the Royal Canadian Mounted Police. He pounded a tree branch into the ground to mark the spot and continued down toward the river.

Cheynne called out to him. "Dakota, I found the title and registration of the car and wallets in the backpacks. I'll send a SatCom message to Jake since I don't have cell reception here. He should still be in Skagway which will have cell towers to call the RCMP." The keys to the car were still in the ignition, so Cheynne started the car to see if the people possibly had a breakdown. If the car wouldn't start, they may have stopped there and gone for help, except they wouldn't have left their backpacks and the boot. Nothing made sense. She sent all of the information she could and sprinted down the path to catch up with Dakota.

By the water's edge she heard Dakota gasp. "Holy

Hell! What happened here?" A mangled woman's body was laying lifelessly on the river bank. They noticed clothing strewn around and all sorts of foot prints including bear paws.

"Oh, dear." Cheynne put her hand over her mouth and tried to stay calm. "Could this be a bear attack? That might explain why the car was abandoned with two backpacks inside? The names on the ID's are Olivia Lambert and Mia Grenier. I'm not exactly sure which one this is, but Olivia has auburn hair as does the victim here."

"This wasn't a bear attack. First, I discovered a small area of matted down grass near the car and a very small piece of clothing and hair with blood on them. If a bear attacked them up there, we would have found a lot more than a small piece, much more blood and bear paw prints at that scene. There were no bear prints up there. Second, there are several different types of footprints down here." He kneeled down to inspect the prints closely, taking photos of them. "There are two other prints, one larger, like a man sized boot and the other is the same print that I found up above, but it doesn't match the boot by the car. The woman was most likely already dead when the bear arrived at the scene. That is a bullet hole in her chest, so someone shot her. If they were all trying to escape from a charging bear, I think we would be seeing a dead bear with bullet wounds, not the woman. This woman isn't wearing a stitch of clothing and here, check this out." He walked over to a pair of jeans laying on the ground about twenty feet away from the body. "No rips or shreds of material. She was obviously struggling while someone removed her clothing, then she tried to run, but was shot before she was able to get back to the car. I don't want to make up scenarios, but I am certain that we are looking at a fatal sex crime." He shook his head in disgust and frowned in anguish. "Well, let's head back to the truck and wait for the RCMP to arrive. We'll show them what we discovered and I'll transfer the photos to them. I also want to look around for tracks and tread from another car. The only problem is that since this is a rest area, we might find many different tread patterns."

As they walked back up the trail, Cheynne said warily, "I agree with you. My gut tells me that we are seeing the aftermath of an abduction. There are no signs of Mia, the other woman. No-one would go for help and leave their gear and wallets in their car and the car started right up so they didn't break down."

Dakota's eyes lowered, "You know what I find disturbing? We seem to run across sex crime scenes often, so why aren't the authorities finding them? Although, I guess we find them because we are looking for them. I bet other people stopped at this rest area, went about their business and left, not having any thought or concern about the abandoned car. If they did, the gear would probably have been stolen."

"Yeah, I think about that sometimes, too. When you look for it, I guess you find it." Cheynne shivered and tried not to think about the horrible scene. She hopped into the truck to see if Jake replied to her message while Dakota searched around. A few minutes later, the RCMP arrived in an SUV and parked beside the truck. Dakota walked over to them, introduced himself and began to review their findings. He showed them the car, the identification of the victims, the torn fabric with hair and blood, boot prints and then walked with the Mounty down the trail to the river.

"My God, what a scene!" One of the Mounties kneeled down to look at the bullet wound in the woman's body. He shook his head in sorrow. "Hey, Jim, run up and get a body bag." He began snapping photos of the body and the scene and Dakota transferred the photos he took earlier to the officer's phone. "Since you're here, would you mind helping me carry the woman's body to my vehicle?"

"No problem." They took care of the lifeless form, bagged her clothing and other evidence and headed up the trail. "Just so that you know, my partner and I are working with an FBI task force in cooperation with your government, hunting sex traffickers. I believe this is another abduction case. I searched the area as thoroughly as I could, but I haven't found any clues to the other person."

"Yeah, I think you're right. Your message to Jake Losato was transferred to me along with your information. I am very familiar with your operation and I have to say, I'm grateful for your help. Not many people go out of their way to help like you are. We have all been well informed about the task force team and what you will be doing and we'll assist you in any way that we can. I have an idea about where the other woman may have been taken, if I'm right. We've had several calls about missing people from rest areas out here in the middle of nowhere, on this highway and if they were victims of traffickers, they would most likely be taken to some city where the traffickers could market them and so on. We will be checking out every town and city all the way up the highway.

I recently had a call from some locals north of here who thought they witnessed a group of people who arrived in an RV, entering a small cabin. They thought something didn't look right, so they called it in. We've already had the cabin checked out and didn't find anything out of the ordinary, but I'll check it out again on the way up the road. The witnesses didn't notice the plate on the RV, but they described it as being a large white model with a gray logo. Unfortunately, they couldn't remember the logo, but we have an APB in place for it." They walked to the abandoned car. "You said the car doors were open when you arrived?"

"Yes. The only thing we did was to look for identification and we started the car to see if it was working, but we left the scene untouched otherwise."

"Okay, we'll take it from here. I'm sure you have to be on your way to make your delivery." He handed Dakota his card. "Detective Jay Lawson. Please call me if you come across anything else. Where are you headed?"

"Whitehorse. We'll be switching loads with a Canadian freight company, then on to Anchorage."

"Drive safely and thanks again for your thorough work here."

"Absolutely." Dakota and Cheynne headed out toward Whitehorse, neither speaking for quite a while. "When we finish up with the load transfer, I'll need to call Dirk to fill him in on what we discovered out here. I sure hope we can figure out what happened to the other woman." Dakota shuddered, remembering how he felt for so many years while he searched for his twin sister, Jillian. He and his team finally located her and brought her home after vanishing forty-one years ago. Now that

Jillian is back in Dakota's life, he has been remarkably content, which has been a new feeling for him since he spent most of his adult life in utter despair. Dakota blamed himself for her abduction because he failed to protect her like he always had, a promise he made to his grandfather when the twins were young. Their parents, Chevyo and Yamka have spent every minute they possibly can with her and Autumn. Autumn is near the age Jillian was when she went missing, so Yamka has taken Autumn into her heart and treats her more like her own daughter rather than her granddaughter. Jillian and Autumn understand this and love the attention and compassion.

Cheynne grimaced. "I hope Mia turns up as well, only alive and uninjured. I'm sure the police will put out a missing person's bulletin right away and we'll be looking out for her." Cheynne and Dakota had both studied Mia's driver's license photo. "I feel certain that we'll spot her if we get lucky enough to locate her." Cheynne's eyes glistened with tears as she described Mia with a trembling voice. "Long black hair, dark eyes, a beauty mark beside her mouth and she's 5'-4" inches tall."

Dakota gently pulled her to him. "Hey, I believe the incident happened recently, so maybe we'll find her. Believe me, I understand your compassion. Our job is unquestionably difficult because we cannot allow our discoveries to affect us personally. I have tried for many years to channel my grief and anger toward locating the villains and taking them down. I hope that works for you as well. Cheynne dried her tears and nodded.

They arrived in Whitehorse three hours later, traded their U.S. load with the Canadian local team and headed to Micco's home. Cheynne was excited to visit with her family and was happy to think about something other than the scene earlier. "You'll love my family. They are really down to earth, hard-working, friendly people. They have plenty of room for us and we can take showers when we get there. How are you feeling?"

"A little tired, but famished. I'm looking forward to a few laughs and a day of R and R after what we just experienced. Our plans with your family and a relaxing day at Hope Ranch for all of us will be a pleasant, well deserved break. I have a feeling that there are a few massive, volatile storms ahead."

21

The weather in Whitehorse was sunny and cool, although a substantial spring storm was headed straight toward Whitehorse, which may cause havoc for the team along the Alcan the following day. The Alcan has been a fully paved road for many years now, but a massive spring storm could dump a deluge of snow requiring chains and focused driving in possible whiteout conditions. Dakota was pleased that he had organized the convoy for safety reasons.

Jake and Zach arrived at Micco's home just in time for breakfast. Mack and Chris were a few hours behind them and planned to join them at Hope Ranch where they would all stay for the day. Jake parked on the side of the lengthy driveway, climbed out of the truck and stretched his arms and legs. "What a beautiful drive. I could never get tired of driving this stretch of the road, right alongside the swiftly moving, meandering Yukon River. I can't wait to toss a line in."

Micco jogged out to greet them. "Welcome. You're just in time for Sylvia's cinnamon apple French toast, smoked bacon and fresh hot coffee. After breakfast, you can shower if you want to."

Jake introduced himself and Zach as he shook Micco's hand. "Thanks for the invite. We're starving and if you can tolerate the smell of wild horses for a bit, we figured that we'd shower when we get to the ranch." Jake and Zach followed Micco into the cozy home where the delicious aroma of breakfast foods filled the air.

Micco handed them each a plate. "Help yourselves. Sylvia, this is Jake Losato and Zach Kahale. And these two sleepy heads are Skye and Daisy." The kids smiled at them shyly.

Sylvia said, "You all must be exhausted. Cheynne reviewed your work with us and I'll have to say, it sounds really dangerous."

Skye looked at Silvia. "What sounds dangerous?"

Dakota answered his question. "We are helping the Mounties find bad men before they hurt anyone. But it hasn't really been too dangerous, yet anyway."

"You mean you can find them in your big trucks?"

They all laughed heartily. "Yes. Would you like to climb up in my truck when we are through with breakfast?"

"Yeah! That would be super cool. Can I drive it?" They all laughed again.

Sylvia said, "Maybe someday, but you'll have to have

a commercial driver's license for that."

Dakota observed his excited eyes. "I'll tell you what. Maybe you could sit in the passenger seat next to me and we'll drive to the ranch together, if that's okay with your mom and dad."

Micco saw the pleading look in Skye's eyes. "Sure. I think that sounds like fun."

"Oh, goody." He shoveled a huge bite of French toast into his mouth, with maple syrup dripping down his chin.

Daisy exclaimed, "I can't wait to ride the horses. Daddy lets us ride the horses at a stable down the road. I like to brush them, too."

Jake chimed in, "You'll love Grace. I bet she would be happy to let you go to her ranch and ride horses any time you want to. I'll talk with her about that. There is a girl there named Jasmine, who is really good with the horses and will probably be happy to ride with you."

She smiled, glancing at her mom and dad. "Will you both ride with me today?"

"Absolutely." Micco grinned back. "I think a little trail ride will be fun. Aunt Cheynne said that they have archery there, too."

Jake finished chewing a delicious bite of smoked bacon. "Grace has dairy cows that might need milking. Do you want to learn how to milk a cow?"

Both Skye and Daisy said at the same time, "Cool!"

"Grace loves children. I bet she has a whole list of fun things for you to do."

Grace always wanted children, but by the time she was finally able to process her grief and put her past behind her, she realized that her child bearing years had slipped away which upset her for quite some time. She was able to overcome her disappointment by taking care of the girls who come to the ranch. Jake knew that she would be thrilled to have the kids there for the day.

The group finished breakfast, grabbed their backpacks and headed to the ranch. While lazily strolling toward the truck, Dakota's cell phone rang. He noticed Mack's name on the screen. "Hey buddy, where are you guys?"

"We'll be at the ranch in about an hour. I could sure use a shower, mate. I hope Grace won't mind."

"She says she has cabins ready for all of us, two bedrooms in each cabin and each with showers. There is also a spacious lodge and plenty to eat. We'll see ya soon and as you Irish boys say, may the road rise up to meet you."

Mack chuckled. "Ye know, two of us shorten the road. See ye soon." Mack O'Donnell and Chris O'Connor are driving partners and both jovial Irishmen men, who speak with delightful Irish accents and often banter back and forth in humorous, quirky dialogues.

Dakota turned to Skye who was tailing right behind him, excited to ride in a big truck. "Are you ready, Pal?"

He flashed an enormous, toothy smile. "You betcha!"

Dakota opened the passenger door allowing Cheynne to get in first. She was happy to ride back in the sleeper while Skye enjoyed the passenger seat. He helped Skye up the steep steps. "Hold on to the side bar while you step up and don't let go until you are safely in the seat." He raised the seat for him and helped him with his seat-belt.

Skye yelled out to Micco, "Look Dad, I'm riding with the big boys." Micco grinned from ear to ear. He was excited to be able to have an adventurous day with the family. Both he and Sylvia had been working long days for the past few months with no extra time for fun family outings.

When the group arrived at the Ranch, Grace was outside on the porch swing snuggled up in a blanket. It was fifty-two degrees with warmer temperatures expected later in the day. She jumped up and jogged out to meet them. Jake hopped out of the truck and hugged her, while twirling her around. "I missed you and I smell like a horse, so I'd like to head to the shower and change clothes."

"Oh, I missed you, too. You know where the shower is and when you get through, I want to tell you all about the fun we had in Miki Tarniq. "

Grace sauntered over to the kids who were already looking around at the beautiful ranch. "And who are you, cutie pies?"

"I'm Skye and that's Daisy."

"Well, I'm Grace and we're going to have loads of fun today. Bring your backpacks inside and we'll talk about what you'd like to do first."

Cheynne hugged Grace. "It's always a pleasure to visit with you. Grace, this is my brother Micco and his lovely wife Sylvia."

As they shook hands, Grace said, "You look familiar."

Cheynne grinned nodding her head. "I bet you have enjoyed her delicious cuisine at her Bistro."

"Oh, yes. Sylvia's Bistro, of course. I love to cook, but your dishes are incredibly tasty. The last time I was there, I ordered your herbed butter elk steak entrée, served with rosemary red potatoes and spiced apple kraut that was out of this world."

"Ah, yes, one of my specialties. Next time you plan to go, dinner is on the house and if you let me know ahead of time, I'd love to come join you."

"That would be really fun, but will you share your recipe for herbed butter, hmmm?" She chuckled.

"Well I don't usually reveal my secret recipes, although I think I can make an exception, but only if you keep it to yourself. I really admire you for helping women in need on this beautiful ranch, so I'll tell you what. How about I bring the kids here a few times a month to ride the horses and we can spend some time in the kitchen."

"I would love that. And you can bring the kids here any time they want to come. I'd love to have them around." Grace beamed with delight.

They all made their way into the lodge to meet some of the girls who were overjoyed to take the kids out to the stable. Jasmine took Daisy's hand. "I know which horse will love to have you ride her but first, I was just getting ready to milk the cows. Do you want to help?" Daisy nodded with a charming toothy grin.

Grace showed Sylvia around her enormous kitchen, complete with top-of-the-line appliances, adequate prep counters and a beautiful two-way stone fireplace which transitioned nicely into the spacious living room..

Silvia grinned. "Okay, get your pen and paper out and I'll give you my herbed butter and elk entrée recipes."

"Oh, thank you. I'm a fast typist, so I'll use my computer."

"Okay, here we go. Blend a stick of unsalted,

softened butter, one teaspoon of lime juice, one tablespoon each of finely chopped parsley, chives, oregano and one teaspoon of thyme. Then place the butter mixture on a piece of waxed paper, roll it into a cylinder and chill it in the refrigerator, while you prepare the elk steaks. I like to slice a thick piece of steak into generous medallion portions and tenderize each piece with a meat mallet and then rub olive oil over the steaks to keep them moist, since elk is very lean. Then combine two teaspoons each of kosher salt, garlic powder, sweet paprika, brown sugar and one teaspoon each of coriander and oregano. Season each steak on both sides with the herb mixture and let it marinate in the fridge for at least an hour. Some chefs marinate the steaks overnight, but I find that it breaks the meat down too much resulting in a mushy meat texture, so I marinate the steak only for an hour or two max."

Grace typed the ingredient list and instructions as Sylvia dictated, not missing a word. "I'll make this dish with Claire and Lorraine who are amazing chefs and who I could never do without. I love to help them while they teach cooking classes to the girls who have interests. Usually, the classes have at least five to six girls at a time and are loads of fun."

"That's marvelous. Even though cooking in a restaurant can be grueling, especially on the weekends when we are absolutely slammed, I like to think of the work as fun, artistic projects where I can allow my creativity to flourish. We always play classical music in the kitchen, which I truly believe inspires creativity and calmness."

Sylvia continued with the recipe. "Okay, so next,

prepare your potatoes or vegetables for grilling and cook them first. Then grill the steaks, which gives them a nice smokey flavor and only takes about four minutes per side, depending on how rare you want your steaks. When they are grilled to your liking, pull out the chilled butter, slice it and place a section on top of each steak, add a sprig of fresh parsley and serve with a delicious Pinot Noir wine and enjoy."

"Oh, I'm so excited! I have several hunter friends who bring wild game to me in exchange for herbs and vegetables which we grow here all year in our green houses. I have a freezer filled with caribou, elk, wild turkey, duck, salmon and halibut to make delicious meals with. I prefer to eat wild game rather than beef or pork since there are no hormones and preservatives added. It just seems healthier and I keep my costs down, since I get the meat for free."

"Wow, that's an extraordinary deal. Since, it's illegal to buy wild game in Canada to sell at restaurants, unless it is farmed and properly inspected, I have limited supplies and I often have to ship it from Alberta, which makes the dinner quite pricey, but well worth it. I am permitted to offer free of charge, what I call taster hors d'oeuvres which usually include elk, caribou or moose, which I plan several times a month. That way, people have a chance to sample some of my delectable recipes. It's a great way to attract more customers who like wild game and they usually come back and order the full meal which I market as my weekend specials."

"That is so interesting. I don't know how you do it though. Running a restaurant must be incredibly difficult and chaotic."

"It sure was at first, but I've been working diligently for many years to finally have everything running smoothly." Silvia sipped her ginger tea. "So, how does your system work here, I mean when the girls are brought here, how long do they stay."

"It's different for each girl or woman. We have young women here now that vary in age from fifteen to thirty. Some just need a week or so to get over a less traumatic situation and some want to stay on for months or even years. I don't have many that stay here indefinitely, however, there are a few girls here that wanted to stay and work here. Jasmine, who was abducted and forced to work for sex criminals for several months was rescued by Sarah and brought here last December. She is a delightful young woman and the other girls respond very well to her, so she decided to stay on.

"Violet and Sofia, who also have been working at the ranch were brought here along with Jasmine. They may stay for a while longer, but I suspect that they will move on like most of the girls do when they feel ready. The girls take classes in several fields, hoping that they will find something they enjoy to specialize in. Once they feel confident, they begin looking for jobs and figuring out where they want to live. Then, they go. It is very important to do everything possible to make the girls comfortable, so that they know they are safe right after they arrive. Most of them as you can imagine, had just experienced extremely traumatic, abusive situations, some lasting for months or even years.

"I was abducted and taken to guarded places which were impossible to get away from, basically hell which I endured for almost ten years until I figured out how to escape. I made it to St. Faith's Anglican Church in Vancouver, British Columbia and worked with a very special woman, Reverend Angelina Lavoie, who helped me sort things out. The church had a program called Compassionate Support Advocacy and Referral Service for people in need or crisis. I was so grateful for her love and compassion that I decided to design and build Hope Ranch, to help women learn to have faith that everything will be okay and that they can feel safe once again. It's also very important that we help the girls find things to do that they enjoy, as well as learning a trade. The longer they stay, the more work hours they are required to put in to help get things done at the ranch."

"Do they participate in therapy sessions?"

"Absolutely. We have several compassionate women who work here every day, either talking with the girls in separate sessions or during group sessions, which most of them really benefit from. The girls take turns talking about concerns and sometimes they share their experiences, but I prefer that the therapists help them focus on ways to overcome their fears and concerns so that they can move on. We've had tremendous success with that strategy and the girls seem to be happy here."

"I can't even imagine how difficult it must be for you to have to listen to traumatized girls which probably causes you to relive your ordeal over and over. My God, I couldn't take it."

"Oh, I am so happy now. I mean, it was a long time ago. I have so much love to share and they feel that love, which is mainly what they need. I don't relive it any more. Seeing the girls smile, hearing them laugh, make friends and learn things makes me feel so content and grateful that I have been able to help."

Grace played lively classical violin and piano music Cd's, which she often did to maintain a harmonious environment. Dakota waltzed into the kitchen with Cheynne who was giggling girlishly. "What are you gals up to?"

"Sylvia was just sharing one of her recipes, which I feel exceptionally lucky to have. Next time you come visit, I'll make a delicious elk dinner for you."

"Oh, love the invitation." Dakota grinned, wiggling his eyebrows. "Micco, Skye and Daisy just learned how to milk a cow and are now waiting for you to ride the horses. I haven't been on a horse in years, so I'm quite excited."

Dakota was grateful that his drivers were enjoying themselves, although the massive spring storm which the team would drive head on into, continued to churn in the forefront of his mind. He tried to suppress his concerns, preferring to participate in the merriment.

Grace said, "You'll love the horses. They are all friendly and gentle, although there are a few that are definitely for more experienced riders. We'll make sure we select the right horse for each person."

Grace sauntered into her bedroom and found Jake resting. She tiptoed around him trying not to wake him, but he heard her and sat up. "Hey, beautiful. What's up?"

"Would you like to ride horses with us or do you need some more rest? The kids are chomping at the bit to get going." She snickered.

"Yeah, sure." He yawned audibly. "Have Mack and Chris arrived yet?"

"No, not yet."

"Well, I think I'll wait for them. Mack is really into fishing and you know I am. The Yukon is calling me. I'm planning on taking anyone who wants to toss in a few lines, so if you guys aren't back after a couple of hours, I'll take Mack, Chris and Zach."

"Okay. There is a pot of caribou red chili in the fridge and garlic French bread that you can pop in the oven. Oh, and there is plenty of cheddar cheese and sour cream to top it off."

"Sounds good, although I ate an ample helping of apple cinnamon French toast a couple of hours ago. But the chili sounds so good that I might have to indulge when the guys arrive." He gave her big, wet smooch. "You guys have fun."

Jake lazily ambled down the hall and peeked in the room that Zach was staying in. He was out cold, enjoying a deep slumber, so he didn't wake him. Jake and Zach drove almost continuously from Vancouver to Whitehorse, alternating every ten hours, delivered their load and barely made it to Micco's place before breakfast. They were both exhausted.

Mack and Chris arrived a half hour later. Jake was hauling in firewood from the covered wood pile when they arrived. The meandering driveway was lengthy and wide, providing plenty of space to park the trucks. Mack strode toward the lodge with his pack of gear. "Grace has ye busy already, aye, Mate?"

Jake chuckled. "Not really. She has things pretty well stocked up around here, but I thought I'd just bring in a few arm loads. How did it go?"

"Well, it took a bit longer to drop and hook than we hoped, because the load from Edmonton was about an hour behind, but no worries. Nice chaps, though. They said they like this drop and hook gig just as much as we do. They also said there is a storm on the way, so they wanted to get going asap."

"Yeah, I saw that on the weather channel earlier. It's supposed to be a doozy. It's headed in from the northwest. I think we should all get as much rest as we can, because we won't be having much fun heading across the Alcan."

Mack nodded and drew in a deep breath. "I was thinkin' about that as well. Possible chain up for hours, mate. So my man, lead me to the showers. I smell like a buffalo."

They both laughed. "Yeah, I felt the same way earlier. After your shower, I'll have chili and French bread ready for you. And if you aren't too tired, we could head to the river to toss in a few lines. Right now, we can catch trout and Dolly Varden."

"I have a bit more energy left in me. Let's have some fun and we'll just hit the beds early tonight. How about you, Chris? Are ye in for a bit of fishing?"

"Aye. I haven't had a chance to fish for over a year. Let's bring back some trout for dinner, mates."

After Mack and Chris showered, they enjoyed mouthwatering, spicy chili while Jake filled them in on the rest area incident. "No kidding. So, they haven't found the missing girl, yet?"

"I don't know, but Dakota said the Mounties were checking out all of the roadside motels and a few cabins along the road that they were suspicious of, so maybe they'll find her. Dirk wants us to check out rest areas and small motels along the way toward Anchorage, so who knows, maybe we'll happen upon some thugs up to no good. Since we'll be hammering down convoy style, there will be six of us ready to take the bastards down if we find them. I don't know about you guys, but I'm ready to kick some ass."

"Aye, let's get it done. I heard from Dakota, that Sarah and her new friend Ethan Sauveur took down a couple of perverts trying to run off with some girls in Anchorage and he also prevented two more idiots from running off with a couple of young girls at the Iditarod. I'd like to meet that bloke. He's the man."

Jake said, "Well, we just might get to meet him soon. Dakota plans to have us stay up here in the northwest working in and out of Anchorage for the next few months or possibly longer. He mentioned that Sarah and Grace want to go back and do a float trip on the Noatak River in mid-June. I talked with Grace about it and she is hoping that we can spend a week up there, rafting, camping and fishing. You know I'm down for that. And his daughter Anji might be attending school with Autumn this fall so, I'm sure the Sauveur family will be visiting Dakota's folks. None of them have ever been to the lower forty-eight and are probably feeling a bit uncomfortable about possibly sending their daughter off to a place that she's never been to before. So, there may be plenty of chances to visit with Ethan. I'd also like to learn more about the Iñupiat culture and their way of life up there in such a remote, wilderness environment."

Chris said, "That's remarkable. What an extraordinary connection for the Sauveurs. I'm intrigued. I definitely want to visit Miki Tarniq and some of the Native American villages. I've done quite a bit of reading about northwest Alaska and have wanted to go visit for some time now. Before we started hunting traffickers, I had been planning to fly into Anchorage, rent a Jeep, tour around for a few weeks and also fly into the northwest. I'm interested in hiking in Denali sometime and checking out the fishing scene in the Kenai Peninsula and then on to Noatak Wildlife Preserve. Since the preserve is such a remote environment, it's right up my ally. I like to go off into wilderness regions every year to find some sense of balance after driving around in noisy, polluted, chaotic areas."

Jake nodded, smiling. "Yeah man, me, too. Grace highly recommends going, so let's work on Dakota. Dirk knows we take off twice a year for some R n R, so let's make it happen. She says the flight from Anchorage to Kotzebue is only an hour and a half and then we jump on a bush plane, seventy to eighty klicks to Miki Tarniq. Easy peasy. The Sauveurs have twenty-four sled dogs." He laughed heartily. "I've always wanted to run a dogsled. I'll have to look into that up here next winter. I really like Huskies, too. I had one for a while when I was living up here more often. I named him Chase because he liked to chase after squirrels and other small animals. He was a funny dog and a great hiking buddy."

Hey mate, where is your cabin?"

"Not far from here. I'd like to check on it, so how about we run my Jeep over there. We could grab some rods and tackle and head down to the river from there. I've been letting a friend of mine stay there, but he's probably at work now. I'll give him a ring to let him know we'll be popping in."

When the guys arrived at the cabin, they were shocked to find a two-story log home with a high gabled, heavy timber roof, supported by heavy timber and stone columns and a deck that surrounded the home. "Mate, this is a family sized log home, not a cabin."

Jake laughed robustly. "It seems smaller inside because the stone fireplace and hearth take up several meters of space and the stairwell takes up another meter and a half. You'll really like the mountain view from the living area."

Chris instantly made his way to the old wood stove in the kitchen. "Dude, do you really cook on this thing?"

"Yep. It's easy. Check this out." He pulled out a large cast iron pot and set it on the stove. "There is nothing like freshly melted snow water to drink and cook with. I throw a few logs in the stove and when it's nice and hot, I fill the pot with snow to melt it. I can cook anything, either on the stove top or in the oven." He grinned.

"Don't tell me you have to heat the pot of snow to take a bath."

"Sure do." He chuckled. "Actually, I have water piped in from my water tank and I have propane heating, but it's expensive, so I prefer to use the heated snow for three fourths of the year. Blake, he's my buddy who stays here and looks after the place, likes to use the stove as well. It's part of the charm. Okay, you're going to love this." The fireplace had a wood stove mounted inside. "See this duct? A pump draws the heated air from around the wood stove, up to the second floor." They followed him upstairs to the bedroom area. "I positioned the floor vents near the beds and one in the bathroom. When it's really cold, I have to turn on the propane heat, but the wood stove takes the chill out of the air so that I don't have to use as much propane."

Mack said, "Pure genius."

Jake pulled aside floor length curtains, revealing a set of French doors that opened onto a deck. "Check out this view. When I lived here full time, I used to sit out here with my morning cup of joe for hours, enjoying the majestic mountain view and the rushing Yukon River."

Mack sat down in one of the deck chairs. "Well that's it, I'm moving in. I don't know how ye ever leave the house other than to do a little fishing." He chuckled. "Next time we are both in or around Missoula, Montana, I'll have to show you, my cabin." He chuckled again. "It's about the same size, maybe a little bigger, but still cozy."

Jake said, "Since Jillian, Liam and Autumn also live in Missoula, we'll know plenty of people there to visit and free places to stay. They have two houses because when Jillian was pregnant with Autumn, Liam built the new home to accommodate the growing family. I'd like to visit them sometime while they are in Missoula and I'm interested in seeing your humble cabin." They all laughed.

"Hey, let's grab the rods and gear. I want to get some fishing in before dinner." They made their way to the river, selecting a spot not too far from the ranch.

After horseback riding, Grace drove Cheynne and Sylvia to the Takhini Hot Pools for a relaxing soak, while the rest shot some arrows, rested and enjoyed the calm before the storm.

After enjoying the adventures of the day, they all met back at the ranch and began preparing dinner. Jake, Mack and Chris were filleting fish for dinner, excitedly discussing who caught the biggest fish. Sylvia had bamboo skewers and sea salt ready and was cutting lemon wedges. Jake whistled as he carried the tray of skewered fish outside.

Grace sauntered out behind Jake and threw her arms around him with a cheerful smile. "Thank you for the nice fish for dinner. You guys did very well." She kissed him on the cheek as he laid the fish on the grill.

Mack walked out with a second tray. "Mmmm! "My mouth is watering. Nothing like fresh catch for dinner." He handed Jake a beer and sneered at him. "My three fish were bigger than your four." He chuckled.

Jake chuckled. "Yeah, but Chris has us both beat. Not only did he catch the biggest Dolly, but he also caught six more using those double hooked lines. I didn't think that would work, but it sure did." They finished grilling and strode back inside to the savory aroma of grilled vegetables and herbed garlic butter melting on the stove.

Sylvia was helping Grace with her special coleslaw. As they shredded white and purple cabbage and carrots, Sylvia said, "Okay, It's all about the secret spices." Raising her eyebrows, she sprinkled in a bit of ginger, nutmeg and cracked black pepper and mixed the slaw with olive oil mayonnaise. "Fit for a queen's table."

22

Sarah arrived at the ranch just before dinner after running errands in Whitehorse and was excited to see everyone. "Bonjour everyone." She smiled at the group and glanced at Dakota and his team while setting two bottles of wine on the table. "I have some interesting news. Trevor did some research for me and found out about an obnoxious man named Axle Heller, who is apparently behind just about every form of trafficking in Anchorage and in many other Alaskan cities. He owns two adult night clubs, which surely offer illegal entertainment behind the scenes. I already have plans to go back to Anchorage. I'll talk with you more about it after dinner." She sat next to Skye and Daisy flashing a wink and a smile. "I'm Sarah." They introduced themselves with giggles and grins. "I bet you two had a really fun time today."

They expressed with dramatic excitement, all of the fun things they experienced throughout the day. Daisy said, "Grace promised we could come back and ride the horses any time we want to. My horse was named Ginger. She's my favorite."

"Oh, Ginger is my favorite, too. I bet she loved having you ride her." Sarah and Grace opened the bottles of Sauvignon Blanc, poured glasses and raised them for a toast. "It's such a pleasure having all of you here. We really must meet here more often."

"Here, here." They all nodded in salute and enjoyed the delicious dinner.

"Save room for dessert." Grace glanced at the kids. "I made my delicious tart lemon bars and Sylvia made Crème Brulee with a twist of lime."

Daisy looked at Sylvia inquisitively. "What's Crème bulay?"

"Oh, you're going to love this dessert. It's a special custard that you light on fire which makes a crackly topping."

Daisy's eyes widened. "Ohhh." She grinned. When the desserts were brought out to the table, Sylvia fired a torch across each Brulee ramekin for just the right amount of time, creating the perfect crackly tops for the delicious creamy dish. "Wow, that's cool." Daisy grinned at her mom. "It smells like roasted marshmallows."

"Yes, it does." She waved her hand over Daisy's dish until it was cool enough to touch. "Let them sit for a minute and enjoy." She beamed. Sylvia enjoys making special dishes and never gets tired of creating. She loves seeing smiles and hearing comments about her tasty, savory gourmet foods.

Sarah said, "Oh, Grace. These lemon bars are scrumptious. You're going to have to share your recipe with me. Just the right amount of lemon and sugar. The last time I made them, they were too sweet."

Mack nodded his head and smacked his lips, then began reciting an Irish poem.

> "In the village of Blarney, there's one magic stone.
> They say when you kiss it, you're put in 'the zone'.
> You talk and you gab and your words are so glib,
> that it matters not least, if it's truth or a fib.
> So, it's lie through your teeth, or it's truth that you own.
> It's all in the gift of the blessed Blarney Stone."

He bowed. "By some crafty Irish man or woman." He raised his glass in salute.

"Hah! I'll see ye and raise ye." Chris stood. "By another crafty Irish man or woman."

> *"My Old Bucket*
> I lost my old bucket so sadly,
> And felt oh so terribly badly;
> Then lo and behold
> A pot full of gold!
> I'd lose me another and gladly."

Everyone laughed. "More. More."

Mack rubbed his full belly and chuckled. "This one is by Jerry T. Curtis." He glanced at Skye and wiggled his brows.

"Now You've Gone and Done It.

> I'd caught me a leprechaun one day.
> He told me to 'Just wish away'.
> So, I wished for 'The Pot'
> And that's what I got,
> Now under me belt's where it stays."

Skye got up and patted his full belly, laughed and rolled on the carpet. Mack picked him up and held him high. "Ye just a wee lad and a wee belly. Wait 'til yer the size of me. With yer mom's good cooking, you'll be growin' out of those pants mighty fast."

Chris stood again. "I don't know the author of this one, but it's called,

Irish Luck

> "Ample food and sturdy drink,
> A clean pillow for yer head,
> And may ye be forty years in heaven,
> Before the devil knows yer dead."

And that's all I have to say about that."

Mack ogled Skye, "I don't know who the scoundrel was that wrote this one, but I'll tell the tale anyway." He cleared his throat and chuckled.

> "There was an old man with a beard,
> Who said, 'It's just as I feared!
> Two owls and a hen,

Four larks and a wren,
Have all built their nests in my beard!"

Mack stroked his beard still ogling Skye. He chuckled heartily causing Skye and Daisy to laugh hysterically and roll on the carpet.

"Okay, you two clowns, give me a hand with these dishes." Grace snickered as they cleared the table. "That's pretty funny stuff. How do you remember those delightful poems? I have tried for years to remember funny jokes and limericks, but I decided it would be best to refrain from telling them, since the last time I tried, I butchered the punch line severely."

"When ye recite the same poems for years, ye remember them like ye wrote them yourself, lass." Mack chuckled.

The weather turned cold with tremendous, gusty winds thrashing against the windows, creating a chill in the great room. Dakota and Jake stoked the wood in the fireplace until the fire was blazing hot while others gathered around the living room. Sarah sat down on the floor with the kids. "I have a couple of funny poems to recite. Would you like to hear one?"

"Make us laugh some more." Daisy giggled.

Sarah cleared her throat. "I have no idea who wrote this one." She grinned at the kids.

"I eat my peas with honey.
I've done it all my life.
It makes the peas taste funny,
But it keeps them on the knife."

Daisy snickered. "Peas with honey. That's funny."

"Oh, you're a poet, too. I know another one which

211

you will surely enjoy." Sarah tickled her sides then stood, animating as she recited the poem.

> "There was a young lady of Kent,
> Whose nose was most awfully bent.
> She followed her nose,
> One day, I suppose,
> And no one knows which way she went."

Everyone in the room laughed as Daisy impersonated the lady with the crooked nose.

"Okay. I can't hold out any longer." Dakota turned and sat cross-legged on the floor. "I've tried many times to find out who wrote this one to no avail, but my dad recited this poem when I was young and I liked it so much that I've been telling it for years." He stroked his chin and lifted his brows.

> "An elderly man called Keith,
> mislaid his set of false teeth.
> They'd been laid on a chair,
> he forgot they were there,
> sat down and was bitten beneath."

Chuckles and smiles filled the room. Silvia and Grace sauntered out of the kitchen, arm in arm laughing hysterically. "We've been enjoying all of the funny limericks. You guys are quite a humorous bunch." Silvia glanced at Skye and Daisy. "I hate to break up the fun, but we have to go home and you two are headed for the bathtub." She held a hand out to help Daisy off the floor.

"Aw, no." Daisy pleaded with pouty lips, "Can't we stay a little longer, please?"

Micco agreed, "Mama's right. It's been a long, fun

day, but the storm is moving in fast and I want to get home while the roads are still clear. Just think dreamy thoughts about your warm, comfy beds." He picked Daisy up and whispered, "We'll see everyone again when they come back from Alaska." He turned to Grace. "Thank you for an amazing dinner and for inviting us here for such an enjoyable day. I'm sure everyone here deserved such a treat."

"Any time and I mean that. The horses love the attention and I love having young ones around." Grace winked at Daisy and shook Skye's hand.

Cheynne hugged her family. "We'll let you know when we're headed back through."

When Micco and his family were gone, Sarah sat down with Dakota's team to discuss Trevor's information and her plans. "Grace and I will be flying to Anchorage right after you guys leave, to do some research and check a few things out. I'd like to meet up with you to organize a major sting operation which of course will include all local authorities and the FBI. I'm counting on them to take us seriously and act immediately without hesitation."

Sarah sipped her wine. "Trevor was able to find out that the men who were arrested at the Iditarod cracked, admitting that they worked for Axle Heller, the organized crime leader who controls a major percentage of the illegal activity in Anchorage. He is in Anchorage now. Boys, let's take him down."

"Lass, do ye know how dangerous that'll be? Jeezum crow!" Mack stared at her wide eyed. "Dirk should be in on your plans now."

"He will be, right, Dakota? I'm counting on you to discuss my plans with him without delay. The FBI is already there and we don't want to interrupt their own operations, however, sometimes a few new faces at just the right time could prove to be the break they've been hoping for. The FBI now has enough proof that Heller is involved in trafficking as well as in a slew of other illegal activities. If we all move quickly and work together, we will be able to finally take him down. Trevor found eighteen businesses operating under various trusts all owned by Axle Heller. The names he used as owners of each trust are fictitious names, but Trevor was able to connect all of the passports to Heller. Each passport has a photo of Heller, but in various disguises which is probably why the FBI hasn't been able to match the profiles, but Trevor has an instinctive magical talent for these things. He aligned all of the photos and played around with the disguises, hair color, facial hair, glasses and so on until he was able to match them all to one look. He uncovered an older photo of Heller, so we don't really know what he looks like now, but we have a pretty good idea, based on age progression software."

She handed the folder to Dakota. "Holy smoke! Sarah this is tremendous. Do you have a computer file that I can send to Dirk? He has an FTP site set up for us to securely transfer files."

"Yes. Here is a thumb drive with everything he'll need, but don't download it to your computer and right after you send it, make sure that you delete it."

"I'll send it to Dirk as soon as we're done here."

She continued, "Heller has dark eyes, dark hair although, he's probably graying to some extent, a large build, 6'-2" tall and a prominent nose. Three of the disguised photos showed him wearing his hair shoulder length, but pulled back in a ponytail. His left arm has a sizable tattoo of a maiden, like the ones you see on the front of ships and he has a killer whale on his right arm. One of the trust companies owns two, 24-meter yachts. Maybe that will be one way the FBI can locate him, and if they do, I bet they find some evidence aboard. Since we understand now that he has been trafficking everything from girls to drugs and assault weapons, there will probably be clues or some kind of contraband hidden on his yachts. Since the authorities haven't been able to locate the yachts yet, maybe because they aren't aware that he has them, checking them out is one of the first things on my agenda. I believe the crafts are in Anchorage. I have a printout of all of the companies, the trusts they are owned under and locations. Included are two adult night clubs, conveniently located right next to two hotels also owned by him, massage parlors and a whole string of cathouses as well as two mansions, one each in Anchorage and Fairbanks."

Sarah poured more wine and continued. "We are planning to stay in one of the hotels when we get to Anchorage. Speaking of disguises, I will not look like myself, neither will Grace." She studied Jake's face. "I promise that Grace will not be involved in anything dangerous. She plans on doing some shopping while I check a few things out."

Jake said with concern, "I'm not sure she should be going with you if you are going to involve yourself like you are planning."

"She wants to go and anyway, I will just be checking things out. There will be no confrontations and I won't ask any questions that will make me look suspicious.

Everything I find out will be shared with you and Dirk and he can decide whether or not to share the intel with the local authorities."

Dakota sat back in his chair and drew in a hefty breath of air, then blew it out slowly. "This operation sounds like it will be considerably larger than anything we've attempted to get involved in. How do you guys feel about it?"

Mack said, "As long as we have a plan which involves the FBI, I'm in. We all agreed to track these criminals and if we can help take down a major crime syndicate, then we are doing exactly what we signed on for. Will it be dangerous? Aye, but," he glared at Jake, "we have to stay together and work as a team. No one goes off and tries to confront these bastards alone."

Jake shook his head. "No worries, I agree. A few men are one thing, but a monster trafficking organization is an entirely different animal."

Dakota said, "Well it's getting late and we all need some good rest. I'd like to roll by six a.m. The major part of this storm has already crossed the Alaskan-Canadian Border. Grace insisted on getting up early and preparing some eggs and bacon for us, so I'll see you all down here for breakfast."

Sarah was in bed doing some research when her phone rang. She looked at the display to see who was calling so late in the evening. "Good evening, Ethan. Is everything okay?"

"Yes, everything is fine. I'm sorry for calling so late. When are you planning to come to Anchorage again? I need to meet with you. I have some information which may prove to be extremely invaluable and we may need your help."

"I'll be flying into Anchorage tomorrow morning. I reserved a room in a hotel that is owned by an extremely dangerous man named Axle Heller. We believe he may be the top dog of an enormous criminal organization. We are still working out our plans but we could sure use your help, so the timing is good. I'll call you when I arrive."

"That would work out well. Thank you and travel safely. Good night."

After the call, Sarah sat up, intrigued. He must have discovered some kind of connection.

23

Tulugaak had a feeling that he and Ethan should talk with Jay Hawkins concerning Ben as soon as possible, since no one had heard from Ben in the past couple of months. If his suspicions were right, Ben might be in serious trouble, surely needing help. For the past several weeks, Tulugaak had been feeling so concerned that he spent most nights in the company of restless, enigmatic spirits, who taunted him to act without delay. The northern lights demonstration became more energetic each night as the weeks progressed and the raven seemed to be persistently calling for his attention. Continuous thoughts of tremendous distress concerning someone close had been entering his mind in waves, each surge with more clarity, immediately following his connection with his raven spirit. Ethan had been continuously goaded by the mysterious spirits as well. He had a nightmare about Anji, running across the tundra, towards a heavily forested mountain area, chasing a mysterious shadow, which turned out to be Ben. He awoke the following morning, realizing that the time to act was now.

Tulugaak and Ethan met with Jay at his pharmacy in Kotzebue. They sipped strong coffee as Tulugaak contemplated on how to begin the discussion. Jay noticed Tulugaak's inquisitive, solemn demeanor. "What is on your mind my friend?"

"Ben." Tulugaak decided to get right to the point, risking a possible confrontation in which Jay would protect Ben at all costs. "I have been considering many scenarios in which Ben may be involved with some of the corrupt activity that has been going on lately. I have arrived at a conclusion that seems to be the most plausible, considering Ben has always been respectful and dedicated to the welfare of the people of Alaska. I think that it's possible that Ben may be posing as an employee, maybe on one of those yachts that were docked in Kotzebue for a few weeks. He went missing right after the yachts departed, so I think that is suspiciously telling. What if he is trying to help and doesn't realize or care about the perils of being in the company of some gravely dangerous criminals?"

Jay nodded. "That makes sense considering his girlfriend, Dalianya went missing from Anchorage last year, while shopping at the market. Ben went to Anchorage to meet with her at a cabin that he rented for the weekend, but she never showed up. He feels certain that she was abducted and blames himself for not accompanying her during her travels. Ben and Akio Ikiaq, Dalianya's father, reported her missing after they found her car in the market parking lot with the trunk wide open and groceries strewn across the pavement. They also found her red scarf on the ground by the trunk. They searched for her for days until Ben discovered that Dalianya may have been kidnapped by the Anchorage mafia. Ben has been a distraught man with thunderous vengeance motivating his every move."

Tulugaak looked confused. "Jay, why didn't you mention this to us a year ago? Everyone we know could have helped him."

"I don't know. I should have, but there was no way to prove that she was abducted. The police investigated, of course searched her car for clues, but came up with nothing. And you are aware that I was dealing with his furious behavior, picking him up from bars, often completely inebriated. I have had so much on my plate this past year, not only dealing with problems with my boys, but trying to run the pharmacy and my bush flight business. Tulugaak, I had been half out of my mind trying to find Ben for almost a year until the first week of March. He showed up at the house, didn't say a word, just hugged me and said he was sorry and that he was planning to make things right. At the time, I didn't really know what he meant by that, but I think I do now."

Ethan said respectfully, "I don't believe he would take a job working for traffickers unless he was working undercover. What do you know about Wily Johns? Did Ben say anything about him?"

Jay hesitated as if he was not sure how to answer. "I

heard about what happened to Wily, but I don't recall Ben mentioning him. Ethan, you aren't implying that Ben had something to do with Wily's death are you?"

Tulugaak and Ethan sensed that there was something Jay was not telling them. Ethan said, "Okay, here are my thoughts about that. We know that Wily was up to no good and was seen back in March in the company of some men in a heated argument out on the tarmac. Ben was here at the same time. Then, the men left on a plane, the yacht departed the next day and Ben disappeared again. I also recalled years back, when he thought about working for the police force to train to become a detective. Then it came to me that he have been trying to solve the mystery of how young Alaskan women were being abducted and now you're telling me that his girlfriend went missing as well. The conclusion seems obvious to me, so we must find him as soon as possible."

Jay looked relieved to have some kind of explanation for what was going on with Ben. He shook his head. "I just don't know what to think, but that sounds conceivable. But he couldn't have killed Wily. He was home with me the day Wily was found dead. And why would he kill him if he was trying to investigate those men and make things right, as he said?"

"To make the criminals believe that he was willing to do what they asked of him and that he could be trusted to work with them. He and Anji used to explore in the preserve together years ago, gathering herbs for your pharmacy. I have to wonder if he knew that Monkshood could kill a man if swallowed, resulting in severe respiratory arrest and heart failure. Could he have taken some from the pharmacy and given it to one of the men who were seen that day? Maybe he wasn't directly involved in the murder, but since Monkshood is native to Alaska, the authorities could be focusing on the people living in this area, who know such things about the properties of various herbs. What if Ben helped them get rid of Wily, not considering that the blame could shift to the innocent people residing in this area? I wouldn't think that big city men would have even heard of Monkshood and would use other methods to murder someone."

"My God, I hope he didn't do that. He doesn't deserve to go to prison. You mustn't share your theories with anyone else until we have a chance to speak with him. He must have a chance to defend himself."

Tulugaak said, "Jay, we have no intention of speaking about this to anyone else and none of us wish to see Ben in prison. He is a good man, but Wily was not, and I believe that an evil man earns his just reward in good time." He paused, holding Jay's eyes intently with his own. "So it seems, the men that Wily was seen with on his unfortunate day must have ended his malevolent life and that is all there is to it." Tulugaak and Ethan nodded fervently to their friend. They sat quietly for a few minutes, each man finding his own peace with Wily's demise. Tulugaak, anticipating the course of the discussion, urged Jay to provide as much information as possible. "Now, about Dalianya. Have you met the girl?"

"Yes. Ben brought her home last year for dinner. She was a lovely, sweet girl and I could understand how Ben would be smitten by her. She was intelligent, friendly and loved to go hunting with her father and uncle. Ben hunted with them the day after we met, completely convinced that Dalianya was his lucky charm and he would surely bring home a fine caribou. I flew them out to her favorite hunting camp at the edge of the tundra, where the great white spruce are clustered. She said that the caribou always knew when they were arriving and that they gave themselves generously to her family. A delightful girl. I sure hope Ben finds her soon and I pray she wasn't abducted as Ben believes she was."

Ethan revealed, "A couple of months ago, Anji was given a gift by a distinctive raven. It was a red scarf with leather fringe and colorful beads. She figured out that it belonged to a friend named Anya, who she has spent time with, as you mentioned, at the edge of the tundra near the Spruce tree line. I have to wonder if Anya is Dalianya. Did Ben ever call her by that name?"

"Oh, I do recall him saying Anya, even though he introduced her to me by her full name and she was wearing a red scarf with beads on the ends. If Anji has seen her, then she must be okay. Ben needs to know this as soon as possible. I also think we should go out to the hunting camp and search around. Maybe we can find a clue that will help us find both of them. I never met Dalianya's father, but Ben knows him well enough. I don't know his last name but his first is Akio and I believe he may be currently residing in Anchorage, or at least he was last year."

Tulugaak said, "Anji has been planning to go on the hunting trip with Ethan and Kaya to find out why the raven brought Anya's scarf to her. I think that is a very good idea, since she knows Anya. She may be able to describe her to you to make sure she is the same girl. I believe she is, since Anji was distressed about seeing a young girl forcefully shoved into a van one day last year, while shopping in Anchorage. Anji has seen Anya recently in Anchorage, Kotzebue and at the hunting camp. She thinks Anya may be hiding from someone who could be actively searching for her. If she was abducted and managed to escape her captors, she could be in a dangerous predicament."

Jay's eyes welled up. "I'll pick you all up at six, Saturday morning and fly all of us up there at no charge." He wiped his eyes with his sleeve, breathing rapidly. His concern for Ben and Dalianya was overwhelming. He prayed that Ben had already located Dalianya and they were together somewhere safe.

Tulugaak embraced him, encouraging Jay to allow his tense emotions to leave his body and mind. "Here, here, brother. We will find resolve together."

"Thank you, my friend. If you two are not already scheduled on a flight, let me fly you home. That way we could leave from Miki Tarniq in the morning."

"Thank you, but I flew here, so why don't you follow us home and you can stay for the night. Hana will be delighted that you will be joining us for dinner."

"That's a good plan. My cooking basically includes microwaving a frozen dinner, so I'm always grateful for a home cooked meal, especially one made by Hana. It's been almost a year now, but I still remember her caribou pot roast." He patted his stomach and smiled widely.

"Jay, you are welcome any time. Just drop in whenever you are nearby. It has become crucial, now more than ever, for all of us to stay in close contact and communicate often."

Hana had elk steaks marinating in olive oil, garlic and rosemary and was preparing sweet potatoes and greens when they walked in. Ethan kissed her on the cheek and she smiled cheerfully, then noticed Jay behind him. "Well what a surprise. I just had a feeling we would need another steak prepared. I hope you brought your appetite." She hugged him kindheartedly, detecting something distressing him. "Are you alright?"

"Yes, ma'am. I've just been at my wit's end worrying about Ben." They shared with her most of what was discussed, leaving out the part about the possibility that Ben was involved in the murder of Wily.

Sophia was sitting at the table, wide eyed with interest concerning Anya. "Well I'll be. I wonder if Dalianya is the same girl that Anji knows. Ben and Anji used to run the dogs out to the preserve to hunt for berries and they always brought back herbs as well." She hesitated, studying Jay's eyes. "I sure hope you find Ben. He's a good man and I'll bet you're right, that he wants to help put traffickers in prison." Sophia suddenly appeared terribly concerned. "But Ethan, can you call Sarah and ask her when her team will be arriving to help so that you are not investigating dangerous criminals alone? I sure hope Ben reaches out to you soon, but I know we'll all feel more comfortable knowing that he has someone looking out for him."

"I called her last night. I just have a feeling that it has become quite an urgent matter to meet with her concerning Ben. Sarah informed me that Dakota's team is on the way to Anchorage as we speak. If Ben did leave on that yacht, they may have sailed to Anchorage. I think we should check the marinas for that yacht and maybe an undercover agent could be posted there to investigate everyone coming and going. Sarah is very resourceful.

After dinner, I'll call her and give her Ben's description and devise a plan."

Jay looked hopeful. "After we search the hunting camp, I will fly to Anchorage with you to meet with this woman. The more people we have searching for Ben, the better chances of finding and helping him. If we succeed in locating him and he is engaging in undercover work, we could put him in serious danger."

Ethan nodded. "I agree." He thought about the powerful spring storm that recently tore through western Alaska which was heading east with enormous force and could cause havoc as it moved across the border and into Canada. He prayed for the team to be safe on the road, although he had an uncomfortable feeling that they may encounter trouble along the way.

24

Grace and Sarah packed meals and snacks at five in the morning while the team hastily devoured a delicious breakfast of scrambled eggs, crispy bacon, potatoes and fresh berries. Dakota sipped his coffee, then addressed the team. "The storm is moving in fast and headed right for us. Keep your CB radios tuned to channel eighteen, since I'm not sure we'll have any cell reception until we get to Haines Junction, where we'll stop for a break and top off our fuel. Our travel distance is 150 kilometers to Haines Junction and 1,133 kilometers to Anchorage. If all goes well, we'll be in Anchorage by six or seven this evening."

The team thanked Grace and Sarah for their hospitality, then rolled down the road toward the Alcan

Highway. So far, the roads were fairly clear with light snow falling and gusty winds. As they got closer to Haines Junction, they could see a massive front so thick that visibility would be extremely difficult. If treacherous weather caused unsafe driving conditions, Dakota planned to have them stop until the majority of the storm passed. He turned on his CB. "Are you guys seeing what I'm seeing?"

"Yeah, buddy." Jake said. "Not looking so good. Get ready to chain up."

"We'll stop if we need to. Mack, do you have your ears on?"

"Aye. This is when I turn on J.J. Cale. I'll be cruisen', mate."

"Sounds good. We've all rolled through spring storms countless times before, so relax but stay focused. I'll join you in the Cale zone." J.J. Cale was a musician, singer and songwriter of the Tulsa genre. His jazzy blues, rock, country amalgamation was a soothing sound, perfect for stressful conditions.

About 100 kilometers down the road, the storm slammed into the drivers like a freight train. Powerful wind gusts wafted the heavily falling snow into a whirlwind, causing a whiteout condition and ice began to pile up on the road. Mack was just ahead of Dakota with Jake bringing up the rear as they slowly rolled down a steep grade. Cheynne picked up the CB. "Time to chain up, boys. There is a turnout in five kilometers." Suddenly, her eyes widened. "Whoa! Hang back, Jake. Mack is in a sideways slide. We're slowing down and moving toward the side where the snow is thicker and covering the ice." They watched Mack as he worked with the slide. "Holy hell! Is he going to be able to pull out of it?"

Dakota observed intently and said calmly, "If anyone can, he can." Mack's rig seemed completely out of control, in a jackknifed position as he slid fast sideways down the hill. Then a few seconds later, he was able to maneuver his truck forward, causing the trailer to swing right and then left each time with less sideways slide. About a minute later, he was beginning to straighten out, rolling and sliding to the south side of the road, right before he reached a steep cliff with no roadside railing. "Damn, that was close!" Mack slowly maneuvered his rig to the right side of the road and came to a stop with Dakota behind him and Jake following.

Abruptly, Mack jumped out of his rig and began jogging down the road. Dakota headed toward him, calling out to him. "Mack, what the hell!" As Dakota began to catch up with him, he saw what the problem was. An RV had slid off the road and was still rolling and tumbling over and over, down the edge of the cliff, where it finally came to a stop upside down, about a quarter kilometer from the highway. They trudged down the steep slippery slope and were almost to the RV, when they noticed a girl running frantically toward them screaming for help. She had no coat, one hiking boot on her left foot and only a sock on the right foot. Cheynne trudged through the thick snow toward the girl to help her back to the warmth of the truck.

Mack shrieked, "The RV slid right in front of me, completely out of control. I saw it fly over the cliff." They continued on down the side of the cliff to the RV.

The girl screamed, "No! They have guns. The driver looked unconscious, but the other man was trying to get

229

out. He'll shoot you."

Suddenly realizing what she was saying, Mack stopped in his tracks and Dakota caught up to him. "Whoa, buddy, hang back." He studied the girl for a few seconds, noticing the missing boot. Then he recalled the incident the previous day and the description of the RV given by the Mounties. They'd been hunting for a large white RV with a gray logo. He scanned the side of the RV and noticed the logo. "It's the same RV that the Mounties described. That girl might be the missing girl from the rest area incident, so it looks like we just stumbled on the traffickers. Cheynne, try to reach the Mounties. We need backup fast and an ambulance."

Cheynne staggered in the deep snow catching up to the girl, noticing her one hiking boot. "Are you okay?"

"Yes," she said shakily. "I hit my head pretty hard and my body is all banged up. We weren't wearing seat belts. There are three more girls in the RV, but I don't know if they are alive, hurt or dead." She began to cry.

Cheynne put her arms around her. "You are okay now and we'll make sure you are safe. Your name is Mia Grenier, right?"

"Yes, how did you know?"

"We stopped at the same rest area and found your driver's license and your other boot by your car. You must be freezing." They headed toward the truck to warm up and call for help, praying that they had cell reception."

Jake had already called for help and managed to reach the Mounties. He gave them the location, then made his way toward the others. When he reached Cheynne and Mia, he asked, "Is everyone okay? I just called the Mounties who are on the way with an ambulance."

The girls shook their heads no as Dakota called out, "Jake, go back and get your Sig Sauer and grab mine. It's in the pouch on the back of my seat and hurry."

Mia anxiously said, "There are four other girls in the RV with two armed men."

Mack had already gone back to his truck to get his rifle, ready to defend them in case they were fired upon. He caught up with Jake and they both hastily trudged down the cliff. "We have to help the other girls get safely out, but there isn't any cover down there."

"Maybe we should wait until the Mounties arrive. Whoa, look! Someone is trying to climb out of the side door. It looks like the door is jammed." They heard a female voice.

"Help, help me."

Jake handed Dakota his gun. Dakota whispered, "Okay, let's go, cautiously. The men don't know that we are aware of the situation. Hopefully, they will think we are just here to help them." Zach followed them with a crowbar, figuring they might need it to pry open the door.

They carefully hiked down the slope and surrounded the RV. The girl was attempting to crawl out of the broken window. Dakota noticed that the door hinges were damaged. "Wait, are you injured?"

"My leg is cut and bleeding, but I'm okay."

As Mack and Zack worked on the door Dakota asked, "Do you know if anyone else is injured?"

"Yes. There are two other girls that are either knocked out or are dead. I couldn't get them to respond to me, but I had to get out. The man behind the wheel looks dead. His head is bleeding and he is upside down in his seat. The other man is injured, maybe a broken arm, so he can't move." She glanced back at the man and began trembling. "He's dangerous and he knows I'm trying to get out." Mack pried the door open just enough so that Dakota could carry her out.

Zach put his arm around her waist and helped her walk up the hill. She eyed him with suspicion and he noticed. "Don't worry, we're the good guys. We have to get you out of this frigid blizzard. We're headed to a warm truck where a nice woman named Cheynne is looking after your friend."

Mack and Dakota crawled in the RV and found two girls slumped over, appearing lifeless. One of them had a bench sofa, that must have broken loose in the crash, on top of her and the other was bleeding badly from her face, neck, head and stomach. They lifted the bench off of the girl and Dakota felt her pulse. He felt a slow rhythm. He was afraid to move her in case her back was broken, so he let her be, hoping an ambulance would arrive any minute. His heart hammered in his chest as he made his way to the other girl, praying she was alive. He felt her pulse and found none. He bowed his head in sorrow, thinking of how unfair it was that so many worthless, egotistical thugs were responsible for the abuse and death of scores of defenseless young women. He felt enraged as he made his way to the man in the passenger seat.

Jake carefully peered into the broken window at the man. "An ambulance is on the way." The man pointed his gun at him with a shaky hand. "Whoa, no need for that. I'm just here to help you." Jake backed off as Mack and Dakota made their way to the front. The driver had no pulse.

Mack reached over the man in the passenger seat and grabbed the gun out of his hand. "So ye tried to make off with these girls and look where it got ye, wretched louse. Since yer buddy is dead, I guess you'll go down for the whole thing. Kidnapping, reckless endangerment, abuse, trafficking, illegal weapons. Don't worry, you'll have a nice, cool cell to think about it in for a long time or better yet, you deserve a lethal injection so the tax payers don't have to pay for your sorry arse. " The man snarled.

The sound of blaring sirens quickly became louder as they arrived at the edge of the cliff above the dreadful scene. A few minutes later, EMTs and Mounties were hiking down the hill with stretchers. Dakota climbed out of the RV to talk with them. "The driver is dead and a man that was armed before we removed his gun appears to have a broken arm. There is also a young girl who is alive, but badly injured, so I didn't want to move her. The other girl is most likely dead. I could not feel a pulse." The EMTs entered the RV to help the injured girl first. Dakota spoke with the Mounties. "These men abducted the girls. A report has been filed including a description of the RV. Detective Jay Lawson met us at the rest area south of Marsh Lake where we found an abandoned car, possibly owned by one of the girls. There are two more girls who we helped get to the safety of one of our trucks where my co-driver, Cheynne DeMarka is looking after them. They both sustained injuries."

"We heard about the rest area case. What a shame. I know Detective Lawson. I'll give him a call and let him know you found the RV and the girls. We sure appreciate you helping out. Rich will go with you to your trucks and pick up the girls." Two more Mounties headed down to the RV. "Hey, by the way, are you guys, okay? We saw the skid marks up there. Looks like one of you slid sideways down the hill."

Mack said, "Aye. That RV spun out right in front of me. I slid sideways for a bit but no worries, it's not the first time."

"Phew! I don't know how you handle those rigs in this kind of weather. I'm sure you're strapping chains on before you head west, right?"

"Yes Sir, we most definitely are."

"Snow plows are on the way up the road. You might want to wait until they clear some of the snow and spray sand before you proceed. Drive safely."

One of the Mounties reached the truck where Cheynne was looking after the girls. Mia asked Cheynne, "Olivia is dead, isn't she?"

"Yes, she is. Can you tell us what happened?"

"We stopped at the rest area for a little exercise. We wanted to go walk around by the river, but while I was putting on my hiking boots, those men walked over to us from their RV and asked us for directions, but then one of them grabbed Olivia and tried to take her to the RV, but she ran toward the river." Mia frantically recounted the incident as tears streamed down her face. "She tried to fight him off, but he hit her so hard that she fell to the ground. Then he picked her up and carried her down to the river. I ran after her, but only made it far enough to see the man tearing her clothes off while she screamed and screamed. It was horrible. The other man grabbed me and carried me back to the RV, tied me up and then he left, locking the doors. I think he went down to the river." Mia was sobbing and shaking. "They might have raped her. Oh, God. Then I heard a gunshot. Why did they have to shoot her? Why?"

Cheynne hugged Mia as she cried in her arms. "I'm so sorry." Cheynne's eyes welled up as she helped the girls climb out of the truck and into the Mounty's SUV.

Mia called to Cheynne, "Wait, do you want your jacket and slippers back?"

"No, please keep them. You need to stay warm."

The drivers put their chains on as the Mounties and EMTs continued to carry out the victims. They had a difficult time with the criminal, who was thrashing and screaming protests. They had to securely strap him to the stretcher and three men carried him up the cliff to an EMT vehicle.

The storm raged and wind howled as it wafted through swaying trees creating eerie, swishing and crackling sounds. Thick, wet spring snow was still falling rapidly and being hurled around by gusty winds with such ferocity that the road was barely visible. The drivers gathered at Dakota's truck. "We'll follow the plows so that we are rolling on the freshly sanded road. Visibility will be greater behind their headlights. Haines Junction is not much farther and if the storm hasn't moved east by the time we fuel, we'll stay put for a few hours until it passes." He shook his head, clenching his teeth. "I'm thankful that we saved those girls, but we should talk more about it at a safer location. Let's roll."

The team made their way safely to the truck stop in Haines Junction, fueled, parked and went in to a restaurant for a warm meal while waiting for the storm to move on as planned.

"Phew!" Mack shook his head, looking sullen and disturbed. "Those poor girls. I'd like to wipe all of those damn perverts off the face of the earth in one powerful sweep. We obviously are making a difference, but my God, there are just too damn many of them. They're like disgusting cockroaches, scurrying up from the depths of hell."

Dakota picked up his cell phone. "I'm calling Dirk to fill him in. If he answers, I'll put him on speaker."

Luckily, he was there. "Dirk Hays."

"Hey, Dirk, I have you on speaker with my team."

"Dakota, are you guys okay? My phone has been exploding with updates."

"Yes, we're all fine. We were able to rescue a few girls, although two others were unfortunately killed, one in an accident and another at a rest area south of Whitehorse." They all filled him in on the recent events, each driver providing as much detail as possible.

"I heard about the rest area incident and because of you guys, we're fortunate to have at least one of the perps in custody. Where are you?"

"Dakota said, "We're in Haines Junction waiting out the worst of the blizzard. We hope to be in Anchorage sometime this evening."

"Hey, you guys know how to manage driving those rigs in severe weather and I respect that, but no need to risk your lives out there more than you already have. I received your information about Axle Heller and I have to say, damn good work. As you know, we have been surveilling him for years, but we needed some solid evidence that he has been responsible for a considerable amount of the corruption in Anchorage, as we suspected.

We had previously figured out that some of the companies on your list were owned by Heller and now, since you were able to find the locations of a few of his hideouts, we may finally be in a position to take that bastard down. We already have field agents in place now who have been following every lead on that list."

"Impressive. You guys don't waste any time. I just sent you that list yesterday."

"No time to waste. I want the whole damn organization to come to a crashing halt, every company, every cathouse, every damn business that he owns, but it won't happen overnight without more help. We need you guys in Anchorage as soon as possible. Our agents will be posing as employees and customers until we find that bastard. He is one elusive son of a bitch! We figured out some time ago that he owns the two X-rated night clubs, had an agent call us with his location at that time, surrounded the club, but damned if he didn't slip away somehow. We searched every person, every space, nook and cranny of the place and never found him. I'm thinking he may have figured out how to get into the hotel next door, but we searched every room and didn't discover any conceivable way for him to escape. Since the hotels are on your list, the theory that he somehow made it to the hotel makes sense. We have two agents working on that as we speak. Those hotels are actually nice, quality hotels separately owned by two different trusts, managed by different people, one from Victoria, British Columbia, Canada and one from Seattle, Washington, which is why we hadn't made the connection."

Dakota said, "Heller began his career in Seattle, so he gave himself away on the one trust. Not too bright, but that probably is how our source began connecting the dots. Heller's disguises must have prevented you from noticing that all of the passport photos of the owners of each company were of him. Our source played around with facial features and hair styles until he was able to find enough similarities to conclude that they were all Heller."

"Yes. When I saw that, I sat there speechless for a few minutes. We should have figured that out by now. What was also interesting is that the finger prints on the passports were all different. A very good forger created those, because all of the names are real people, most of them deceased, but somehow not recorded as deceased. One of them we discovered was a teen-aged boy who passed away over fifty years ago, with no death certificate issued or filed. Sly son of a bitch. Well, I'd like to know who gave you your information, because we could use a brain like that on our team."

"If I told you, I'd have to kill you."

"Come on, Dakota, I'd at least like to pick his or her brain a bit. Maybe he could teach a course at Quantico."

"All I can tell you is that I received it from an anonymous source. I don't know the person who sent it, but I did review it extensively to make sure it all made sense. I didn't want to send you someone's conspiracy theory."

"Yeah, right. Well, no matter for now. I want you guys in Anchorage until we can bring Axle Heller down, which may happen in the next day or two. Since the two perps that were arrested in Anchorage confessed to abducting the girls for Heller, I'm hoping the percentage of missing girls including Native Americans declines considerably after we apprehend him and everyone who works for him.

My philosophy is to know with absolution that I will take down the entire organization, not just a few and I won't quit until I have succeeded. Otherwise, it's similar to the planarian flatworm that grows another head when its head gets chopped off. The organization starts all over again, basically continuing with new leadership."

"You're a force to be reckoned with, Dirk."

"You know it."

Dakota, you and your team drive safely. Those Yukon storms can be treacherous as you have just experienced."

"Thanks, Dirk." They ended the call. While Dakota and his team were waiting for their meals, they discussed the recent events. Dakota eyed Mack with concern. "We were very lucky on that bust and rescue, even though you were in danger of sliding over that cliff along with the RV. I hope you aren't too shaken up. I've experienced a slide myself but dude, you handled your rig like the finest pro."

"Aye. The problem with most drivers is that they're afraid to die, mate. I don't have a death wish, but fear could take you over the edge. The trick is to stay calm and work with the slope. As soon as ye see the tail of the trailer begin to realign, ye slowly turn the wheel to get back under it. I could see that the road was not solid ice and I was fortunate to roll again on a snow packed road with a few dry patches, so the wheels grabbed the road again. What concerned me was the RV. The driver obviously had no winter driving skills and most likely poor tire tread. I went into a slide to avoid smashing into him. He spun around a few times before he slid off the road with tremendous momentum. That RV tumbled down the cliff like the hand of the devil clutched it in its fist. I think Chris wet his pants." He chuckled while grinning at Chris.

Cheynne put her arm around Chris. "I know I would have wet my pants if I was in the front seat witnessing what you did."

Chris laughed. "I will admit that my eyes were as big as saucers and I didn't breathe for a minute, but I didn't wet myself. I'm just glad that you were driving."

Mack said, "I'm proud of ye for not freaking out. That would have made it harder for me to maintain control. Yer alright, Lad."

Jake said, "In all of my years of driving, I've only experienced a sideways slide one time, on black ice. I was headed west on the downgrade right after the Vail Pass summit. That first curve is a doozy if you hit black ice. But right after the curve, is a straight section and I was able to straighten it out with quickly enough. Actually, the pass that is super sketchy is Cabbage Pass in Oregon. Headed west, right after the summit is the beginning of a steep downhill, curve after curve. I drove that stretch right after an ice storm and witnessed my trailer slide left and right the whole way down. The cliffs are so steep that a truck going over the edge, would probably keep moving all the way to the bottom of the cliff and you wouldn't live to see another day."

The meals arrived and everyone ate quietly, with little conversation. They were all deep in thought, reflecting on the day's events. Dakota checked the weather radar for the area. "Looks like we'll be fine in another hour. The majority of the storm has passed." They all glanced out of the window to see lighter falling snow. "I'm sure the plows have been keeping up with it, but I suggest we keep our chains on until the road is dry, even though Canada isn't too happy about truck chains after May first. I guess this is an unusually late spring storm, like the occasional storms we experience in the Colorado Rockies."

"Kluane Lake." Jake beamed while he studied a map of the Yukon Territory. "One of my favorite stops for breathtaking views and fishing. We'll be driving along the Lake which is seventy kilometers long and beautiful cobalt blue."

Cheynne smiled and said, "You are in your element aren't you."

"Yes, Ma'am. I've been driving this stretch of highway for thirty years and I love everything about it. Whenever I've been lucky enough to haul loads with plenty of time to make my delivery appointments, I stopped to fish and just enjoyed the trip. Maybe we can stop more often on our way back." He grinned deviously at Dakota.

"Well, Dirk said we'll be working up here through June, so I'm sure we'll find opportunities to enjoy a few exceptional areas along the drive. We'll be in Anchorage for a few days, so by the time we head back, maybe the weather will be a little warmer. The days will be about a half hour longer every five days until summer solstice. Driving during the daylight is much more preferable for everyone, I'm sure. We'll just have to dodge the RVs." They all sighed and groaned. Dakota liked hearing his drivers share pleasant experiences and planning exciting activities.

Mack said, "We'll have to be on the lookout now, knowing that traffickers are using RVs to transport girls. Damn pervs. I wonder if those traffickers we saw earlier also work for Axle Heller, since they seemed to be on the way to Anchorage."

"Yeah, I was wondering the same thing." Dakota looked down at his empty plate, thoughtfully. "Maybe the authorities can get the perp they have in custody to spill the beans. If we keep locating the idiots that are working for Heller, maybe there will be fewer abductions. We just have to stay ahead of his game."

Mack said, "I've never been interested in patronizing those X-rated clubs, but I wonder if a few of us should check them out, maybe wander around a bit to see if we can discover how he gets out. Maybe there is a hidden door somewhere."

"I believe Sarah's plan is to disguise herself and saunter around the bar as she searches for Heller's offices and other private areas." Jake sipped his coffee. "Maybe a few of us could meet up with her so that we look like a group interested in the entertainment. That way, there will be more of us for safety reasons, but we could split up as we search. I don't like the idea of Sarah going in alone. If Axle Heller's organization is as colossal as Dirk believes it is, then he's going to be one, dangerous beast."

"I agree." Dakota glanced at Cheynne. "Would you be okay going into a club like that? I think that if all eight of us, including Sarah and Grace, go in as a group and spend some money on dinner and drinks, we would blend in with other patrons and a couple of us could sneak away from time to time. Sarah thinks there might be a secret passageway from the club to the hotel. That makes sense to me, because the Feds have not been able to locate him when they search his clubs."

"Dodgy bastard!" Mack scowled. "I bet the lass is right. She mentioned that the hotels were under construction immediately after the clubs were built. He could have very easily designed a tunnel leading from the basement directly to the hotel basement. The question is, where is the door to the tunnel and is it in a guarded area? He may leave it unguarded, because he probably figures no one knows it exists other than a few of his own men."

"I hope you're right." Dakota glanced at his calendar. "Okay, here's the plan. Let's drop our loads and park our rigs at the truck stop in Anchorage. Pack a small overnight bag including a few self-defense items and possibly some kind of disguise, a ball cap, glasses, makeup and so on. I think Sarah's idea to conceal her identity is clever, so that she could return at a later time with no one the wiser. We may need to check out several of his establishments without anyone remembering our faces."

He sipped his coffee, then continued. "We'll book a few rooms in one of the hotels and search for a passageway door from the hotel side, which may be easier to find than from the club side. We'll plan from there so that I can include Dirk and his men. I really don't want Dirk's men blowing our operation, by increasing the numbers of men who look like Feds, so I think that if we have our plan worked out, once everything is in motion we can coordinate with them. Finding the tunnel will be tricky because Heller might have the tunnel and the entrances monitored. Possibly, a lost maintenance worker with a cart of supplies could work."

Zach said, "I worked in the H/Vac field for a while and the commercial ducts are large enough to crawl through if you're super skinny like me. Chris may be able to help us with a set of plans for each building, right, Chris?"

243

Chris already had his computer out and was searching the Anchorage permit and building department databases. Since he previously worked for the police department as a computer specialist, he is amazingly skilled and expedient at locating information needed. Dirk had preapproved an access identity clearance for Chris, even though he is also an information junkie and a super hacker. Chris has used his special skills on many occasions, to locate criminal networks, personal and commercial information for special projects and has assisted in bringing down drug lords, mafia members, traffickers and other criminals, particularly if they use the internet regularly.

"Here we go." He turned his screen around so that everyone could see as he panned around the blueprints. "This is the basement level of the Monarch Bay View Hotel which is located just west of the Sweet Gems strip club. I didn't expect to find a tunnel on the plans, since that could have been a concealed plan addition, cash paid directly to the contractor, who probably works for Heller anyway, but here is where I would locate it." He drew a red line from the hotel to the club and showed the club plan side by side with the hotel plan.

He downloaded the plans into a folder and opened up the second hotel and nightclub plans. "These are the Golden Empress Hotel plans about a mile away from the Monarch, with the Sea Maiden strip club right next to it. He drew a red line on that plan where he thought a tunnel may be located as well."

"Good work, Chris." Dakota patted him on the back. "Now all we have to do is figure out how to find the bastard, lure him in and trap him in the tunnel. I think that if we have any luck finding him in one of his clubs, we could have Dirk's trap in place with all entrances guarded and move in to bust him, which would prompt him to head directly for the tunnel. If that plan works, I don't want any of you anywhere near the tunnel, because I'm sure there will be one hell of a gun battle with possible fatalities. Our job is to locate the escape and deliver the plans to Dirk and let him send his men in." Dakota glanced at Mack and Chris sensing that if they were needed at during the bust, they would be there and he would as well, but he didn't like the idea never the less. "I haven't discussed any of this with Dirk yet and don't intend to until we can determine if we are correct."

Chris also downloaded the sitemaps of the buildings and pinned them on a map of Anchorage. He then referenced the list of businesses that Sarah had given them along with the addresses and pinned those locations as well, so that a coordinated operation could be designed to take down all of the businesses at once. If Dirk and his team could accomplish this, Axle Heller's organization would at least be crippled substantially. "When I get back to the truck, I can print these plans."

Zach said, "Did you find Mechanical, plumbing and electrical plans? If you print those, I can work on verifying the location of your tunnel using those plans. Even though the construction floor plans are not recorded in the Anchorage building permit set, the M.E.P plans, may show air and electric to the tunnel if there is one."

"On it." Chris already downloaded the entire folder and copied and pasted the plans that they needed to a file ready for printing.

Dakota glanced around to each driver. "Before we

leave, I'll call Sarah with our plan and arrange to meet up with her at the Monarch. I just have a feeling about that particular hotel, so we'll start there. If we don't have any luck, we'll try again at the Golden Empress. She mentioned that she and Grace were planning to arrive sometime today, so Jake, you and I should keep in touch with them and we'll meet up in Anchorage."

"Definitely." Jake looked troubled. "I really don't like Grace being involved, but she so badly wants to help with a possible rescue of girls and she really wants to accompany Sarah. I don't think she plans on being involved in the more dangerous part of our work, so that's a good thing, but Dakota, I'm worried about her like always. If anything happens to her, I'll never forgive myself for not doing more to talk her out of going. Axle Heller has to be taken down and soon."

"Here, here, my man." Mack raised his coffee cup in salute.

They all joined in. "Here, here."

Jake said, "Let's go kick some arse!"

Dakota raised his cup. "I'm not going to let Heller get away with more innocent young women if I can help it. I really think that along with Dirk's team, we have a conceivable chance of taking Heller out." He swallowed the rest of his coffee. "Okay, let's head out. It looks like the snow and wind have died down substantially. Let's have a look at the road ahead and check out the conditions. Maybe we could go ahead and remove the chains. I'd sure like to get into Anchorage this evening but our delivery schedules are loose, so there is no need to rush. For those of you who are driving second, get some rest. Keep your ears on so that we can all stop together."

They all headed out to the trucks.

Dakota said, "I'll be right be out. I missed a call from Jillian. She probably wants to discuss her plans to visit the Sauveurs in June. I really hope we have cleared out some of the trash in Anchorage before Jillian and Autumn arrive. I can't even describe how nervous I'll be otherwise."

25

Jillian was cooking in the ranch lodge kitchen with Autumn and Brooke when Dakota called. "Hey, brother, how's it going out there?"

"Much better now. We just enjoyed a badly needed break and a nice hot meal in Haines Junction after rolling through a massive storm which included, you'll be excited to hear, rescuing some girls from a couple of creeps that the RCMP had been searching for." He didn't want to discuss the details of the incident with Jillian, yet he knew she would be elated to hear that they saved more girls from a possible, devastating fate.

"Oh, fantastic. I sure hope you guys were not involved in a dangerous situation."

"One of the traffickers was arrested and the other

died in a crash." He quickly changed the subject. "Sorry, I missed your call. What's up?"

"I wanted to discuss our trip to Miki Tarniq with you. I've been looking into airfare, but we'll have to figure out how to time it right, so that you will be there at the same time. I figure Autumn and I could stay in a hotel near the Anchorage airport for a day until you arrive if need be and then we could fly to Kotzebue together and arrange a bush plane from there."

Dakota thought about Jillian and Autumn in Anchorage and felt immediately disturbed. He would not allow them to walk around in Anchorage alone. "Sarah and Grace are planning to visit sometime in June and I'd like to be there at the same time. I plan on talking with Ethan about camping near Miki Tarniq so that only you, Autumn, Sarah and Grace would need to stay with them in their home. I certainly don't want to overwhelm them."

"Yeah, right, but I think it would be a blast to camp with you, okay? We can figure that out later, but I'd like for you to get a hold of Ethan and let him know that we want to come out there then so that he can plan. Can you work with Dirk to make sure you can be there at the same time?"

"I see no problem. Our team is working on a significant mission, which we hope will be wrapped up way before then. Jake, Zach and everyone else who wants to join us will be thrilled to plan an exciting camping, rafting vacation. I'll be talking with my team about this soon. I'll call you tomorrow when we arrive in Anchorage and I've had time to get a hold of Ethan."

"Sounds good. Dakota, please be careful."

After the call, Jillian smiled at Autumn who was

listening to the conversation. "Are you excited?"

"Oh, yes! Maybe I can help by calling Anji. She emailed me her phone number yesterday. I'm really looking forward to speaking with her. Maybe I can let her know what we are planning and ask her to pass the information and Dakota's cell number on to Ethan."

Jillian handed her the phone. "Why don't you call her now?"

Autumn rushed into her lodge room, opened up her email on her laptop and located the phone number. She sauntered back to the kitchen and dialed Anji.

"This is Hana Sauveur. Who is calling?"

"Mrs. Sauveur, I'm Autumn. Anji must have talked with you about me, right?"

"Oh, yes, Autumn. Anji has been so excited to be corresponding with you. We are all looking forward to your visit."

"Thank you. I'm also excited to meet you all and to get acquainted with Anji. I have never been to Alaska and I'm thrilled that you are interested in having me stay for a few weeks. I was hoping to speak to Anji. Is she there?"

"Yes, she is in her room. I'll go get her."

A minute later, Anji was on the call. "Autumn. I'm so happy that you called. When can you come visit? I have so many things planned."

"Well, we we'd like to come out some time in June. My mother, Jillian, will be coming with me and from what I understand, Grace and Sarah plan to be there at the same time. We don't want to overwhelm you and your family, so my Uncle Dakota and a bunch of his employees are planning to camp nearby. Do you think you will have room in your house for me, my mom, Grace and Sarah?

If not, we can all camp."

"Oh, we definitely have room for all four of you, but we might want to go camp with them, at least for a couple of days. That will be super fun. We all may want to do a river float trip and camp along the way. I'll talk with Papa as soon as he gets home and I'll let you know what he thinks will work out."

Autumn was smiling ear to ear. She had the call on speaker phone so that Jillian and Brooke could listen. "Well, I can't wait. I graduate on May 29th, so I'll be excited to celebrate the end of high school with you. I'm also looking forward to talking with you about CSU and when your parents might allow you to come here to tour the campus and our living arrangements. I know that I'm jumping ahead a bit, but I'm hoping that you have made the decision to go to CSU with me. I don't know anyone here except my family and Brooke, so after we spend time together, hopefully we will both feel more comfortable about attending there."

"My feelings exactly. I have decided and I've already written them back and accepted a scholarship award. I'm also applying for more scholarships and grants. It's exhausting work, because most of the grants require papers outlining my interests, accomplishments, skills and knowledge in my chosen field, which is botany. Papa says he has the money to pay for my tuition, but I want to pay for as much of it as I can. Alina and Kaya will be attending universities as well, and I know it will be a struggle for my family if they have to pay for all of us."

Autumn glanced up at Jillian and smiled. "My parents said they want to cover all of the tuition costs, but I feel the same as you do. I want to pay for as much as I can, which is why I will be working on the weekends and during the summer at Brooke's ranch. I am also applying for scholarships and grants in the psychology field. There are many women's organizations that need help, caring for and assisting girls who have been through tragic situations. In fact, even though it isn't your field of study, I bet Brooke would be happy to give you a job here at the ranch. My mother is a landscape artist extraordinaire and might really benefit from your knowledge of plant species. She will be assisting in the maintenance of the grounds and has planned the landscape surrounding the entire ranch including many edible plants, flowers and fruit trees. I feel certain that she could use your help, especially since she will also be living in Montana for several months each year. That's where our home is."

"Oh, I thought you lived in Colorado."

"My Grandparents live here and my parents will be sharing their home when they come out here for visits. Wait until you see their home. They have a beautiful heavy timber and stone home with decks surrounding the house and the most beautiful gardens I have ever seen. My mother and grand designed the gardens and worked on them together for many years when she was young." Autumn frowned and went quiet for a minute, recalling Jillian's tragic years away from home, but quickly shook herself out of it as she hugged her mother. "You will love visiting here. Uncle Dakota lives about a mile away from my grands' house so we will have his house to stay in as well, if needed. Also, I have been researching the area and found several beautiful hiking areas and a few other fun places to visit, that is, when we can take breaks from studying."

Anji was beaming as she listened. "I'm excited and very grateful that we have such an amazing opportunity to create a sensational friendship. I also feel more comfortable about going to college with a friend, since I have never been in the lower forty-eight states. I really can't even imagine what to expect, except for photos and descriptions that I studied in articles. I have done a lot of research about Colorado and I already have a list of places I want to visit and explore. I'm especially interested in areas like Rocky Mountain National Park, Waterfall Loop, Hanging Lake in Glenwood Canyon and Chautauqua Park in Boulder."

"What a terrific list. We can explore those area together, because I haven't been there either. After I graduate, I'll have much more time."

"I have already graduated, which is why I have extra time to apply for grants. I hate to end the call so soon, but I have to run to Papa's shop to pick up some things for Mother. Do you have Dakota's phone number? I'd like to give it to Papa. He wants to call him to discuss his visit and a few other things."

Autumn gave her Dakota's number. "I'll keep in touch and Anji, you can call me anytime. I'll be here at the ranch for a few more days and then I'm going home for graduation. I'll call you with our flight plans as soon as I can." The girls ended the call. Autumn felt absolutely elated that she was communicating so well with Anji.

Jillian hugged her. "I'm so happy that you have a new extraordinary friend and so many exciting experiences ahead of you. Dakota plans on being at your graduation and of course, your grands will be driving home with us. I'm really excited to be able to introduce them to Nicholas and Chrys and to show them around Missoula. I think they'll love it and will want to visit us often just for a change of scenery. Both Missoula, Montana and Evergreen, Colorado mean so much to me and I just can't imagine giving up one for the other. Your Papa and I plan on keeping at least one of the homes in Missoula and Mom and Dad really want us to share their home when we are here." She smiled contentedly. "I'm eager to meet Ethan and Hana and I do hope we all become good friends."

"I'm excited to be graduating soon and I hope Uncle Dakota can make it, but his work is very important. If he can't, I will absolutely understand.

"I believe Dakota will make it because he is also planning on being here to celebrate Brooke's grand opening, three days after your graduation." She grinned at Brooke.

"Dakota better be here." Brooke took the roast out of the oven. "I'm counting on our entire team to be here if possible. I want a full house of happy people all donating to the cause. I even invited Dirk Hays and Kate Lindt, who are the FBI agents in charge of the task force team. I asked them to invite anyone they could think of who may be either interested in providing funding or who might be able to help me find grants and other resources. And, I still have to hire people to help."

Autumn looked at Brooke thoughtfully. "Have you thought about calling CSU and CU to find out if there are graduates who are looking for work? I know I would jump at the chance to work here for a first job, right out of school."

"I do have both schools on my list to call, but I've

been so busy with the construction, that I haven't had time to call or send out employment opportunity letters. I have a standard letter typed up and ready to go, so maybe I'll be able to get to that tomorrow."

"Would you like help? I could post the opportunity on all Colorado jobs web sites. Do you have a list of the jobs that are needed?"

"Oh, you are so smart and quick as a whip. Yes, I have a list including two psychologists, a Chef, Sous Chef and at least three other kitchen staff members, housekeepers and so on. I'll give you the list."

"Okay, on it. I'll get all of that done tomorrow and can help you review the applicants as they come in. After I graduate, I could come back here to continue to help until we go to Alaska."

Brooke gave Autumn a huge hug. "You are my shining star. I don't know what I would have done without you and your mother." She smiled at them both. Well, I'm hungry. The chicken roast smells delicious."

Jillian took a large bowl out of the cupboard. "I'll make a salad. Mom and Dad will be back here with the quilts any time now." Yamka has a collection of twelve quilts that she skillfully made over the years, which she generously agreed to donate for the beds. Brooke wanted the lodge rooms to feel homey and comfortable and was overjoyed to learn that Yamka wanted to donate them.

Autumn grinned. "Grand and I have already started a quilt. I selected evergreen, sage, purples and a bit of grey blue in all sorts of floral patterns. I will donate it to you when I'm finished. Hey, I just remembered, Anji and her mom also make quilts. I bet they are beautiful and maybe we could buy some of them. Anji told me that many of them illustrate scenes of the Alaskan environment, like moose, caribou, bears, fish, mountains, local flowers and trees. What treasures they must be."

Brooke said, "Oh, I would love to have a few. I think I'll call Sarah about that. Maybe she would be interested in buying a few to donate. Maybe you and Sarah could bring them back with you this summer."

"Sure. I have a feeling that our two families are going to be good friends. Anji told me that Alina, one of her sisters, makes clothing and plans on studying fashion design. Maybe she could come out here as well. She could teach the girls to sew and make clothing. I can't wait to see her creations. The whole family seems to be creatively skilled. Joie, her other sister, works with wood, designing bowls, boxes and tables and Kaya, her brother, knows how to build houses and buildings. He will be studying Architecture in Anchorage this Fall."

Jillian tossed the salad and flipped the asparagus in the sauté pan coating them with garlic, butter and fresh squeezed lemon. "I also have a good feeling about the Sauveur family. I am really looking forward to spending time with them and I want them to visit here as often as they like, especially while you two are here together at school. There will be so much that you could learn from each other."

They suddenly heard footsteps, then Chevyo and Yamka strolled into the kitchen. "Ho, ho, ho! Merry spring Christmas," Chevyo bellowed, flashing an enormous smile as he set down the stack of gorgeous handmade quilts.

Yamka smiled at him coquettishly. "He's always so proud of my work. She kissed him on the cheek and winked at him flirtatiously.

Brooke sighed. "Oh, I so hope that Rhys turns out to be the love of my life, so that we could share a magical, soulful love like you two have." She smiled thoughtfully with a sparkle in her eyes. "Now, lets' look at these beauties." She and Autumn each unfolded a quilt. "Yamka, these are remarkably lovely. They must have taken years to complete."

"Oh, no. Not that long. What else do I have to do? A little cooking and cleaning which Chevy and I share and a little gardening. I can make a queen size quilt from start to finish in one month." She held up the latest design. "This one took me three and a half weeks."

"But it looks like it took years. The detail and stitching are so fine and I love your choice of colors and patterns." Brooke's eyes began to water as she sauntered over to hug Yamka. "Thank you. The girls will love them. I will use each quilt to determine the colors of pillows, rugs and other décor planned for each lodge room. After dinner, let's go put them on the beds."

After an evening of delicious food and laughter, everyone retired to be well rested for a busy day at the ranch. Brooke gazed at the ceiling, her heart fluttering as she thought about Rhys. She wondered where he was and hoped he could make it back in time for the opening in less than two weeks. She talked with him the previous day when he informed her that he would be driving through Canada and into Alaska to help with the current war against Axle Heller. Hearing that frightened her, as she thought about everything that could go wrong with such an enormous operation. Brooke was normally a positive thinking, glass half full kind of woman, strong and confident, but she had been lonely for so many years that she didn't want anything to hinder the glorious momentum of their newly found love relationship. She was surprised that she cared so deeply for him in such a short period of time. They had been working together, but as separate drivers at Dakota's company for many years and had only just begun seeing each other romantically five months ago. And now she wondered how often she would get to be with him since she would soon be retiring from the company to manage Harmony Ranch.

Rhys is a jovial Scotsman who has been in love with Brooke for quite a while now. She smiled at the thought of his quirky dialect and his amusing, compassionate demeanor. He had recently mentioned his desire to quit driving, with plans to acquire a few horses and dairy cows and spend the rest of his years ranching. He lives in in a charming log home with plans to expand the home on a four-acre parcel of land in Winter Park, Colorado, not far from Brooke's ranch in Granby. She wondered if he would be interested in helping her run Harmony Ranch rather than investing in his own ranch. She sighed contently and finally drifted off to sleep.

26

Rhys MacAllister and Nash Chavez had just exchanged a load with a Canadian team in Ft. St. John's when Dakota called. "Hey, how's it going?"

"We're headed out with our load to Anchorage, but the question is, mate, what's going on up there? We've been hearing about the massive storms, both weather and crime related."

"Oh, you heard right. We need you up here. I've already spoken with Grace about your stopping at the ranch in Whitehorse for the night if you need a break. I'll text you the address. There will be a cabin ready for you with a nice shower room and comfortable beds. I highly recommend taking her up on that."

"Well, okay. We're on it. So, what are Sarah and Grace

up to?"

"They will be leaving in the morning for Anchorage. Sarah is planning one of her infamous schemes to rescue some women and will be joining us in a major operation to locate and take down Axle Heller." Dakota gave Rhys the low down, filling him in on the details of Heller's colossal organization and their plans to locate him. "Dirk and his men of course will be working with us and he feels extremely positive that they finally have enough intel on this guy to wipe him off the map. From what I hear, trafficking in Anchorage is rampant, but the government and many other gallant individuals and groups are doing everything they can to join in the fight. I just think we're going to need your skills and extra man-power and with our expertise, we might just win this battle."

"Right on, Dakota. We'll keep in touch and thanks for arranging the stay over at the ranch. I've been interested in checking it out since Brooke's ranch is modeled after Hope Ranch." Rhys paused and cleared his throat. He intended on bringing up his retirement plans earlier, but there never seemed to be the right time, so he decided to go for it. "By the way Dakota, if things work out between Brooke and me, I may be retiring from the company soon. She is going to need help on the ranch and I've been chompin' at the bit to get into ranching myself. I have plans to expand my cabin and ye know how I feel about the lovely lasse."

"Yeah, I know. I've been expecting this. We've been working together for so many years, it will feel like I'll be losing a brother and certainly one of the best members of my team, but we all have to retire at some point, so give me all that you've got until then."

"Aye, my head is still in the game. Dakota, ye won't be losing a brother. We'll be in touch and we'll be pestering ye to get off the road and come for barbecues and such. If Brooke's plans for Harmony Ranch work out the way she hopes, you'll be rescuing girls and bringing them to us to look after. We'll still be on the team, just in a different way."

"Thanks, Rhys. Also, Autumn will most likely be working with Brooke and Jillian on the weekends and during her summer breaks, so we'll all be spending time together. I'm really pleased about the way things are shaping up. We'll talk more about this soon. I'll see you two tomorrow night."

"Aye, on the way."

Rhys described the work ahead to Nash and filled him in on the particulars. Nash exclaimed, "Alright! I was hoping we'd get called up there. It does sound like we will be involved in some risky business, but I'm ready to roll." He jumped in the driver's seat and headed out while Rhys moseyed back to the sleeper to rest after an eleven-hour shift.

Rhys wondered what criminal activity they might encounter on the way through Canada. If Axle Heller's criminal empire in Alaska is as monstrous as Dakota described, that could explain why there had been so much corrupt activity in Anchorage. It sickened him to think about the innocent young girls and boys who fall victim to Heller. It also made sense to him that a large percentage of the trafficking going on between the lower forty-eight states, Canada and mainland Alaska could be as tremendous as it is because of several main corrupt organizations. It reminded him of the older days when known mafia rings, master-minded and controlled all types of trafficking in almost every large city in most countries. The main difference between the old mafia gangs and the current ones is that most of them operate underground and are unknown to the public who believe mob gangs are a thing of the past. Rhys knew otherwise.

Rhys was extremely proud of Brooke for building Harmony Ranch to help the innocent victims of sex traffickers. When he had worked as a detective on the Denver police force many years ago, he specialized in trafficking, abduction and domestic abuse cases which is the main reason he was interested in working on the FBI task force team with Dirk Hays. He has had tremendous success in tracking and capturing sex criminals including being a major player in the recent arrest of a major mafia crime organization responsible for the abduction of Jillian, over forty years ago.

Jillian had escaped her captors many years ago, however, the two men responsible were still at large until December of last year. Jillian didn't feel that she was safe until her captors and several others involved were arrested. Ray Giordano had seriously threatened and stalked Jillian's family resulting in her decision to change her identity and live away from them for twenty four more years in order to protect them.

Rhys shivered as he recalled the arrest of a revolting group of traffickers who he and Nash tracked from Texas to a corrupt freight company in Oklahoma City the previous year. After witnessing traffickers remove a group of horrified women from the back of a trailer, Rhys had no alternative other than involving himself with the criminals directly, resulting in a brutal battle in which he was fired upon. At the time, he felt as if those would be his last moments alive, so he fearlessly had given it his all and managed to take down his assailants.

For the past few years, Rhys has felt like the days of tumultuous excitement in his life should cease and has been ready for the next journey in life. He liked being in the middle of the action, knowing that he was a part of correcting a major wrong in the world but at sixty years old, he has felt the need to move on. The possibility that he and Brooke could develop a beautiful relationship together thrilled him and was the push that he needed to get off the road and begin living a less stressful, more peaceful life.

Dakota and his team of truck drivers are some of Rhys' closest friends, which had prevented him from leaving his truck driving career sooner. When Brooke made her move to leave, he decided the time was right for him as well, especially since she reciprocated his feelings of compassion and attraction. Now, Rhys feels deeply within his heart and soul that Brooke is his soulmate and she has shown him likewise. With these comforting thoughts, he fell asleep as Nash rolled on.

After a few hours of travel, Nash received a phone call from Dakota. "Hey buddy, what's going on?"

"Just checking in with you. After you deliver your load tomorrow, park at the Anchorage Truck Corral on eighteenth street and call me. I will come pick you up and get you checked in at the hotel. Keep in touch and let me know if you run into any trouble on the way."

"Got it. Thanks, Dakota."

After the call, Nash reflected on the past work, feeling grateful that the team had been able to assist in locating and arresting several large trafficking cartels as well as rescuing nearly thirty young women from horrible, abusive situations. He enjoyed being part of such an elite, significant team of brave U.S. military and police veterans, each possessing significant skills, which have proven to be useful in tracking and taking out criminal gangsters. Nash also felt lucky to be a partner with Rhys, who has been in the foreground of most of the major busts. He has felt safe and confident knowing Rhys is a well-known decorated veteran of the Denver, Colorado Police Department. Most of Dakota's employees share similar thoughts and feelings about the dangerous, but vital work they have been involved in.

Nash prayed the team would be able to rescue young women while in Anchorage. He continued to think about the upcoming events which he thought could go two ways. Either the team proves to be successful in taking down Axle Heller and his organization with no one suffering injuries or someone ends up wounded or killed and the gangster eludes the task force once again. If the latter occurs, Heller could immediately initiate an aggressive war against the authorities. He whispered to himself, "Who knows how monstrous this criminal is and what he is capable of?"

Nash decided to think positively about the operation, knowing that all precautions will be arranged. He thought about the Sauveurs and the other Alaskan people who may also be involved. He understood their rage and suddenly felt extra motivated to help.

27

Anji

Papa, Kaya and I boarded Jay's plane and headed for the hunting camp. I was beside myself anticipating the possibility of seeing Anya at the camp with her father. There was no way of knowing if they'd be there, but it was imperative to find out why the raven carried her scarf to me. I feel certain the peculiar bird wanted me to help her. I guess I'm beginning to believe that there could be some kind of spiritual connection between Anya and the raven. Maybe I am starting to loosen the restraints of my stubborn scientific convictions, but I figure if that is what it takes to find Anya and discover what happened to her, then I guess I am willing to accept it as a possibility.

If Anya is with her father, then she will be protected unless they left her alone again, which will frustrate me

265

to no end. I have never ventured further into the woods at that location, so I've never seen the camp. I figured maybe they built some sort of shelter for her to stay in on days she wasn't up to an arduous Caribou tracking event. She mentioned that she is skilled with a rifle and hunted with them often, so I am hopeful that she'll be there and we will finally be able to solve this frustrating mystery.

Jay landed the plane on the tundra, not far from the edge of the trees. We gathered our gear and walked the rest of the way. It seemed extraordinarily quiet except for the sound of our boots crunching in the crusty spring snow. As we approached the edge of the forest, sudden bursts of gusty winds caused eerie creaking sounds as the tall spruce trees swayed against each other. I sensed that something wasn't quite right and chills rushed up my spine. "Papa, the raven!" I pointed to the mysterious black bird perched on a snow-covered tree branch.

The raven gazed down at us and vocalized resonantly, "Kraaah, Kraaah." The bird seemed angry and it began pacing back and forth on the branch while bobbing its head.

"We have to go into the forest." I jogged toward the group of trees as the raven continued to observe us, cawing as if it was pleading with me to understand its message. I turned back to see Papa right behind me. I suddenly experienced a bone chilling shiver as we approached the edge of the woods. My heart drummed ferociously and my stomach felt like a bundle of knots. I couldn't help but feel that Anya was not okay. I clutched my jacket with my arms wrapped firmly across the front of me as if I could protect myself in that way.

"Wait here." Papa held my eyes sternly with his own. "I will go ahead to make sure the forest is safe and I'll wave you on after I check it out." Papa observed the raven for a minute while it bobbed its head and fluttered its wings as if to say, go on. When Papa entered the woods, he scouted around and located a tall, hunting lookout with clear sight through the trees to the open tundra, a perfect view point. Then his eyes were suddenly drawn toward the ground. Below the lookout was a grave marked with a beautifully carved wood headstone. His heart dropped as he immediately understood even before he read the name on the marker. Dalianya Ikiaq, loving daughter of Akio Ikiaq 2000 – 2018.

Ethan stood still in his stance as he pondered the significance of Dalianya's grave. His eyes welled up and he shook his head as he realized that they were too late to help this young girl. He wasn't sure how Anji would react to her grave. How had Anji seen and spoken to Anya? Ethan was in a state of quandary. He thought of the raven, Anya, the red scarf, then he caught a glimpse of a shiny, colorful bead on the ground and remembered the beads on Anya's scarf. He picked up the bead and walked out to the clearing where the others waited.

Papa's eyes were watery and his face was pale. "Is everything okay?" I rushed up to Papa with his hand held out presenting the jade bead. I took it feeling perplexed for a moment. "It's Anya's, look." I pulled her scarf out of my pocket and raised it up so that Papa could see the matching beads. Jay stared at the scarf with furrowed brows as he recalled Anya wearing it. I dashed into the trees to see for myself. Was Anya there? I searched for her and called out her name. "Anya, are you here?" I received no response and then I noticed the lookout and trudged through the deep snow toward it.

"Wait, Anji." Papa, Jay and Kaya followed me into the woods and toward the lookout.

And then my eyes fell on the grave. "I don't understand. What does this mean? Dalianya Ikiaq. Whose grave is this?"

Papa whispered to me. "Anji, look at the letters in the name closely."

My eyes welled up and my legs weakened barely supporting me. With blurred watery vision, I read the name carefully spotting the name Anya, hidden in her full given name, Dalianya. "Oh, no! No! How can this be? Anya's name is Dalianya? This is her grave? B… but how? Why? I don't understand." I fell to my knees and tears streamed down my face. "But she talked with me and she has shown herself to me many times. How can this be?" Then I recalled researching the names of the girls who went missing. I couldn't find Anya's name and I now understood why.

"I spoke to her grave with a trembling voice. "Dear, sweet Anya. You were the girl I witnessed in Anchorage, but I thought you escaped. I'm so sorry." I felt so ashamed of myself that I could do nothing else but cry.

Jay kneeled down in front of the grave beside me and put his arms around me. Then he picked up a lovely carved wooden box that was positioned in front of the gravestone and opened it. There were two letters, neatly folded and tucked inside the wooden box. He read one of the letters aloud; "To my beloved Dalianya. I'm so sorry I couldn't keep you safe. I promise I won't rest until I find and kill the man who took you away from me. I love you from the bottom of my heart and soul. Until we can be together again, Ben." Tears soaked our eyes as we held each other, both in utter hysterics. "This is why Ben has been so troubled. He must have found her lifeless body and buried her here."

I dried my tears with my sleeve and held the scarf close to my heart. I leaned over Anya's grave in prayer. "Anya, I'm so sorry. If I had only informed someone of what I observed that day in the parking lot, you might still be alive. I beg your forgiveness." I carefully wrapped the scarf around her gravestone, then began weeping uncontrollably, completely unhinged.

After a moment, I gained control of my emotions. "Thank you for finding me and leading me here. I understand now. You wanted me to find Ben and the slugs who ended your life so needlessly. I promise we will." I felt enraged and wanted to plot a deadly revenge with Ben and Anya's father.

Kaya held me in his arms as I continued to weep. "Shhhh. We'll find him. I'm so sorry, Anji."

Papa pulled another letter out of the box. He read; "My sweet daughter, a part of my heart has gone with you. Keep it safe until I join you in your harmonious new home. Please keep watch over me and love me from above. I love you with all of my heart, Papa."

I glanced up at the raven. "Thank you for leading me here." I turned to the grief-stricken faces of everyone. "Anya was trying to show me where she was buried, but I didn't understand that, I mean how could I when I thought she was alive." I tried to stabilize my trembling voice. "Ben and Anya's father must have found her and decided to lay her to rest here, in a place she loved. She

269

must have known that Ben and I used to come out here many years ago which could be why she showed herself to me. We have to find Ben. I'm certain he is seeking revenge on the men who killed her and I believe that he may be in serious trouble. And Wily Johns must have been involved somehow, because she made an appearance when we were in Kotzebue. She wanted us to put the pieces together and was worried about Ben."

The wind kicked up and the raven flew in circles around us. I shivered, feeling overwhelmed by spirits hovering over Anya's grave. For the first time, I really felt a connection with the spirits of our loved ones and I finally understood why Papa and Grandfather were so completely entranced by the whispers of the northern lights. Anya appeared in the distance and beamed at me. I turned to Papa to see if he could finally see her, too.

"No, Anji. She came to you only, although I do feel her spirit."

I was grateful for that. I put the bead and the letters back in the box and placed it on her grave. I held her lovely eyes intently with my own. "We will find and help Ben, I give you my word." Suddenly the raven swooped down and circled Anya, then her image faded away. I heard my voice quiver with grief as I spoke, "Now that we know who her father is, let's go find him."

Papa said, "Jay and I are going to Anchorage tomorrow and will meet with Sarah and Dakota's team. If Akio Ikiaq is still living in Anchorage, maybe we can locate him. I bet he has been in touch with Ben. In light of what we have all just experienced, I think we should head back and plan another hunting trip in the fall. We have a lot to do."

Kaya was disappointed, though he understood. He wanted to help as well, but he knew that Papa would not let him go. Papa would want him to take care of the shop and the family while he was away.

As we trudged through the snow toward the plane, the raven flapped its wings and circled above us, then soared away. We boarded and headed home. I could not move my eyes away from the lookout tower, Anya's small corner of the world, until it was finally out of sight.

Mother, Grandma and Grandfather were sitting at the kitchen table when we arrived. I revealed the details of my shameful discovery with my head bowed toward the floor. Grandma got up and wrapped her warm, loving arms around me. "You were her only hope to find Ben and solve her mystery. We may never know what happened to her, but at least her soul can now rest."

"I don't think she will rest until we find Ben. They were in love. I wonder if she will continue to appear until she knows Ben is okay."

Grandfather said, "I agree. Her work is not yet complete. Love is a powerful thing." He looked at Papa. "When are you leaving?"

"Jay and I will leave first thing in the morning. When we arrive in Anchorage, the first thing we will do is find Akio Ikiaq. He will be happy to discover that others are helping to find the malicious men who murdered Anya. I just hope he has not gone out on his own to try to find the criminals himself. If anyone harmed one of my daughters, I know I would not rest until I found the beasts responsible."

There was fury in Papa's eyes. I understood that he will not come back until he and Jay locate Ben. He will help the FBI team hunt the traffickers down, but I pray they will be very careful. "Will you please tell Grace and Sarah about Anya? I'm feeling uncomfortable, because I truly believed that she was really here in an earthly form. They will think I'm crazy, seeing ghosts."

Grandma said, "No, they will not think you are crazy. They will understand that you have a very special gift and you were able to help Anya in ways that others could not. Many people who live out here in such a remote environment possess the unique ability to connect with the spirits of our loved ones, but you have the ability to believe in someone so completely that you can truly help them. The raven also knew this."

I was stunned. Here I am, a mortal soul who believes in pure science, not in ghosts, lost spirits or troubled souls. Maybe I had to learn to understand that we are more than just mortal beings, that we are energetic spirits temporarily trapped in material bodies until our work here on earth is complete, whatever that might be. I'm absolutely overwhelmed just thinking about it, but Anya's spiritual presence proved it. I saw her and felt her presence as surely as I exist. Mentally exhausted, I retired to my room to rest. I didn't want to think about it anymore. I also knew that I could not tell anyone about my experience with Anya. This would have to be my secret and I will have to cope with my feelings about it.

I picked up my violin and began to play, but the only sound I could make was the sound of sorrow, a reflection of my grieving heart. I put the violin down and laid on my bed, staring up at the ceiling. I wondered if Autumn was able to talk with the dead. I cringed at the thought and then I remembered that Autumn is half French

Native. I learned from our Alaskan native friends that most of them are very spiritual people and I began to wonder what the differences and similarities are between the native people of Alaska and Canada are compared to the French Native people. Are they also connected with the spirits of their ancestors, the earth, rivers, mountains, wild animals and so on or have they been simulated into the population of the norm, whatever that might mean?

I just want to be a normal girl, who is studying her field of choice at a good university along with everyone else who is trying to understand where they belong and what they are supposed to be doing. I love botany and can't imagine studying anything else. I have to admit that I'm not quite sure yet, how I could best help the world with what I will learn, but there are many options and I want to keep myself open, at least to the entire field of botany. I do know that I want to focus on the study of plants that help people with sickness and health. There are so many plants that have immune strengthening properties, for instance, Echinacea, garlic, turmeric, Holy basil, Astragalus and cinnamon. I continued to ponder over such things and finally drifted off, lost in a dreamy cloud of confusion.

When I awoke just before dinner, I realized that I had slept all day and had not helped with any of my chores. I moseyed out to the kitchen, smelling sweet aromas of fruit, spices and other sweet, savory foods being cooked on the stove. I ambled toward Mother and hugged her. "I'm sorry I slept all day. That smells delicious."

"I knew you needed extra rest with all of the things you have been going through lately. I'm making one of your favorite meals, halibut with lemon hollandaise sauce over sauteed spinach and for dessert, blueberry custard tarts with fresh berries on top. And your grandmother is making a fresh green salad with lousewort, greens, taproot and salmon berries." She met my eyes with an enormous smile and gave me a tender squeeze.

"I love you, Mother. I'm okay though. I feel grateful that I helped Anya find people who will be able to help Ben, even if she is now living in a world beyond as a beautiful white lily, growing on the other side of the mountain. I wish I had known her when she was living on this side. I kind of feel cheated. I can feel her personality somehow within me, but," I lowered my eyes to the floor in humiliation, "I felt so alone and I really wanted her friendship, so maybe my yearning mind gave life to her."

Grandma studied me intensely. "You do know her in a way. She came to you, because she shared something unique with you. Maybe you should go with Papa, just to meet with Anya's father. Maybe you could sit down with him and inquire about her. Speaking with him may help you both come to some compassionate resolve about her very nature. I'm sure he is feeling tremendous loss and possibly regret which is why he has been spending his time hunting for the beastly souls who took her away from him. He might be absorbed in hatred and revenge like Ben is, which is never a good place to be in."

"Oh, I hadn't thought about that. And maybe visiting with him would help us find Ben, so that Anya's soul can finally rest in the peaceful place that she deserves. I can't seem to let her go yet. I'll talk with Papa about it. Grace will be there and we can meet with Anya's father and then go our own way while the others hunt for Anya's killer.

After dinner, I spoke with papa. He said I could go under one condition, that I work it out with Grace to go do something together that is far away from any of the areas that they will be working in until they locate Ben or Mr. Ikiaq. "No problem." I thought about going to a few art galleries, because Anya mentioned that she loved paintings and sculpture by local artists. I researched a few of the artists that she cited and discovered that I really liked a few paintings by Theresa Gonzalez, Courtenay Birdsall Clifford, Byron Birdsall and Nathalie Parenteau. Many of the paintings were absolutely exquisite and there were a few that I would love to hang on my bedroom wall or on my dorm room wall at the university. I thought that maybe visiting a few of the galleries might help me know her better and every time I gazed at the paintings Anya admired, I would think of her.

I feel lucky that I still have many years of my life ahead of me and I am grateful for my life here on earth. I wish more than anything that Anya had been able to experience many more years. I began to understand that life is precious and there's no way to predict when mine might end. I will try earnestly to appreciate everyone and everything that I encounter on my journey through life.

Papa informed me that we would be leaving early in the morning, so I packed a small suitcase and prepared to retire for the night. I then called Grace to make sure she would be in Anchorage and to let her know approximately when I would be there. She said that the plan would work for her as well because she wanted to accompany Sarah, but she didn't want to be around the team while they were involved in dangerous work. Counting on Dakota's team to triumph over the despicable criminals, she did however, intend on being nearby to assist frightened girls who would certainly require safe refuge.

I really admired Grace and Sarah for working so devotedly to help girls like Anya. I wish all people would find ways to protect young people from being savagely plucked like beautiful lilies from the garden, left to bruise, wither and die. I hope to witness scores of unselfish people assisting those who had to endure the tragic suffering that evil criminals forced upon them. And lastly, I'd like to live in a world where pathetic, selfish sex criminals are dealt with so severely that they decline in numbers until they are an extinct species.

28

Dakota and his team arrived in Anchorage, delivered their loads and parked their rigs at the truck stop. They checked into the Monarch Bay View Hotel and met in Dakota's room for a meeting. Dakota outlined how the team should proceed. "I'm exhausted and I'm sure you all are as well, so I recommend that we rest until dinner, at oh, say 1900 hours. We'll have dinner at the night club and then begin exploring, leisurely. Mack, I'd like for you, Chris and Zack to try to talk with some of the girls to see what you might find out, maybe posing as interested men, looking for a good time."

"Aye, no problem with that task and with my good looks and charm, it shouldn't be too difficult." He displayed a devilish grin. Chris stayed quiet but also grinned in his charming way.

Zach chimed in, "Aw, darn. You mean I have to hang around the beauties? What a gnarly task. I'm so bummed." He chuckled.

"Yeah, I didn't think you'd have a problem with this assignment. Cheynne, Jake and I may stay at the dinner table together, but we could take turns wandering around, scoping things out. Cheynne, you may fortuitously walk into the area where the girls are preparing for work. You might ask one of the girls if the owner of the club ever hires middle aged beauties such as yourself and who you should talk with if they do." Dakota flashed a wide toothy smile. "You look twenty years younger than you are, so you might actually get to talk with someone." She wiggled her brows and kissed him on the cheek. "We'll work out what to do if you are able to get that far tonight."

Dakota chuckled. "Jake, you know how to spot a creep a mile away. Study the faces of the bouncers, bartenders and so on. One of us might notice where certain people go, areas not open to the public. Remember, tonight is only a precursor to the real work in the next few days, unless we get really lucky. We'll be meeting with Dirk and a few of his men who are already here and have already been engaging in undercover work at the hotels and nightclubs.

Sarah will be arriving tomorrow and she will have some ideas as well. We are just getting the lay of the land, sort of speak. Don't make the girls or wait staff suspicious of you and drop some dollars for the dancers, gamble a bit and so on. We'll be getting a nice bonus for our work, so you will all get paid back and more. Come to me if you need some money, but don't overdo it. We just want to blend in with regular guests, no special attention and please keep the drinking to a minimum. We are working, so if any situation out of the ordinary arises, we will need to be alert and on game. Listen for disgruntled comments by the staff or by the dancers. Okay, off to your rooms to rest."

Dakota was sleeping when his phone rang, startling him. He didn't recognize the call, but decided to answer it anyway. It was Ethan Sauveur. He introduced himself and asked if he would be available to meet with him in the morning concerning Ben Hawkins. Ethan reviewed the past few days with him so that Dakota could understand that Ben might be in Anchorage and that he may be in grave danger. Dakota thought for a minute and said, "Maybe we could try to locate Akio Ikiaq and meet with him first, in case he has been in touch with Ben."

"I agree. Do you work with someone who could do a search on the man, maybe find out where he might work and live?"

"Yes. I'll call you in the morning and let you know what I come up with." Dakota told Ethan where he was staying and informed him about Axle Heller, his organization and what the team was planning.

"Anji is coming with me to talk with Akio about Anya if we succeed in locating him. She planned to join Grace so that she will be in good hands after we meet with him. Jay Hawkins, Ben's father and I want to help the team. We realize that it could be dangerous, but we are coming to help Ben and you and your team may need the extra eyes and muscle. Jay and I will drive to the harbor to try to locate Heller's yachts. I think it's a good idea for you to accompany us unless you have other plans for tomorrow morning. Would that work for you?"

"Sounds like we have a plan for tomorrow. I'll organize everything with my team."

"If we find Ben, we'll have to figure out how to talk with him without blowing his cover. We also have a plan to check out all of the small airplane hangars. Jay flies the same type of plane, a DHC-6 Twin Otter, which is mentioned one of the investigative reports from Kotzebue, a plane that might be owned by Axle Heller. We think that he may have been there the day Wily Johns was murdered. Jay will be able to find it if it's the same plane and if we can locate the correct hangar. Jay and I will do that when we arrive, since we will be at the airport anyway."

"I'll need to inform Dirk Hays who is heading up this operation. We might need backup if we locate Heller at his yacht or at his hangar, but I have a feeling that we may find him at one of his clubs. Ben might very well be the link that we need to locate Heller. Ethan, I sure hope he is okay and that he has managed to play his role carefully. He is obviously a brave man."

"Brave yes, but he is out for revenge, which could cause him to do something foolish. If he thinks that Axle Heller had something to do with Anya's murder, who knows what he may be planning. Okay, I'll let you rest and I'll call you when we arrive."

Before heading out to the nightclub for dinner, Dakota called Chris. "Hey, buddy. Can you do a quick search for me? I'm looking for a man who hopefully lives and works in Anchorage."

"Yeah, sure thing." He turned on his laptop and within a couple of minutes, he was in the Alaska records database. "Okay, name?"

"Akio Ikiaq. I'm looking for a current residential address as well as a possible employment address."

Chris quickly searched through various records. "Okay, found him. Latest residential address is 18 Spruce Street, Anchorage and it looks like he works at a cannery, called Deep Ocean Seafoods." He gave Dakota the address. "He has earned a substantial amount of money for the past two years for that type of work, so he must work a lot of hours. I also found a second address near Kobuk." He gave him that address. "I suggest going to the cannery first thing in the morning because if he still works there, he'll be there. Fishing vessels will be lined up at the docks, waiting to unload king salmon, lingcod and halibut so cannery workers earn most of their money at this time of year."

"Thanks, Chris. See you at the club." Dakota decided to call Ethan back since it wasn't too late yet. Hana answered the call. "Mrs. Sauveur, this is Dakota Hunt. I hope I'm not calling too late."

"Oh, well hello, Dakota. I've heard so much about you and I look forward to meeting you soon. Let me get Ethan on the line."

"Thank you."

Ethan was anxious, figuring that Dakota had already discovered some information about Akio. "Dakota?"

"I found Mr. Ikiaq's home address in Anchorage and he works at a cannery." Dakota gave him both addresses.

"Excellent. I appreciate that. I'll call you as soon as we land in Anchorage around eight in the morning. Let me know if anything else comes up that would help."

"The cannery is near the airport, so we could meet

you there. How about at ten, which would give you time to check out the hangars. I called Dirk about the yachts and the airplane hangars. He is planning several surveillance operations, probably beginning sometime tonight. Dirk is preparing an organized mission that may include the seizure of every boat, plane and establishment that Heller owns, all at the same time. We need to locate Ben before that happens. I think it would be best if he is nowhere around when that goes down."

"Yeah, no kidding. We sure don't want the authorities to think he is involved with the criminals. He will surely have a difficult time explaining what he is doing with them. Well, have a good night and I'll see you tomorrow."

Chris and Zach discreetly wandered around the lower levels of the hotel, making their way down to the basement level, hoping to locate a door that might lead to the tunnel. Zack said, "Since the plans show electric and ventilation ducts along the route you charted, the tunnel must exist. There would be no other explanation for them otherwise." They opened a door which turned out to be a janitorial closet. They each grabbed a janitorial cart with cleaning supplies and strolled down the corridor.

Zach quickly jumped on top of the cart and unscrewed a light bulb which effectively lessened visibility near a locked door at the end of the corridor. Chris pulled out a set of tools to try to release the lock. After a few minutes, he was able to get the door open, although they hadn't planned on triggering a high pitched blaring alarm. They hastily peered down the hallway, confirming that there was indeed a tunnel. "Holy, bejeesy!" Zach quickly closed the door and they bolted up the stairs and down the upper corridor to the main lobby. Once in the public space, they slowed down and casually strolled through the lobby doors. They were both wearing dark sweatshirts with hoods and ball caps covering their evening attire. They hid behind some cars in the parking lot, quickly stuffed their disguises in a plastic bag and tossed them into a trash can. "Phew! That was close. Maybe we shouldn't have opened the door, because now Heller will be guarding the tunnel much more carefully."

"Chris said, "Well, at least we know the tunnel exists. We'll get the info to Dirk, asap."

The team met at the club, ordered dinner and drinks and began scouting around as planned. Chris and Zach recapped the details of the incident with Dakota. He contemplated several scenarios for a minute, then nodded. "Good work, but I think you jumped the gun by opening the door. It will probably be okay because the hotel is fully booked with guests walking around and hotel staff cleaning, but we'll now have to move quickly. I'm sure you were caught on camera, but you guys wore disguises, right?"

"Yep. We took them off as soon as we made it to the parking lot. There was no one around when we removed them and tossed them into a bin."

"Okay. I'll need to get a hold of Dirk right away, because he may have to move up his plans. Chris, come with me to confirm the location of the tunnel with Dirk. I just wish we knew when Heller may be at the club or hotel. Damn! We're not even sure what he looks like."

Dakota glanced at everyone at the table and whispered, "Start scouting around inconspicuously, please. We need to find someone who knows what Heller looks like and if they know when and if he will show up here tonight."

Dakota and Chris stepped outside of the club and called Dirk. Meanwhile, Cheynne was able to make her way to a hallway where she noticed a door that most likely was a dressing room for the dancers. She opened the door as one of the girls was on her way out. "Oh, excuse me. I was looking for the restroom, but I guess I'm a bit turned around."

"Down the hall and to your left, honey." One of the girls kindly explained.

"Thank you. By the way, how do you girls like working here? My daughter expressed an interest in working here for some extra money, but I wanted to check it out first. I used to dance when I was younger and made very good tips, although as you know, it's all about the management."

Several girls turned to her with obvious astonishment. One of the girls asked, "You would allow your daughter to work here? Wow! If my mother knew I was doing this, she would kill me. Most of us don't have a choice, you know. We either dance for that wicked man or we have to do other things, if you know what I mean."

"Who is the owner of the club? Maybe I should speak with him." One of the girls shook her head no. Her eyes met Cheynne's with a look of terror. She was the one Cheynne needed to talk with. She slyly walked over to the frightened girl and slipped a note into her palm and turned back toward the door.

"Miss, you had better go on out before that bull moose finds you in here. Forget about your daughter working here. There is only one way in and no way out, I can promise you that."

"Okay, thanks for the heads up. Sorry to disturb you." Cheynne left the room and walked down the hall to the restroom. She had previously written a note with hope that her plan would work. So far so good, she thought.

A few minutes later, the girl walked into the restroom and said, "If I get caught talking with you, it'll be the end for me."

Cheynne pulled out a wig, some glasses and a change of clothing from her bag. "I can help you if you want to get out of here, but you have to follow my instructions carefully. Act now and don't hesitate. Put these on now and please don't argue."

She was thankful that the girl did as she was told without saying a word. Cheynne took the girl's clothing and stuffed it into her bag. "We are going to walk right out of here and to my hotel room. After that, I will take you somewhere safe. We will be walking right by my dinner table, where a good friend of mine will escort us right out of the front door. Do not make eye contact with anyone and maybe improvise a bit. When we get to the table, I'll hand you a drink. Take a swallow and laugh a little, maybe some small talk, but don't overdo it. What's your name?"

"Lana." She looked terrified. "I sure hope this works because if we get caught, we're both dead."

"My friends and I are here to help. You can trust us." Cheynne sauntered through the club with her, arm in arm as if they were good friends. They made it to the table where Dakota was sitting with Jake. She eyed Dakota and Jake sternly. Cheynne handed Lana a glass of wine and Lana took a swig as they planned.

Jake eased himself out of his chair and put his arm around Lana and walked toward the door with Cheynne. He got it. The scenario was not planned and Cheynne hoped that the guys would figure out what was going on quickly. Jake said, "Well, darling, I hope you enjoyed dinner. We have just enough time to get home before the kids have to go to bed. We'll find another sitter next time who can stay longer." He grinned at Lana as they walked out of the club, right past the bouncer.

Lana was quick to improvise. "The steak was delicious. We will definitely be coming back."

The three made their way casually across the parking lot to the hotel. They continued the charade until they were in their hotel room. Cheynne felt enormous relief. She turned toward Lana. "You can relax now. Please have a seat." She brought Lana a glass of water. Sorry about how that played out. I didn't really have the whole thing planned and was not sure if it would work but thankfully, it went well. Are you okay?"

"Yes, believe me, I'm okay that is if you can keep me safe. I have been working at that horrible place for three years, praying for an opportunity to escape. Who are you?"

Jake answered. "We are here to find out about the owner of the club. Do you know who he is and what he looks like?"

"Yes. I overheard him talking to the bull moose one day, that's what we call the bouncer. I think he called him Axle. After the bouncer called him that, Axle grabbed him and stuck his gun in his side and whispered something in his ear. I don't think that he was supposed to call him that. We thought his name was James, but I think I'm right.

They didn't see me behind the bar. I thought he was going to kill bull moose."

Jake hoped that Lana would continue to answer his questions. "What does he look like?"

"He is very tall with graying, dark brown hair that he keeps pulled back in a ponytail. He sometimes wears a black leather hat and he has a tattoo of a yacht on one arm and a maiden on the other."

"That's great. Do you know if he will be at the club tonight?"

"He probably will be, later. I...I don't want to be around here when he arrives. He might be here in the hotel now. I can't be here. I want to go home. Please, can you take me home? I haven't been able to talk with my family for a long time. They must think I'm dead or something." She started to cry.

Cheynne said, "Yes, we can take you home, but will you help us with a few more questions first?"

"Okay." She sniffled and Cheynne gave her a tissue.

"Jake smiled at her. "Do you know what days Axle shows up at the club?"

"About four or sometimes five days a week and always on Saturday nights, he plays poker at nine o'clock. I sometimes serve drinks to them during the game. All of the girls take turns bringing the drinks in so that the men can have a look at each of us. Then the men choose which girls they want to accompany them for the night and we have to dance for them and, and, sometimes we have to go with them to their hotel rooms." Lana began trembling and tears streamed down her face.

Cheynne hugged her, rocking her slowly. "It's all over now. You don't ever have to go back there." She thought for a moment. "Does Axle know where you live?"

"No, I don't think so. I was younger when I was kidnapped and didn't have a driver's license and of course I still don't. I live in Noorvik and there would be no way for him to know that." I was with some friends at the shopping mall in Anchorage when some nasty thugs grabbed us and forced us into a dark van. They brought us here to the hotel, where a man named Lex Scorpo threatened us and drugged us. We call him Scorpion because if you make him angry, he unleashes his wrath and stings like a scorpion."

"Can you tell us what happened when you arrived?"

"I remember waking up several days later in some hotel room. There was a man there who gave me flimsy dance clothing and high heeled shoes and told me to show him my moves. He forced me to learn how to dance really provocatively. When he was satisfied that I was skilled enough to dance in the club, they brought me here. He said if I disappointed James, that's what he called Axle, I would be killed. So you better believe, I danced. I don't know what happened to my friends who were with me when we were taken. The men did not bring them here."

"Maybe we can find them." Cheynne handed Lana her phone. Please call your family" Lana took the phone, sobbing. I don't even know what to say. It's been so long." She dialed the number, hoping that her family still had the same number and still lived in the same house.

Her Mother answered the call. "Hello?"

"Mother? It's Lana." She listened to her mother weep causing her to drop to her knees and cry hysterically. "I want to come home. Please come get me. Some nice people rescued me. I'll tell you all about it, but can you come? Are you still living in Noorvik?" They were still living at her home and they told her that they would set up travel arrangements for an early morning flight. She asked her mother to hold for a minute while she made arrangements to stay somewhere safe for the night.

Jake said, "Ethan and Anji are flying out in the morning. Maybe after Anji talks with Anya's father, Lana could fly back with her. Grace will accompany them for safety reasons." He studied Lana's eyes. "We have a friend who is on her way here. Her name is Grace and she helps girls in need such as yourself. Would you like to wait for her and travel with her? I would feel more comfortable if you would. There will also be a girl with her named Anji who lives in Miki Tarniq, who will travel with you as well. I think you will need to talk with the authorities eventually, but getting you home safely is our first priority."

Lana thought about it and continued speaking with her mother. "It's late and I believe I can trust the people who rescued me, so I will come home with them tomorrow." She ended the call with her mother, then dried her eyes. "Thank you so much, but I am afraid to stay here. What if he searches for me here? Someone may have already noticed that I am not at the club for work and they could already be searching for me."

Cheynne said thoughtfully, "I don't think he will search the guest's rooms. You can stay here with me. Jake, you could go back to the club and let Dakota know what's going on and find out if they have discovered that Lana is missing."

"Okay, but I have one more question, if you're up to it." Lana nodded. "Have you ever seen Axle leave through a door that may be concealed from the public areas?"

"No, but I do know that he leaves somehow without going through the main door or the rear emergency door, but I have never watched him leave. I remember watching him open a door at the end of the south hall and walk down some stairs. That door stays locked, so I don't know where it goes."

"Excellent." Jake remembered the building plans that Chris printed out. The possible location of the tunnel was on the south side of the building. He wondered how they could get through a locked door undetected and without sounding the alarm again. "Okay, I'll head back, but don't go anywhere. If you are hungry, we could bring something back from the club."

"No, thank you. I have already eaten. Thank you for helping me."

Jake went back to the club and let the others know what was going on. Dakota grinned like a Cheshire cat. "That's my amazing woman. I would have never guessed that she would be able to just walk right out with one of the girls. We had better leave now, before someone gets suspicious. I told Dirk about the alarm incident at the hotel. Now that he knows that the tunnel exists, he'll be moving fast to prepare a major sting. We'll either come back here tomorrow night or we'll head over to the other club to scope it out and to try to locate the other tunnel."

Dakota wanted to get back to the hotel room to arrange to have Grace prepared to meet with them as soon as they located Akio and Anji had a chance to speak with him. Grace would take Anji and Lana home with the help of Jay, who would arrange a safe flight back with a trusted pilot. Dakota felt like everything was falling into place. He wanted to take Axle Heller out as badly as the FBI did and he hoped that Heller wasn't already getting spooked since the alarm went off at the hotel earlier.

When Dakota opened the door to the hotel room, Lana shot up, wide eyed and startled. He quickly said, "It's okay, I'm Dakota. The hotel is fairly quiet and I didn't see any kind of search going on, so don't worry. I give you my word that you'll be okay. We'll make sure you are safely disguised when we leave in the morning." Dakota observed that Cheynne had given Lana some clothing to wear which would work fine until they could pick something up for her in the morning.

Dakota's phone rang and he noticed that it was Rhys. "Hey, where are you guys? We may need you sooner than we expected."

"We can be there early tomorrow night. We won't stop at the ranch, because it will take too much extra time. The weather is clear so I want to roll on, just in case another storm rears its ugly head. What's going on?"

Dakota reviewed the recent events and discussed the plans for the next day. "When you get here, we will probably be ready to move into action. Call me as soon as you arrive so that I can fill you in on the latest plans. We will be working with Sarah which should be very interesting. She apparently has some plans of her own, so I'll be coordinating with her tomorrow morning. Keep in touch and be careful out there."

Dakota called Grace next to confirm her plans. She was already prepared and happy to be able to help. "I will make sure Lana and Anji get home safely. I'm sure Ethan knows a pilot that can take us to Miki Tarniq and I'll just spend the night and return the following day."

"Thanks, Grace. We are all grateful that you will be here to help."

"Nothing pleases me more than to help young women stay safe. See you tomorrow."

29

Dakota decided that the team should have breakfast somewhere other than the hotel. He thought it would be best to minimize the number of times they were seen. He rented a travel van and they headed to a restaurant near the airport. Dakota called Ethan to let him know where they were. "Good morning Dakota and right on cue. I was just about to ring you. I have some good news. The plane is here and Jay is ninety-nine percent certain that it is the same plane that was seen in Kotzebue. It doesn't appear that anyone is preparing to take off anytime soon."

"Okay, I'll let Dirk know. Have you eaten breakfast? We are at Blue Sky Café, near the airport."

"Yes, but I'll meet you there. Since it's not far from

the cannery, we'll follow each other there. I have a strange feeling about that cannery. The thought came to me that if Ben has been working with Axle Heller, then maybe Akio is as well. Can you find out if Heller owns that cannery?"

"Yes, hold the line for a minute." Dakota set Chris to the task.

Chris searched all of the phony identities, passports and the list of companies that they previously discovered were all owned by Heller. "Aha! Here's one that most likely is the cannery we're looking for. Deep Ocean Cannery, listed under an affiliate trust owned by James McKillian, one of Heller's phony identities."

Dakota gasped. "Well, I'll be. I wonder if Akio figured that out and has been trying to get to Heller through the cannery management. "Chris, look back into Akio's work history and see how long he has been working at that cannery."

"One year."

"Ethan, Akio has been working with the cannery for one year." Dakota didn't hear anyone on the line. Ethan?"

"Yes, I was just thinking. Ben's girlfriend was murdered a year ago and Ben went missing after that. We just stumbled onto her grave in the forest, east of the tundra. We think Ben and Akio must have buried her there and may have decided to work together to find the men responsible for her death. And now it appears that they both may be working for Heller for that reason. Dakota, I'm concerned. Let's get to the cannery asap. I'll meet you there at the restaurant in ten minutes."

A few minutes later, Grace and Sarah walked into the restaurant. "Good morning." They sat down at the table next to the others.

"Good morning." Dakota said. "Have you eaten yet?"

"Yes, we were up early this morning."

"Good, because we'll be meeting with Ethan in a few minutes and we'll need to head out as soon as they get here." He filled them in on the plan.

Sarah said, "I'll take a cup of java to go." She turned to Grace. "Would you like a cup?"

"Yes, thank you." She beamed at Lana. "You must be Lana. I'm Grace and this is Sarah. How are you doing?"

"Oh, I'm okay. I'm just overwhelmed and ready to go home."

"You are a brave girl. We'll get you home." She turned to Dakota. "Is Anji with Ethan?"

Dakota frowned. "Yes, however, I'm beginning to feel concerned that they are going with us. Why don't you and Sarah take Lana with you and follow us in your car." He glanced at Sarah. "We'll check out the cannery and if Akio is there and everything is safe, we'll bring him out to the car so that Anji can talk with him about Anya."

Lana looked puzzled. "Who is Anya?"

Grace said, "Anya or rather Dalianya is a young girl who was also kidnapped like you were, but I'm afraid she wasn't rescued on time." Grace's eyes welled up, threatening to spill over.

"Dalianya Ikiaq? You mean she is dead?" Lana began to cry.

Grace dried her tears with her napkin. "Yes, did you know her?"

"Yes, she worked at the club for a while, but she tried to escape and they caught her and took her away."

The whole group gasped in horror. Grace hugged Lana. "I'm so sorry. Anji knew her as well, in a sense, and she wants to talk with her father, who is the man we are hoping to find this morning. If you would like to, you could talk with him as well. I'm sure he would like to know what happened to her. We'll take you home shortly after that."

The air was emotionally intense and nobody said a word for a few minutes. Dakota noticed Ethan and Jay pull up in the parking lot as he paid the bill. "Let's all head out."

Grace and Sarah walked out with Lana to the car and Sarah greeted Ethan and quickly let him know about Lana, the plan to get them all back home safely and that they wanted Anji to ride with them. He gladly agreed.

When they arrived at the cannery, Sarah parked the car and Dakota, Jake, Ethan and Jay headed into the building. Dakota showed the rest a photo of Akio that Chris had printed earlier. "Ethan, why don't you and Jay go talk with the receptionist, maybe inquire about working there, ask who the manager is and find out if you can tour the facility. Jake and I will head over to the dock side to see if we can find him there."

"Sounds good. Text me if you find him and we'll meet you back by the cars."

Ethan and Jay were able to meet with the operations manager, who was happy to show them around. "I'm Dean Brinks." They shook hands and introduced themselves. "We are shorthanded and are hiring now. You fellows showed up at the right time." He handed them hard hats. "Put these on. Safety code requires it. We are looking for machine operators and catch unloaders on the docks." Brinks escorted them to the machine area while Jay and Ethan searched for Akio, but none of the men matched his description. They made their way to the rear of the facility toward the docks, where several men and women were unloading the fish from the icy hold of a large vessel. Brinks said, "We receive vessels all day, all year long, filled with salmon, crab and other types of fish. These unloaders work quickly and efficiently to unload each vessel so that they can be on their way to go catch more."

Jay thought he spotted Akio on the boat handling a large vacuum unloader, so he walked up a bit closer, then turned to Brinks. "I'm interested in working as an unloader. Can I talk with that man for a minute?"

Brinks whistled and nodded to the man. "Akio is one of our best. He'll be able to answer any questions you may have. I'll be back in a minute. I have to take a phone call."

Brinks walked back into the building. As soon as he was out of earshot, Jay said, "Akio, I'm Jay Hawkins and this is Ethan Sauveur. We'd like to talk with you about my son, Ben. Can you get away for a few minutes?"

"Ah, Jay Hawkins. Ben has told me a lot about you. Sure, I can take a break for a few minutes. I'd shake your hands but believe me, you don't want this stuff on your hands. You'll stink like I do for the rest of the week. Good job, but the fish smell lingers even after a lemon wash." Dakota and Jake noticed Jay and Ethan walking with, who they figured must be Akio. Dakota caught Ethan's eyes and nodded, then glanced toward the side of the building.

Akio asked, "Are you looking for Ben?"

"Yes, I have been for quite a while and I'm extremely worried about him. I think he may be in serious trouble."

"No trouble yet, but that boy is bound and determined to take down Axle Heller and by God, I hope he does. I took a job here so that I could try to find out where the son of a bitch is. I discovered that he most likely was responsible for murdering Dalianya. He owns a night club where I believe she was working after the son of a bitch snagged her from a grocery store lot."

Akio's eyes welled up. "The last time I saw her alive was when she flew from Kotzebue to the Anchorage airport with a pilot named Wily Johns which was a grave mistake." Ethan glanced at Jay. "She had been staying at our cabin with my brother and a friend. I picked her up from the airport in Anchorage and brought her home to get her car and some clothing for a weekend away with Ben. She said she was headed to the grocery store to pick up some food to cook and then on to meet Ben at the cabin near Anchorage, but she never made it. Ben said he waited at the cabin for half an hour, then went looking for her. They must have passed each other somehow because he said he looked for her car in the lot and it wasn't there. I figured she may have been running late and probably arrived at the store after Ben left." He shook his head and tears trickled down his cheeks.

"When Ben found out that Wily was the pilot that flew Dalianya here, he went through the roof. He had arranged for her to fly with Ujurak Moon, but she apparently went to the wrong hangar and ended up with that wretched, sorry soul. That's when he told me that Wily worked with Axle Heller and explained who he is. Ben thinks that Dalianya may have talked about her plans, not realizing she was putting herself in danger. Then Wily probably discussed her with Heller, who then had her followed and abducted possibly by Wily himself, the snake." Akio chugged some water and glanced toward the boat harbor. "I went looking for Wily, meaning to kill him in cold blood, no questions asked. A shot at close range, right between the eyes."

Ethan stared into Akio's eyes. "Did you kill him?"

Akio looked off into the distance again, shuffling his feet. "Ben informed me that he got a job on one of Heller's yachts in order to get close to him, to learn as much about his operation as possible." Tears began streaming down his flushed cheeks. He dried his eyes with his sleeve. "Damn it! I miss her so much. She was such a caring thoughtful girl and she surely didn't deserve what happened to her. I aim to help take the bastard down as soon as I can figure out how. The Yacht that Ben is working on is called, The Pretty Girl. Son of a bitch." Akio dropped to his knees, utterly unhinged.

Jay put his arm around him. "Akio, Ethan and I, along with a few other brave souls who are working with the FBI are going to find Heller and take him down. This is Private Detective Dakota Hunt and Jake Losato." They all nodded to each other.

Dakota said, "Mr. Ikiaq, we need to talk with Ben. Can you tell us where the yacht is located?"

Akio showed them where the yacht was usually docked. "Ben is going by the name of Inuksuk Yuka. Dalianya used to call him that. Her 'bright star'." Don't blow his cover. He has been keeping his head down while trying to figure out Heller's patterns. Heller makes his way to each of his main operations on a weekly schedule. He showed up here yesterday and I swear on my daughter's grave that I almost went after him planning to slit his throat, but I held back. I made a promise to Ben that I would not let my rage get the best of me. Patience, Ben says, patience. I'm sure I have run out of patience!"

Ethan asked, "Do you know if Ben has figured out where Heller might be in the next few days?"

"He's usually at the Monarch club on Saturday around seven thirty. I guess he plays poker every Saturday night with some high stake's players." Dakota nodded to Jake, since Akio's information confirmed their previous discoveries. "I thought about getting in on one of those games, but I don't have the funds yet. I've been working my backside off to save every dollar possible. Vengeance for Dalianya is worth every cent I have and I don't care if I lose or get killed, as long as I can get close enough to kill him first."

Jay said, "Akio, you just gave me a great idea. Dakota, do you think you can get your FBI contact to back us up with 50K, which if we play this right, they'll get back when we take the bastard down? I am a master poker player and I feel like luck is on my side?" He grinned ear to ear.

"I'll see what I can do. I'll speak with Dirk who wants Heller more than any other criminal in the U.S. Akio, there are a couple of girls that I would like for you to meet. Can you spare a few more minutes? They are in a car in the lot over there." Dakota pointed to the car.

"Okay, but I have to get back to work before Brinks thinks I left for the day."

The men walked to the car where the girls were waiting. Grace had assured the girls that everything would be okay if they got out of the car to speak with Akio, so they cautiously and nervously did. Dakota said, "Akio, Anji and Lana knew your daughter."

Akio was emotional and seemed to be troubled when he saw Lana. "Are you the girl I saw at the nightclub one night about three weeks ago? We talked for a minute and you said you knew Dalianya, right?"

"Yes, I remember you." Lana hugged Akio. Her eyes welled up and her voice trembled. I… I'm so sorry Mr. Ikiaq. Oh, I'm so sorry. Dalianya was so sweet and very brave. She wanted to escape and she tried to get me to go with her, but I was so afraid that I couldn't go. One night, she put on a wig and a nice dress and tried to get one of the men at the bar to escort her out, but I think the man knew Axle. He wasn't there that night, but she succeeded in leaving with the man. I'm afraid he might have taken her to Axle, because she never returned. At least, that's what I believe might have happened. We were all warned that if we tried to escape, we would be killed. And when Cheynne told me that Dalianya was dead, I felt certain that she was murdered. Mr. Ikiaq, she was a good girl and surely didn't deserve that."

He nodded. "Yes, she was a good girl. Thank you, Lana."

Anji ambled toward Akio, anxiously. "I didn't know Anya the way Lana did, but I knew her in an exceptional way even still." She looked down and tried to summon the nerve to tell him how she knew Anya. "Please don't think I'm crazy, but Anya came to me in spirit form. I thought for a long time that she was alive. She talked with me and showed up at certain places, as if she was trying to lead me to the truth. I carried around her red scarf with colorful beads for a long time and then to my complete astonishment, my papa, Mr. Hawkins and I discovered her grave." Tears filled her eyes as she recalled the events of

301

her earth-shattering experience. "We read your letter in the wooden box. You see, Mr. Ikiaq, I believe she was trying to lead me to you and Ben. She was in love with Ben, wasn't she?"

"Yes, they were very much in love. They were planning to get married. Ben is a good man and I would have been proud to have him as my son in law. She wore that scarf all the time because Ben gave it to her. Thank you for finding me, Anji. I am very lucky that you are so in tune with your spiritual nature."

Jay was listening intently. "Ben hadn't yet informed me that he was planning to marry her. I only had chance to spend time with her on one occasion, when Ben brought her home for dinner." He held Akio's red, swollen eyes with his own. "I would have been proud to have her as my daughter in law. She was a special girl and I could see why Ben was so smitten with her. Ben lost it for a while and I didn't know why, but now I understand. He changed drastically when Anya passed on. We must find him and let him know we are here to help. He has become vengeful and as you said, he means to do whatever he can to take Heller out with little concern for his own life."

Ethan said, "Let's go check out the yacht and see if he is there. Jay, can you get in touch with Ujurak? I trust him to get the girls back safely. Lana lives in Noorvik and hasn't seen her family in many years and I think Anji should return with her. Grace has agreed to go with them to make sure they are safe. Akio, we will do everything we can to make sure justice is served. Anya's killers will pay with their pathetic lives, mark my word. I will keep in touch with you. In fact, I'll give you my address in Miki

Tarniq. Please come visit whenever you like."

"Let me know if there is anything I can do to help. I will not be working for Axle Heller much longer. I just wanted to take him down, but it looks like I'll just be in the way at this point. If his operation goes down soon, I don't want to be anywhere near here."

Ethan nodded. "Yes, you might want to tell your boss that you have an emergency and you will need your paycheck now. The FBI is planning to seize all of Heller's businesses sometime tomorrow. Please come visit us in Miki Tarniq when you are ready. My son will be going away to college soon and I will need some help at my shop. We would all welcome you and help you get settled, that is, if you are interested."

"I'll think about that. Dalianya loved living near the preserve, so I might take you up on that. There surely is nothing holding me here anymore. My wife passed away many years ago and my brother is a nomad, but he would be very grateful if I moved somewhere near the Noatak Preserve. We hunt near there every year, so I'll be in touch."

Jay said, "I just spoke with Ujurak. He is picking up some goods in Anchorage and could meet you gals at the airport in an hour and a half. Could you find something to do until then?"

Anji said, "I would like to visit a few galleries to see some art that Anya described. Then we could meet him at the airport." They agreed and Lana, Grace and Anji left together in Grace's car, while the others took off to find Ben. Anji understood how dangerous the mission would most likely be and was worried, but she hoped for the best and prayed for them to be safe.

30

Anji

Grace located an art gallery that specialized in the work of local artists. We were delighted to view some exceptional work by artists Anya had mentioned such as Theresa Gonzalez, who paints with vivid bright colors. A painting of brilliant pink lupine flowers with a glowing cerulean sky above was one that I particularly liked. Next to it, was a painting that really captivated my attention titled The Guardian, by Dee Carpenter. A painting of a raven depicting a regal, confident aura, reminded me of the uncanny raven I seemed to have a mysterious connection with. I instantly thought of Anya when I saw it. What was really interesting was the sly position of the bird in front of a colorful turbulent river background, with salmon swimming upstream. I wondered if the artist planned that or if she was initially painting the salmon in the river and then changed her mind, turned the canvas sideways and then painted the magnificent raven. I wished that I could have it, but I didn't have enough money for such an exquisite piece of art.

Lana stood in front of a colorful floral painting, gazing at the beauty of the piece. "I feel so free. I can't believe I am in an art gallery enjoying paintings. I didn't think I would ever be able to do anything as a free woman again." She smiled and her eyes glistened with tears. Both Grace and I hugged her. I was certain that Grace understood what she felt like when I noticed a tear drop on her cheek.

Soon it was time to go, so we made our way to the airport where Ujurak was waiting by his plane. Grace made arrangements to park her car for a couple of days, then we boarded the plane and headed home. Noorvik was on the way so we stopped there first and accompanied Lana to meet her parents. I wept as her father and mother sprinted to her and hugged her tightly. I felt such love and yet such grief at the same time. I could not imagine being abducted with the possibility of never being able to speak with or see my family ever again. I shivered and thought, when I go away to school, I will make sure that I call my family often and I will go home every summer.

Lana's folks walked briskly toward us and thanked us for bringing her home. We exchanged addresses and I asked them to come visit anytime they liked. I wanted to keep in touch with Lana and I thought maybe we could become friends. I looked down from the sky as we were flying away and I saw Lana still waving at us.

Ujurak said, "On to Miki Tarniq, ladies." I thanked him for going out of his way and asked him to join us for dinner. He was happy to accept the invitation. "I wouldn't miss an opportunity to enjoy Hana's cooking."

I thought about Papa, Jay, Sarah, Dakota and his team and wondered if they had located the yacht and Ben yet. I was worried, but hopeful appreciating that Papa will not stop searching until they locate Ben and remove him from danger.

It's only about eighty miles from Noorvik to Miki Tarniq and not a long flight. Kaya was waiting for us when we arrived at the air strip. He jumped out to help us with our luggage. "Papa called to let us know what was going on. Sounds like you had an eventful day."

I presented a slight smile feeling emotionally exhausted. "Yes, we sure did. I'm sad and yet happy at the same time if that makes sense."

"I understand. Hey, I'm sorry about Anya. The whole thing was really strange and I haven't yet wrapped my head around it. I know you wanted her to be alive. Is that why you are sad?"

"Yes, and my heart is shattered to pieces for Ben and Mr. Ikiaq. They were both grateful to hear that so many people are helping to take down the beasts who murdered Anya."

When we got home, I gave everyone the details which made Mother very concerned. Of course she doesn't like Papa involved in such dangerous missions, but he's the kind of man who will not sit idle while others are fighting a battle that he feels is vital to the safety of our Alaskan people. We enjoyed dinner and talked about our upcoming plans concerning Autumn and her mother, school and summer visitors who will begin arriving soon.

The next morning, I heard the river calling my name. I felt overly stressed about my future journey in an unknown world and all of the emotional events that had recently occurred. I pulled on my wetsuit and hauled my kayak down to the river. I gingerly paddled while I observed schools of fish darting left and right, tightly packed together as if they were attached by invisible strings, which made me laugh. There is nothing like the feeling of gliding through the swiftly flowing river. I laughed heartily as a large Dolly Varden jumped high out of the water to catch a mosquito. It felt good to laugh.

When I'm unsettled about something, paddling my kayak is usually the perfect peaceful activity for working through my troubles. It seems to be impossible to hold on to negative thoughts and emotions when you are surrounded by such natural splendor. I focused on dipping my paddle gently into the water, then I pulled the paddle back with adequate strength while the kayak glided more smoothly as my speed increased. I proficiently maneuvered around boulders, using my paddle to shove away from the rocks as the water swirled around my kayak. A heavy rapid section of the river forced my kayak briefly sideways, then backwards, then by holding the paddle deeper in the water in the direction I needed to go, I found myself headed forward, once again floating swiftly down the river with all of my troubles and concerns vanishing into the swirling depths of the water.

When I returned from my peaceful kayak excursion, Grace and I talked more about school. She caught a glimpse of a small tear threatening to drip down my cheek. "You feel that you will miss your home terribly, don't you?"

"Yes. I'll be away during autumn which is my favorite season. I love being here when the salmon spawn and bears and birds congregate in the shallows of the Noatak River to enjoy delicious salmon feasts. I like to get as close as I dare to watch grizzly and black bears splash around as their mighty paws hastily swipe up the sluggishly flopping chum salmon, filling their bellies in preparation for a long trek to their dens to hibernate for the winter. I love the turning of the leaves in the Preserve when the colors are brilliant gold and orange."

"Colorado has spectacular color in the autumn as well and there are many rivers and lakes where you can paddle your kayak. I have a feeling your family will come visit you often and Miki Tarniq isn't going anywhere. You can return whenever you want to." Grace put her arm around me and at that moment, I felt truly grateful to have such compassionate friends.

31

E than, Jay and Dakota's team arrived at the harbor to search for the yacht. It was docked right where Akio said it would be. They noticed Ben on board working on the rigging with a few other men. They decided not to go all at once which could spook the men on board, so Jay and Ethan walked down the dock on the side where Ben was working.

Jay called out to him by his under-cover name, "Inuksuk Yuka. How are you, my man?"

Ben was startled to see his father, but he quickly realized that Jay must have figured out what was going on since he knew his phony name. He waved at him, whispered something to one of the other men and hopped off the boat. As Ben approached Jay, he subtly shook his head. Jay understood that it may not be a good idea to show any sign that he was a family member. Jay and Ethan followed Ben down the docks, far enough away to be out of sight and ear shot. Then Ben hugged Jay. "What are you doing here? You do not want to be seen with me."

"Ben, we know what is going on. Ethan and I just had a discussion with Akio Ikiaq and we understand what happened with Anya. We found her grave and your letter in the wooden box. We're here to help you and before you say anything, look over there." Jay pointed to the car where Dakota and the team were waiting. "Those people are working with an FBI task force that is here in Anchorage to take Axle Heller down. They have organized a major sting operation which will include the seizure of all of Heller's businesses that they are aware of, including his jet and his two yachts. You do not want to be here when that happens or you will go down with them."

"Well, it's about time. That no good, pathetic beast had Lex Scorpo, his right-hand man, murder Anya. I've been prepared to put a bullet right between both of their eyes as soon as I had the chance."

"That's exactly what Akio said. Ben, step down and let the authorities take over. The best way you can help is to work with us to make darn sure the FBI is aware of every faction of Heller's organization. Private Detective Dakota Hunt discovered a long list of businesses and establishments which are being observed as we speak. They want it all to go down at the same time, including plans to trap Heller. I'd like for you to come with us right now and take a look at the list, think hard and let us know anything else about him that might be helpful to us."

Ben looked back toward the yacht, trying to decide if he needed to go get anything on board, anything that would tie him to Heller. "I've been careful to keep very little on board and my wallet and passport are in my pocket. I guess I could just disappear, but you had better be right about the timing of this. You know Heller will run the second he gets suspicious of anything that doesn't feel right to him, although I think he has become a bit complacent. The self-righteous bastard thinks he's untouchable. He has certain corrupt police officers in his bulging, green pockets eating right out of his hands. They protect him by looking the other way when he snags girls."

Ben's fists tightened as he clenched his teeth. "They give him tips when detectives start snooping around his businesses. Low and behold, right when the authorities go in for the bust, Heller disappears along with girls, drugs, weapons and anything else that could tie him to the business. He then takes off and lays low until things calm down again. That's why the authorities haven't been able to take him down."

Jay nodded. "We also know about his phony identities. Ben, we should get out of here, now. Don't hesitate, just don't go back."

"Okay, let's roll. I told the guys on the yacht that you were some businessmen, hoping to get hooked up and that I would send you to one of Heller's partners. So have you figured out where the other yacht is yet? Because that's the one Heller will run to when he finds out that this one has been compromised."

"Take us there now."

"Alright, you're not kidding about moving without

delay." They jumped in the SUV and headed down the road to a small, private harbor where Heller's second yacht was located. Ethan introduced Ben to the others who all let him know that they were grateful to support and assist him in any way possible. When they arrived at the marina, Ben pointed to the yacht which seemed to be vacant at the moment. It's called Camelia. That's his girlfriend's name. She lives in his mansion here in Anchorage." He gave them the addresses of both homes.

Dakota handed Ben the list of businesses that Chris had previously discovered and all of the fake identities that they were aware of. "Check out that list and let me know if you can add to it." Dakota dialed Dirk's cell number. After a few rings, Dirk answered.

"Dakota, what's up?"

"I have a source who has just identified the locations of Axle Heller's yachts and homes, unless you've already figured that out. My source is scrutinizing the list and will be adding to it if he can. He said that as soon as Heller gets wind of anything out of the ordinary, he will beeline it to the Camelia yacht and disappear. We are heading to the yacht now." Dakota texted the addresses to Dirk. "Are you guys ready to move on this? It seems we had better act tonight. I have recently learned that he plays poker tonight, as he apparently does every Saturday night at nine-thirty, at his Sweet Gems night club. You have the tunnel locations of both clubs, the location of his private jet and now you have the locations of both yachts. Since we know he's here in Anchorage, let's move, buddy."

"We've been in meetings all morning and have been in direct contact with every man we have out there. Every business on our list is being observed as we speak. Hang on for a minute." Dirk put Dakota on hold. After a minute, Dirk said, "Okay, I just arranged for my men to stake out the yachts and his mansions. At nine this evening, it's going down. Every damn cathouse and business will be seized and we'll have our men, including your team at both sides of each tunnel, choppers overhead, you name it. Oh, and thanks for the info about the cannery. We didn't have that one on our list. We have undercover agents posing as wealthy business men who will be throwing cash around at the clubs, ready to act at a moment's notice."

"I have two guys that can try to get in on the poker game, but we need you to help us with 50 K, which you would get back right after we take him down. Is that possible?"

"Yes." Dirk's partner, Kate, began making the arrangements. "I'll meet you at six o'clock in your room. I want your team impeding both sides of the tunnel. I'd like to crash the poker game, but he will most likely make a run for it, hopefully right into the tunnel where we'll all be waiting for him."

They reviewed more of Dirk's plans and ended the call. Dakota shared the news with the rest, who were all a little anxious about being in the middle of what could possibly be a fatal nightmare. Ben said, "I'm not resting until this is over. I've worked way too hard for it all to blow up in our faces and the bastard has a chance to elude the authorities once again."

Sara said, "I sure hope none of the young women get injured in this mess. I will be ready to assist them but until then, Ben, I need your help. Describe what Lex Scorpo looks like. I have a plan to get rid of him without any of us doing the dirty work."

Ben stared into her eyes, then grinned conspiratorially. "He is a large, muscular man, about six feet tall, dark eyes and shoulder length salt and pepper hair, which is usually held back in a band. Oh, and he has rosy cheeks, like his blood pressure is always elevated. So what's your plan because they call him scorpion and believe me, he lives up to the name."

"Let's go check out the Camelia yacht. Lex Scorpo just sold it to me for $300,000 and I plan on letting Axle Heller know all about our fantastic deal."

"Oh, no. Heller paid over a million for that yacht. He'll kill Scorpion."

"Exactly." She grinned. "Do you know if anyone is on board at this time?"

Ben said, "I'm not sure, but Heller trusts me to look after the yacht." He grinned again with narrowed eyes. Come to think of it, Heller just asked me to bring it around and dock it next to The Pretty Girl, which is what I will tell anyone who might be watching the boat. But we will really be sailing it the other direction, right into the hands of the FBI. Let's go."

Sarah chuckled as she schemed. "I will wear a lovely disguise and a carry a large bundle of money, which will be visible in my handbag. Heller may not allow me to get in on the game, but I bet he'll meet with me to discuss it once he sees the cash. Then I'll unleash the news but first, I'll have to make sure Lex Scorpo is at the club."

On the way to the harbor, Dakota called Dirk. "Meet us at the harbor with one of your men who knows how to sail a seventy foot yacht. We need the boat to disappear." He reviewed the plans with him, including

Sarah's strategy.

Dirk chuckled. "I like it. I will have some undercover agents covering the lady's back. I sure hope she knows what she's doing. I can see a scenario where an enraged Axle Heller unleashes his fury on her. I hope she is very careful and expects the worst. Have your man walk away when my agents arrive at the boat slip. We'll take care of it and I'll let you know when we have the yacht out of sight."

"Thanks, Dirk. On the way."

When they arrived at the harbor, Ben walked down the dock to the slip where the boat was anchored and climbed aboard. He checked all of the rooms and luckily, no one was around. He figured that since it was Saturday, most of Heller's men would be working at one of the night clubs. He started the engine and prepared the boat to be moved. A few minutes later, Dirk's men showed up. Ben gave them the keys and made sure they were okay to go and headed back to the car.

Dakota sped away toward the hotel, looking dreadfully uncomfortable. "Are you sure you want to do this, Sarah? I'm concerned for your safety. You have a reputation for pulling off many daring, risky schemes, but this formidable man may be gravely determined to get his boat back at all costs, even your life."

"Jay and Ethan will be working on getting in the game which will occupy Heller's attention, then I'll walk up to him and unleash the bomb and then, hell hath no fury! If we're lucky, Axle will walk right up to Lex and blow him away, one less cockroach over running the planet. If anything goes wrong, Dirk's men will be there."

"Okay. You'll have plenty of backup. Just do not

under any circumstances go with him somewhere alone."

Ethan's phone rang. He saw that it was Anji. He decided to ignore her call for now. "As soon as we get to the hotel, I'll call her back. Anji has been very concerned about you, Ben."

Ben smiled. "Anji is a special girl. I'm grateful and amazed that she was able to connect with Anya. It's quite strange because she never really bought into the whole spiritual, nonphysical world. You know her, she's all into the science of things."

Ethan looked off into the sky. "I have reflected on the matter carefully and I believe Anji connected with Anya, not realizing she was doing so. Since she witnessed Anya being abducted in the parking lot, she felt so tremendously guilty that she didn't tell anyone or do anything about it. At the time, she didn't really understand what was going on. When she learned about our girls being abducted by traffickers she began to feel so upset, that all she could talk about was Anya. She saw her many times here and there and even spoke with her on several occasions. As you said, since Anji has been so thoroughly immersed in the science of things, she would never have believed that Anya was coming to her in a spiritual form. She also had the help of a very mysterious raven, which dropped Anya's scarf in front of her one day when she was outside by the barn. This peculiar raven seemed to be observing Anji and also had some kind of spiritual connection with her."

"Sensational. However, I'm not too happy with her for not saying anything when Anya was abducted."

"Don't blame her for what happened. She didn't understand what was going on and she did everything she could to solve the mystery. She is very upset, Ben."

"I understand. I'm just so damn angry. It's Heller's doing and not the fault of Anji. I'll speak with her and I promise I won't upset her. I'll just let her know that I don't blame her. I'm still just so sad and heartbroken." Ben's eyes welled up. "Anya and I were going to get married. I loved her so much and now she's gone, maliciously eliminated from my life."

Jay studied Ben's eyes. "You know you could choose to keep her close to your heart. Wouldn't she want you to feel that way?"

He dried his tears and responded reflectively. "Yes, of course. She'll always be a part of me, the good part." The silence was deafening as Dakota drove toward the hotel, each person reflecting in their own way.

The clock was ticking. When they arrived, they noticed that everything seemed fairly quiet and ordinary. Dakota called Rhys and learned that they had just delivered their load and would be at the hotel shortly. "Check in and then meet me in my room. You'll be receiving a quick review of our plans. You and Zach will be positioned on the hotel side of the tunnel with Chris."

Dakota rested for few hours, until it was almost time to go. He found himself anxiously pacing back and forth as he reviewed his plans. Cheynne comforted him, reassuring him that they were ready and extraordinarily capable. Wind gusts whistled at the windows and the environment seemed surreal. Within a few minutes his team convened in Dakota's room as planned. They reviewed each post and prepared to head out. Dakota murmured, "It's almost time." He received a text on his cell from Dirk. It read; It's going down. Make your way to the club.

Dirk answered Dakota's call immediately. "As soon as Heller's poker game starts, we'll be moving the girls and other guests out of the club. He'll get wind of it and go out to find out what the problem is. Everything will go down fast. At the same time, Heller's yachts and jet will be seized along with every business, cathouse and home on the list. His cell phone will be exploding with concerning calls and he'll run right into our hands."

Everyone took their positions as Jay and Ethan distracted Heller with fifty thousand dollars. The plan was working. Heller was escorting the players into a back room where he held the games, when Sarah strolled up dressed in a low back scarlet gown, appearing as a gorgeous, wealthy, blonde woman with sulky brown eyes and pouty ruby lips. Sarah naturally has long, dark chestnut hair and hazel eyes, so her disguise was astonishing. Ben had mentioned earlier that Heller was attracted to women in red.

Sarah put her hand on Heller's arm. "Why you must be Mr. Heller, the previous owner of my lovely yacht. I just wanted to personally thank you for your very generous offer."

Heller appeared to be drooling over Sarah at first until he realized what she was saying. "Excuse me, what did you say?"

Sarah spoke with such a syrupy sweet, southern voice, that people began to gather around to listen to the discussion. "You know, the Camelia, the yacht that your buddy Lex Scorpo sold to me for $300,000. You're really an impressive business man, selling your yacht to me for such a nice low price, making sure I'd spend all the rest of my money right here at your casino." She opened her purse and pulled out six large bundles of cash. "I thought maybe you might have a need to fill another seat at your poker table."

Heller's face was turning bright red in contrast with his sinister black eyes, which were glowering at Sarah as he attempted to remain calm. "What did you say your name was?"

"Roxie Eris." Sarah held out her hand to Heller. "I'm pleased to make your acquaintance, Mr. Heller." Dakota and Dirk's men were standing around the corner, ready to rescue Sarah if her plan went awry. "Oh, look. There he is now." Sarah waved at Lex Scorpo and called out to him. "Oh, Mr. Scorpo." Lex turned and walked toward Heller and Sarah.

Heller gritted his teeth, seething, then narrowed his eyes. "Lex, my man. Miss Eris was just telling me how you sold Camelia to her for $300,000." Heller grinned ominously at Lex.

Lex, looking completely perplexed uttered, "What was that?"

Heller glanced at Sarah's ring finger, which was adorned with a large glittering ruby. "Miss Eris, would you please wait here. I'll be back in a minute." Sarah smiled devilishly. He walked with Lex upstairs to his office. Once the door was closed, Heller pulled his cell phone out of his pocket and called one of his men to check on the yacht. After a few minutes he said, "Oh, you say the Camelia is not in the harbor? Well find out where in the hell it is!" He slammed the phone down on his desk, opened his top drawer and pulled out a gun with a silencer attached. While keeping his sinister black eyes trained on

Lex, he walked toward him aiming the gun between his eyes and pulled the trigger. Heller stomped back down the stairs in search of Miss Roxie Eris, who was nowhere in sight. Shaking his head furiously, he briskly walked to the poker room, sat down and grinned confidently to the other players, showing no tell tail sign that he had just murdered a man in cold blood, a perfect poker face. Heller bellowed, "Double Belvedere with a lime twist and make it snappy."

Two girls took the drink orders while the players introduced each other. The first round of the game was almost finished when Heller bellowed, "Where in the hell is my drink, damn it!" No one responded. He got up to go see what the holdup was. He opened the door and walked out noticing an alarming stillness. No one was anywhere to be seen. The club was empty. Several FBI agents had escorted the patrons and employees out while Sarah quickly helped the women who were working at the club, escape into vehicles which were prepared to take them to safe homes.

Axle Heller immediately ran toward a door at the back of the club, swiped a card in front of an electronic device and bolted down the stairs toward the tunnel as planned. He was half way down the hall when an earsplitting alarm began blaring, echoing in the tunnel. He stopped in his tracks when he heard footsteps approaching. Rhys, Dakota and four agents were cautiously moving toward him, guns at the ready. Heller panicked and ran back the other way, right into Dirk, Ethan, Mack and a team of agents. Heller fired wildly, but the bullets missed and ricocheted off the cement block walls. Rhys and Dakota tackled Heller to the ground before he was able to fire another shot.

One of Dirk's men cuffed Heller while Dirk held his gun to the side of his head. "I should just blow you away right here and now, but I'm actually looking forward to hearing the judge sentence you to death for abusing and killing scores of women."

"You don't have any proof that I did any such thing. I run legal establishments. If someone I work with killed people, that's not on me. My hands are clean."

Dirk shook his head. "Axle Heller, you are under arrest for the murder of Lex Scorpo, trafficking everything under the sun, money laundering, kidnapping, abuse, torture and murder of many young women and a whole slew of other offenses." Dirk stared Heller down with such deadly intensity that Dakota thought he just might pull the trigger. "Just in case you're curious, three of your men just confessed to a number of serious crimes naming you as the man behind the whole damn organization. Your wife, Camelia is also in custody and eighteen of your businesses, yachts and your jet have been seized. The girls who you forced to work for you are being questioned as we speak. I'm sure every one of them will help us convict you and identify more of your cohorts."

Heller scowled and narrowed his eyes. "It ain't over until it's over, you'll see."

Dirk laughed. "Oh, I forgot to mention, your two police buddies are also in custody. Who knows, maybe you'll get to spend some time with them in USP ADX Florence, Colorado while you wait for your trial and sentencing. We'll be asking for Judge Arnette Baridam, one of the toughest judges in the country, who has no tolerance for human traffickers, particularly sex traffickers. This ought to be the trial of the century." He glared at Heller, then escorted him to a helicopter which was ready to transport him to ADX, one of the most secure prisons in the country which housed some of the most notorious, violent criminals.

Dakota called Cheynne. "Axle Heller is in custody. Look outside. Cheynne ran to the window and observed three helicopters circling above.

There was live coverage being reported on every channel. A reporter outside of the Sweet Gems Night Club announced, "An FBI task force team has just arrested organized crime leader, Axle Heller, and has seized his homes, yachts, a private jet and approximately twenty corrupt businesses in a major operation which they have been planning for months, according to the Anchorage authorities. They have also captured sixty-six offenders who were all working as part of a massive criminal organization, which engaged in every form of corrupt activity from drug and sex trafficking, to the trafficking of illegal weapons, money laundering and unfortunately, the abuse and murder of many young women and boys."

Cheynne was in the hotel room watching with immense relief. She turned the channel, finding a report from the Mayor of Anchorage, who was overjoyed with the success of the operation, but explained to the public that this was only the beginning of what he hoped would be a continuous, daily, energized effort to prevent trafficking in Anchorage as well as in the entire state of Alaska.

Sarah had taken several young women to a safe location before the club was besieged by the authorities.

She was able to arrange for them to speak with a couple of FBI agents who allowed them to give recorded testimonies and call their loved ones to pick them up shortly afterwards.

Dirk Hays thanked Dakota and his team for assisting in another successful major operation. He also thanked and acknowledged Ethan and Jay, letting them know that he would be continuing to search persistently for sex criminals in the state of Alaska and would do everything he could to prevent more Alaskans from falling victim to the clutches of such murderous criminals. Ethan felt grateful, but he comprehended that the war was not over.

Dakota and Ethan walked away from the others to talk about visiting Noatak. Ethan said, "I've never met such fearless people and I'd like to consider us good friends." They shook hands. "You just let me know when you want to come out and I'll make the arrangements. We have a lot to celebrate, my man."

Dakota grinned. "Looking forward to it. My employees are all looking forward to camping, fishing and floating on the river and we all are very interested in getting to know you and your family."

Jay and Ben walked up to Dakota holding their hands out to Dakota. Ben said with a confident, yet relieved voice, "I want to thank you for coming up here to help us take that demon down. My sweet Dalianya will be able to rest peacefully now that her killers have been apprehended." His eyes welled up.

Dakota embraced Ben. "Heller will most likely be penalized with a death sentence and Lex Scorpo is dead, so Dalianya has been avenged. I realize that doesn't necessarily make you feel any better since she is gone but as your father mentioned, she would want you to live on holding her memory close to your heart."

Jay hugged his son. "I'd really like for you to come home for a while if you will. I miss having you around and I need your help with my bush flight business this summer, if you are interested.

Ethan said, "If you don't have enough work flying tourists around, I could use another hand at the shop. In fact, maybe you could do both. I asked Akio if he wanted to help as well, which I'm really hoping he will take me up on. With Kaya and Anji leaving for school in a few months, I'll have plenty of work available. I'd really like for all of us to stick together to continue to take care of the young people of Alaska." Ethan nodded to Ben. "I'm relieved that you are okay. You're a good man, Ben."

Dakota felt elated, yet still concerned for the safety of the Alaskan people. He could sense that much more work would need to be accomplished in order for the state to be purged of the evil that continues to broil beneath the concrete camouflage. He shook off his gloom, preferring to perceive the victory as a robust step forward. He forced himself to smile. "Let's all go out for dinner, on me. I'd like to end this day on a good note and we surely have a lot to celebrate. My team will be staying in a more pleasant hotel for the night and we'll be heading out in the morning. Autumn graduates next week and Brooke has her Harmony Ranch opening gala on June first, so we'll be busy for a few days with that, but we'll be making our way back here by mid-June."

Ethan smiled. "Anji and Autumn will have a good time getting to know each other. I can't tell you how comforted I feel about her attending school in Colorado near your family. I will miss her tremendously, but I feel that she will be safe. Hana and I will be making regular visits, you can count on that. I'm actually really enthusiastic about visiting another state, since I've never had the interest or reason to do so until now. I think I might like Colorado. Anji has shared her research with me including many extraordinarily beautiful mountain areas."

Dakota smiled. "My house is always open to you. Just give me a ring whenever you are planning to visit and I'll arrange to be there, brother."

The group headed out to a nice restaurant with tasty surf and turf and enjoyed light hearted conversation and good company. After they said their goodbyes, Jay, Ben and Ethan decided to head home rather than staying for the night. They were exhausted, but they were feeling like their world was a little safer and wanted to rest, peacefully in their own homes.

When they arrived in Kotzebue, Ethan addressed both Ben and Jay with concern. "You both can trust that I will keep your answer to myself, but I must put the subject to rest. Did either of you kill Wily Johns?"

Ben started to speak, but Jay cut him off. "I know Ben wants to protect the man responsible, but I can't let him take the blame. Wily caused his own demise by abducting Anya on behalf of Axle Heller. I believe it should go down in the records, that Heller is guilty for both deaths, however if you really must know, Akio Ikiaq was responsible for poisoning Wily with Monkshood."

Ben bellowed with concern, "Akio should not go down for that. He did what he had to do and as vengeful as it may have been, it was a necessary evil. When I found out that Axle Heller was going to get rid of Wily, I informed Akio, although he was already planning his revenge. I begged him to wait a little while longer, because I knew that Heller would have one of his men do the dirty work for him, but he wouldn't listen. We should leave well enough alone and take what we know to our graves."

They all agreed. Ethan said, "If we are questioned by the authorities, we must tell them that we believe that Axle Heller was to blame, but I suggest that we not divulge any information other than that. I also believe that Akio is a good man and in all honesty, I may have done the same if Wily was responsible for the kidnapping and murder one of my daughters." Ethan bowed his head, nodding assuredly. "It is done."

32

Anji

Papa came home smiling and whistling, which meant the mission was successful. He described the day's events, detailing the main incidents. I was so happy and feeling so much better about myself, knowing that they were able to locate Ben and kept him safely out of harm's reach. I know if I ever see anything out of the ordinary again like I'd witnessed with Anya, I will not hesitate to inform someone immediately. She will be with me in spirit always, reminding me that I must protect myself at all costs.

I now understand why Papa and Grandfather feel so connected with the spirits of our ancestors. I understand that having faith and trusting people are good qualities, but being alert to my intuitions could save my life someday. I also realize now, that I cannot control everything in life and I feel that I will be ready to deal with outside forces that try to hinder my journey as they arise.

Since Grace was here, I talked with her about things that we had all recently experienced. She said she felt strongly that things will work out well for me in Colorado and assured me that I will experience many treasured moments there. I'm really looking forward to working with Autumn and Brooke at Harmony Ranch. Jillian sounds like a lovely woman who has some amazing proficiency working with plant life that is native to Mountain areas. I would like to learn how to grow many more varieties of plants and vegetables and I'm sure that Jillian will be a fun person to learn from.

Working and sharing with girls who have suffered through situations like Anya had, would make me feel closer to her in yet another way. I don't feel guilty anymore and I don't believe that Anya ever wanted me to feel that way. She only wanted me to help her with her unfinished business as they say, so that she could finally move on to live peacefully in heaven, surrounded by her ancestors who love her.

We all retired to bed, although even though it was quite late, I was not sleepy. I stared at the ceiling thinking and pondering for hours. I glanced at my clock, noticing that it was two thirty in the morning. The wind was slightly gusty causing the leafy branches on the tree outside my window to swish and snap, scratching at the window pane. I got up and peered out of my window, amazed to see a slight wave of purple and green in the sky. We don't normally see the northern lights at this time of the year since the sky is not dark but in the twilight hours, the mysterious lights were visible tonight. Suddenly, Anya appeared and began dancing among the waves of light, twirling and smiling down at me. Maybe I was dreaming, but I saw her never the less. My eyes welled up and I placed my hand over my heart and waved back.

Epilogue

Our Inupiat friends invited us once again to the Nalukataq festival along with Autumn, Jillian, Dakota and his friends, who all enjoyed attending with us. We all had so much fun that no one wanted our time together to end. Papa, Kaya, Joie, Alina and I played a few lively tunes while everyone danced, laughed and enjoyed a fun-filled, safe celebration. There were no shady criminals lurking around, no stress and no disturbances of any kind. I was grateful for that.

During the next week, we camped, rafted down the river, fished, shared stories, laughed and thoroughly treasured the company of our new friendships. Autumn stayed after everyone else left as planned. I took her hiking with Kodiak, Nukilik and Piper and showed her all of the flowers that were blooming along the tundra as well as in the Noatak Wildlife Preserve. I showed her Anya's grave and recounted my story with just enough detail so that she understood. I revealed my inner most secrets about seeing and feeling Anya's presence somewhat reluctantly, but I figured that if we were going to be friends, we had to be able to trust each other. Autumn surprised me by telling me that she also feels the presence of the spirits of her ancestors, particularly the spirits of her great grands, Jonoche and Chenoa. She said that they come to her sometimes in her dreams, which I was relieved to hear. She made me feel comfortable about my experiences and my spirituality and she suggested that I never let anyone try to suppress my special gifts.

Papa, Mother and Grandma flew with Autumn and me to Colorado a week before school was to begin. I was really grateful that Grandma was able to come with us. She has been my best friend all throughout my life and I couldn't imagine beginning my next chapter in life without her by my side.

The Hunt family are truly caring, compassionate people as I'd hoped. Mother and Grandma had a wonderful time getting to know Jillian and Yamka. Chevyo, reminded me of my Grandpapa, Tulugaak, both very wise, peaceful, compassionate men. Papa enjoyed getting to know the Hunt family as well, which was very important to me. He informed me that he felt comfortable about me going to school there, knowing that the Hunts would be fairly close by.

Autumn and I ventured out together to check out Colorado State University and spoke with the housing office to arrange our living quarters. We were both truly excited and I could tell that Autumn was happy to have me as her friend to attend the university with. The campus was beautiful and felt secure. We toured around making note of the locations of all of the buildings where our studies would take place. Our apartment was close by, so we walked along the beautiful treelined path and checked in with the office. A friendly, helpful woman showed us where our living quarters would be, the laundry room, study lounge and a gorgeous garden patio with tables and benches. I could see myself studying outside in the warm sunshine.

I was excited to see the mountains in the distance and longed to go for a hike, which is just what we did after returning to Autumn's family home. Jillian, Dakota and Papa went with us probably to make sure we were safe and we didn't mind a bit. It was actually quite enjoyable just spending quality time together. While climbing a steep stretch of the trail, I noticed a beautiful raven gracefully drifting with the gentle air currents above us. I breathed in deeply and smiled.

Bibliography

1. Corral, Roy. Journalist and photographer. Mayo, Will, Introduction. (1946, 2002) What The Elders Have Taught Us, Alaska Native Ways, stories written by Natives of Alaska. Publisher: Alaska Northwest Books.

2. Schreiber, Melody. (Nov. 27, 2019). Why human trafficking is a serious but mostly invisible problem in Alaska. Arctic Today

3. PACT-Ottawa's Truck Stop Campaign (Persons against the Crime of Trafficking in Humans) https://www.pact-ottawa.org/truckstop.html

4. TAT (Truckers Against Trafficking) https://truckersagainsttrafficking.org/

5. Hensley, William L. Iggiagruk. (2009) Fifty Miles from Tomorrow. Publisher: Farrar, Straus and Giroux, LLC.

6. Jans, Nick. (August 29, 2013.) The last Light Breaking: Living Among Alaska's Iñupiat Eskimos. Publisher: Alaska Northwest Books.

7. Jans, Nick. (May 1, 2009.) A Place Beyond: Finding Home In Arctic Alaska. Publisher: Alaska Northwest Books.

About the Author

D eb D. Donohue lives in the Colorado Rockies where she enjoys writing, reading, drawing, dancing and hiking. Her son and extended family live in various parts of the country.

She earned a Bachelor of Science Degree in Architecture from Gerald D. Hines College of Architecture at University of Houston and three years of Interior Design studies at Design Institute of San Diego. She studied literature, writing, poetry and philosophy at Mesa College and Houston Community College, which prompted her to begin writing fictional stories within a concerning social context.

Her first two novels, Jillian, A Dakota Hunt Novel Book One and Anji, A Dakota Hunt Novel Book Two are fictional stories, however, certain incidents and events which occur in both novels are based on actual circumstances in the criminal sex trafficking trade. Many of the stories of her heroic characters are based on her own experiences and travels throughout the United States, including mainland Alaska and northwest Canada.

The idea for the books occurred to her after she reviewed the Truckers Against Trafficking (TAT) website and materials. She wanted to get involved in the fight against sex trafficking and hopes her books will help create more of an awareness that our world continues to struggle with modern-day slavery, human trafficking.

The books are meant to encourage hope for the young people who were victims of sex crimes and for their families who may have suffered tremendous losses.

The stories are also meant to encourage young people to be alert to suspicious behaviors of possible offenders and to protect themselves while in public.

Deb also hopes that many more people find ways to get involved in the fight against trafficking and in the rescue of young people from such a devastating plight.

www.ingramcontent.com/pod-product-compliance
Lightning Source LLC
Chambersburg PA
CBHW020358260626
47156CB00007B/2167